T0065239

Doc Charlie

Doc Charlie

Robert Callis

DOC CHARLIE

This is a work of fiction. All of the characters, names, incidents, organizations, and dialogue in this novel are either the products of the author's imagination or are used fictitiously.

iUniverse books may be ordered through booksellers or by contacting:

iUniverse
1663 Liberty Drive
Bloomington, IN 47403
www.iuniverse.com
844-349-9409

ISBN: 978-1-6632-2728-7 (sc)
ISBN: 978-1-6632-2729-4 (e)

Library of Congress Control Number: 2021945953

Print information available on the last page.

iUniverse rev. date: 08/24/2021

DEDICATION

This book is dedicated to my daughter, Christine Marie Arndt. She is an Assistant Superintendent of a school district in Illinois. She began her career as a teacher, achieved her master's degree, and moved into school administration advancing to her current position. She is a strong woman with strong opinions. She has made her own way, and she has done a fine job of creating a career and of raising her son. This story is about a strong woman like my daughter.

CHAPTER ONE

The sun was halfway to the horizon when Kit drove his truck north from Kemmerer towards the Fontenelle Reservoir. Swifty slouched in the passenger seat, his cowboy hat down over his eyes. Both men were looking forward to this brief trip from daily reality. They were headed north from Kemmerer to a campsite near Fontenelle Creek on the old Herschler Ranch. Their agenda including fishing, relaxing and whatever.

"I heard you hooked up with an old girlfriend from high school. Some gal named Ann?" said Kit.

"Who told you about her?" demanded a suddenly alert Swifty.

"I called your Aunt Judy, and she filled me in on most of your adventures up in Cody," replied a grinning Kit.

"You can't believe anything that woman says," retorted Swifty.

"That's not what I heard," said Kit with a slightly smothered laugh. "So, tell me what really happened."

"Nothing to tell," replied Swifty. "I went to the ranch, saw my mom and sister, attended my dad's funeral, and ran into someone I went with in high school. End of story."

"The story I heard was a lot longer, a lot more colorful and a lot more interesting," said a smug Kit.

"What the hell did my Aunt Judy tell you?" asked Swifty.

"She told me to call this Ann who is a vet in Cody. So, I did, and Ann told me a funny story," replied Kit.

"What did she tell you?" said a suddenly guarded Swifty.

"She told me a lot, but I'd rather hear it from you," replied Kit.

Swifty sat up in his seat, alert and angry and looking like a small boy who got caught with his hand in the cookie jar. He sat silently for several miles and then he started to relax. Finally, he turned to his friend and spoke.

"I guess it can't hurt none to tell you, but you gotta promise me you'll tell no one else. And I mean no one, not even Big Dave," said a now less aggressive Swifty.

"I promise to tell no one," said Kit.

"All right," said Swifty, sighing in resignation. Then he started talking. He told the story of his trip to Cody with as few words as possible, but even then, it was a lot of talking for someone like Swifty who uttered words like each one was a hundred-dollar bill being removed from his savings account.

"I think you left out a few things," said Kit.

"What things?" snorted Swifty.

"How about that fight you got into at that bar in Cody where Dr. Ann saved your bacon with her tranquilizer gun," replied Kit. "Or the time where she enticed you into her bedroom, stripped naked and then when you started to disrobe, she tossed cold water on you and left you standing in her bedroom with your britches down around your ankles."

"How the hell did you know about that?" asked a surprised Swifty.

"I told you, I talked to Ann, Dummy," said Kit. "You should learn to pay more attention when I speak. You might just learn something."

"That'll be the day," retorted Swifty.

Neither man spoke for another ten miles. Then Swifty broke the silence.

"Promise me something, Kit," said Swifty in a slow and evenly paced voice.

"What?" asked Kit.

"Promise me you'll never tell anyone on this planet what you just told me you heard from Ann," said Swifty reluctantly. It was obvious he was having trouble asking Kit for a favor.

"Look, I'm having a bit of fun at your expense, but I've repeated her story to nobody except you and I have no reason to," said Kit. "You're my best friend and I'd expect the same respect from you."

After a few minutes of silence, Swifty finally spoke.

"Thank you," he said.

"You're welcome," replied Kit.

They drove in silence for another ten miles.

Then Kit broke the silence.

"But it sure as hell was the funniest thing, I've ever heard about you," Kit burst out.

"I gotta admit," said Swifty. "She nailed my ass to the wall. I never saw it comin' and I ain't been that embarrassed since I was about ten years old."

Both men burst out in laughter, and they continued to laugh for another five miles. About half an hour later, they

3

turned off the paved road and went through a wire gate, after stopping to open it. After they passed through and stopped, Swifty got out and closed the gate behind them. They drove for another fifteen minutes and came onto a flat area right next to Fontenelle Creek.

Kit parked the truck and both men got out. After a quick inspection of the site, they kicked away some old dry cow pies and some sticks and tumbleweeds. When they were satisfied with the site, they unloaded the truck. They put down air mattresses and blew them up with a hand pump. Then they set rolled up sleeping bags on top of the mattresses. Swifty cleaned out an old fire circle and Kit went looking for firewood. By the time Swifty had cleaned out the fire pit and replaced stones around it, Kit had returned with an armload of firewood. Swifty laid out wood in the pit for a fire and placed two large rocks on two sides of the pit. Then he hauled an old grate out of the truck and set it on the rocks, so it was elevated from the top of the firewood.

Kit brought a large cooler from the truck and placed it near the firepit. Then he pulled two large folding camp chairs out and set them on either side of the cooler. He went back to the bed of the truck and checked on the food box and the utensils crate. Everything on his checklist was there.

When Kit returned to the firepit, Swifty was pulling two cans of cold beer out of the cooler. He tossed one to Kit, and the two men sat in the folding chairs and popped the top of their beer cans. They each had two beers and took turns telling stories, some true, some not, and some absolute prevarications.

As the sun was sinking in the west, they made a supper

of burgers and baked beans washed down with fresh coffee. Swifty noticed Kit was now using honey instead of sugar.

"You changed to honey in your coffee?" asked Swifty.

"Yep," replied Kit. "I read it's healthier for you than sugar."

"Next thing I know you'll be eatin' dried cow chips dipped in humus," said Swifty.

"Do you even know what the hell humus is?" asked Kit.

"Sure, I do," retorted Swifty. "It's that crap that those granola heads on television tout that surely tastes as bad as it looks."

Kit just shook his head and grinned at his friend.

When they finished supper, they used water from the creek to wash their few dishes and set them on some canvas in the bed of the truck to dry. Kit produced a bottle of bourbon from the Buffalo Trace Distillery in Kentucky and they each had a stiff drink. By then the fire had died down and it was dark out. Both men undressed and slipped into their respective sleeping bags. Within minutes, the campsite was quiet except for the occasional snore, and pops from the fire pit embers left from the supper fire.

Both men were up before the sun the next morning. Kit placed firewood in the fire pit and started a fire. Then he left to search for more firewood as Swifty grabbed the old coffee pot and proceeded to make cowboy coffee. He filled the coffee pot with fresh water and placed it on the fire. He lifted the top of the pot open and tossed in a handful of ground coffee. He followed that up with some clean eggshells and replaced the top. When the coffee came to a boil, he lifted the coffee pot off the grate, added a bit of cold water to take the coffee grounds to the bottom and then set the pot on a flat rock.

He poured hot coffee into two large metal mugs and set one in front of Kit. Kit added honey and dried creamer from a small container while Swifty took his coffee the way he liked it, hot and black.

Kit looked up from his coffee cup and pointed at the creek. "You're in charge of breakfast this time, remember?"

Swifty nodded and got up and grabbed his fishing rod and a plastic bag of earthworms. He walked over to the narrow creek which was barely three feet wide. The creek ran slightly downhill and Swifty positioned himself next to a small pool formed in the creek. He baited his hook with a worm and cast it upstream and let the bobber float down into the small pool. Two seconds later the bobber was pulled roughly under the water and Swifty reeled in a small trout, known as a "brookie" for its size. Within minutes he had a half a dozen brookies and he laid his fishing pole down on the ground.

He cleaned the trout and washed the split carcasses in the creek. Then he brought them back to the side of the cook fire. He laid the fish out on a flat rock. Then he produced a large plastic bag partially full of corn meal, salt and pepper. One at a time he dropped a cleaned trout into the bag and shook the bag, coating the fish with the bag's ingredients. When he had all six done, he put them on a metal plate. Then he produced an old black cast iron skillet. He went to the cooler and grabbed four slices of long, thick bacon. He put the bacon in the skillet and then placed the skillet on the grill. When the bacon was done, he removed them and placed them on a paper towel laid on a flat rock. Then he slipped the coated trout into the bubbling bacon grease. He turned the trout occasionally as they were fried over the cook fire and when he was satisfied, he placed three trout and several pieces of bacon on each of the two plates and handed one to Kit.

Kit refilled his coffee cup and Swifty's and handed the full cup to his friend. Both men sat on the folding camp chairs and dug into their hot, fresh breakfast as they enjoyed the warmth of the bright Wyoming morning sun.

When they were finished, they scraped the few remains on their plates into the fire pit, and Kit took the few dishes and washed them in the stream. Then he set them out on an old towel on the bed of the truck to air dry. The old iron skillet was another matter. Kit washed it out in the stream, then took sand from the stream bottom and cleaned the skillet, then rinsed it out in the stream and set it next to the plates to air dry.

When he returned to the cook fire, Swifty was in his chair, with a fresh cup of coffee in his hand. Kit poured himself a still hot cup of coffee from the old coffee pot, doctored it with creamer and honey to his satisfaction, and took his seat in the chair next to Swifty. Kit reached in his shirt pocket and produced two cigars. He handed one to Swifty and each man bit off the end of their cigar. Swifty produced a long stick from the fire and used it to light both their cigars. The two men rested in their camp chairs and spent the next few minutes, drinking hot coffee and enjoying their cigars.

After an hour and a half, Kit got to his feet and looked over at his old friend.

"Time to go already?" asked a puzzled Swifty.

"Yep, time to go," replied Kit.

"What's the rush?" asked Swifty.

"I have a possible new client coming in this afternoon," replied Kit.

"What kind of client?" asked Swifty.

"A lady from back East made an appointment to see me," said Kit. "She's flying into Salt Lake this morning, renting a car, and driving up to Kemmerer."

"How in the hell did some lady from back East hear about us?" asked a puzzled Swifty.

"She said she was referred to us, but I have no idea by whom or why they would refer her to us," replied Kit.

"What's her name?" asked Swifty.

"Her name is Marie Andropolous. She's a widow lady from Ohio. I looked her up and she's about sixty-three years old," said Kit.

"Hmm," mumbled Swifty.

"You have a problem with a new client?" asked Kit.

"She's interruptin' my quiet time," mumbled Swifty.

"You never had a quiet day in your entire life," laughed Kit.

"Well, crap," said Swifty. "We might as well break camp and get back to town if you're so set on bein' a respectable businessman."

Kit laughed and emptied his coffee cup. Swifty soon followed, and they proceeded to break camp and clean up the campsite. Thirty minutes later, they were out of the gate and headed south to Kemmerer. It was a beautiful morning in Wyoming, but Swifty slumped down in the passenger seat, pulled his cowboy hat down over his eyes and slept all the way back to Kemmerer.

CHAPTER TWO

Kit pulled to a stop next to Swifty's truck and helped him transfer his gear from Kit's truck. He left Swifty in the parking lot and drove to the old bank building that housed his business Rocky Mountain Searchers on the first floor and his apartment on the second floor.

The unloading of the truck took about ten minutes. After stowing everything away in the building, Kit went to his office. He sorted through his mail and checked his electronic messages. Nothing important jumped out at him. There was an email from Mrs. Andropolous. Kit pulled up the email on his computer. Her email was notifying him she would be landing in Salt Lake City by one P.M. local time and would be renting a car and driving to Kemmerer. She said she anticipated she would be at Kit's office by early in the afternoon.

Kit ran the distances in his head and thought her estimate was accurate. He looked at his watch. It was a little after noon. He could use a cup of coffee. He could make a new pot, or he could run across the Triangle Park to the café and get a cup there. He decided on the café and was almost out the front door of his building when he heard his name yelled out.

He stopped midstride and looked to his right where the sound had come from. Coming down the sidewalk were two of his oldest friends and his father. He turned to greet them and shook hands all around.

"What can I do for this distinguished body of city elders?" he asked.

"Elder my ass," said Big Dave.

"That'll be the day," added Woody, the leading attorney in the county.

"Be careful who you insult so early in the day," said Kit's father Tom Andrews.

Kit threw up both hands in a form of mock defense and said, "Oops, so sorry."

"Try again," said Big Dave.

"How can I help you distinguished gentlemen?" asked Kit.

"We came here for a good cup of coffee," said Woody.

"A free cup of coffee," added Big Dave.

"Follow me," said Kit and he led the trio into his office. After they were seated, Kit excused himself and went to the small kitchen and made a fresh pot of coffee. He returned to his office with a tray containing the pot of coffee, large mugs, a container of milk, one of sugar and a plastic squeeze bottle shaped like a bear full of honey.

"What the hell is with the damn plastic bear?" asked Big Dave as he poured a large mug full of black coffee.

"I switched from sugar to honey," said Kit.

"Honey is probably better than sugar," said Woody.

"God knows what the kid will try next," snorted Big Dave.

Kit's father had to stifle a laugh with his hand over his mouth.

Very shortly everyone had a mug full of coffee, and Kit listened intently as the three older men discussed what was going on in Kemmerer and basically how the country was going to hell in a handbasket. The discussion went on for about half an hour and included two refills of coffee. Out of breath and out of coffee, the three older men thanked their host and disappeared out the front door in the direction they had magically appeared from in the first place.

Kit looked at his watch. It was just a little before one. He cleaned up the coffee mugs and supplies and returned them to the tiny office kitchen. He returned to his office and did a final Google search on his new female client. He found nothing new had been added since his last search. He heard a knock on the door jamb of his office. He looked up and saw a short, dark haired, attractive older woman dressed in a stylish skirt, blouse and jacket. She wore no-nonsense black leather shoes on her feet.

Kit got to his feet and introduced himself and offered his hand. The lady took his hand and spoke.

"I'm Marie Andropolous. I had an appointment at one o'clock, but I am a bit early. Is that all right?"

"Of course," said Kit. "Please come in and have a seat."

Mrs. Andropolous entered his office and took a seat in one of the large chairs facing Kit's desk. Kit retreated behind his desk and seated himself there.

"How can I be of service to you?" asked Kit.

"I'm not sure where to begin," said Mrs. Andropolous.

"Just start wherever you feel comfortable," said Kit. "We can always return to any point you feel was left out."

"Thank you," said Mrs. Andropolous. She closed her eyes and bowed her head slightly. After a couple of minutes, she looked up and opened her eyes. Her eyes were dark. They weren't brown and they weren't black, they were just very dark.

"I need to tell you a story about me first," she said.

Kit remained silent and nodded his head in encouragement.

"When I was finishing high school in a small town in Ohio, I became involved with a boy most of my friends considered reckless, even dangerous. I fell head over heels for him. We had an affair, and I became pregnant. When I told him, he was silent. Two days later he left town and disappeared. In those days there were no legal abortions. I told my family, and we went to the family doctor, and he confirmed my pregnancy. I was sent to another town where Catholic Charities had a place for unwed mothers. I stayed there until the baby was born, and I agreed to release the child for adoption. I only saw my baby for a few minutes. The nurse told me the baby was a girl.

Afterwards, I returned home, finished school, and enrolled in college. There I met my husband, Walter. He was studying to become an engineer. I was studying to become a teacher. After we graduated, we got married and had two children, a boy and a girl. Both grew up, graduated from college, got married and moved away. Walter was successful in his career as an engineer, and we traveled to places all over the world where his work took him. Walter retired and we settled into a retirement community in Florida. Three years ago, Walter passed away. About six months later, I began to read about other young women like me who gave their babies up for adoption when they were noticeably young."

Mrs. Andropolous paused and reached in her purse for a tissue. She dabbed her eyes and returned the tissue to her purse. She looked up at Kit, paused for a moment, and then continued her story.

"A lot has changed with adoption laws and the secrecy that surrounded them back when I had my child," she said. "Now, lots of sealed records can be opened and many questions can be answered. I began to try to learn what had become of my baby. I didn't mention any of this to my children. I wasn't sure what I would do if I did learn what had happened to my child. I still don't know if I would even try to contact the child if I did find out where she was, if she was still alive."

She paused again and tears were streaming down her face. Kit handed her a box of tissues from the credenza behind his desk which she gratefully accepted.

"I'm so sorry," she said.

"Don't be," said Kit. "I understand how hard this is for you."

Mrs. Andropolous composed herself and she continued with her story.

"I hired a private investigator about two years ago. He was highly recommended by my attorney, and he was very thorough. I told him I wanted to know what happened to my daughter but was not sure I wanted any contact and he understood," she said.

She paused, and Kit remained silent and motionless behind his desk, as he silently encouraged her to continue with her story.

"His report was very thorough. My baby was adopted by an older childless couple who were Catholic. They were of modest means but had desperately wanted children the wife could not have. They were good parents, and my daughter did well in school. She was bright and physically active. When she graduated from high school, she received an ROTC scholarship to college. She graduated with honors, majoring in pre-med, and began her service obligation with the United States Air Force. She was commissioned as an officer and the Air Force sent her to several schools during her career. She became a registered nurse, a surgical nurse specialist, and then a physician's assistant. She was stationed on Air Force bases all over the country and a couple of other countries. Her final posting was to Warren Air Force Base in Cheyenne, Wyoming. Are you familiar with that base?" she asked.

"Yes, I am," Kit replied.

"She was stationed in Cheyenne for the last four years of her military career. She served twenty years in the Air Force and then she retired," said Mrs. Andropolous.

"When did she retire?" asked Kit.

"She retired almost two years ago," said Mrs. Andropolous. "Then we lost her trail."

"Would you like something to drink, Mrs. Andropolous?" asked Kit.

"If you have some bottled water that would be wonderful," she replied.

Kit left the room and came back with a cold bottle of water and handed it to his guest and then resumed his seat behind his desk.

Mrs. Andropolous took several drinks from the bottle and then replaced the cap and set it down on Kit's desk.

"Thank you, Mr. Andrews. I guess a combination of stress and doing more talking than I normally do made my throat feel very dry," she said.

"You're welcome," said Kit. He waited for her to continue, but she remained silent. He decided to try to get her restarted. It seemed odd to him that a retired Air Force medical officer could just step off a base and disappear in the United States.

"You mentioned you lost her trail," said Kit. "Do you have any clues as to where she might have gone?"

"She just seemed to disappear into thin air," said Mrs. Andropolous.

"With no trace?" asked an incredulous Kit.

"Well, I guess there was a trace," she replied.

"How so?" asked Kit.

"According to my investigator, she drove off the base in her car and drove to a used car lot in Cheyenne, where she sold her car for cash. She called for an Uber car. The Uber driver picked her up at the dealership and drove her to an old motel in Cheyenne," she said.

"How long did she stay at the motel?" asked Kit.

"According to the investigator's report, the motel has no record of her checking into the motel. From the moment she got out of the Uber car and walked up to the front of the motel lobby, she just disappeared," said Mrs. Andropolous, who began quietly crying again. Kit slid the box of tissues to her, and she took one and began to dab at her eyes.

Kit waited patiently until she resumed control over her emotions. When he felt she did, he began asking her some basic questions, taking care to jot down her responses on a small note pad.

"Were you able to trace her Air Force retirement checks?" asked Kit. "I assume she would be receiving a pension from the Air Force after twenty years of service."

"That information is all classified," replied Mrs. Andropolous. "You need a court order unless the military retiree is deceased."

Kit put down his pen and sat back in his chair. He thought about what Mrs. Andropolous had told him and then asked what to him was an obvious question.

"Mrs. Andropolous, I have to ask you, why come to me here in Kemmerer, Wyoming?" asked Kit.

"Because the last place I know she actually was seen was Cheyenne, Wyoming," she said.

"Kemmerer is a long way from Cheyenne, Mrs. Andropolous," said Kit. "Wyoming is a big state."

"Wyoming is the last place she was seen," said Mrs. Andropolous. "My investigator told me you were the best in the business at finding someone in the state of Wyoming."

"Your daughter could be anywhere, not just in Wyoming," replied Kit.

"Mr. Andrews, this is all I have to go on and that's why I'm here. I'm out of options and my investigator is stumped. If my daughter is not in Wyoming, she went somewhere, and I believe you are my best bet to find where she is," said Mrs. Andropolous.

Kit sighed and looked down at the file the woman had brought with her and placed on his desk.

"May I make copies of this file, Mrs. Andropolous?" Kit asked.

"The file and everything in it are for you," she replied. "I have other copies."

"All right then," said Kit. He pulled out his standard agreement and fee sheet and showed them to Mrs. Andropolous. She read them and did not blink at the cost. She asked no questions. She signed the contract and wrote out a check for the retainer amount. Kit took the signed documents and the check and placed them in the file containing her copied documents.

Kit thanked her and told her he would be in touch by email and would keep her informed of his progress or lack of it. They shook hands and Kit walked her out of the building to her parked car. She got in her car and rolled down the window and looked up at Kit. She was crying again. She dabbed her eyes with a tissue and then looked at Kit.

"I'm not a crazy old woman, but I am a determined old mother. Please find my daughter," she said. Then she composed herself, rolled up the window and drove off, heading south towards Salt Lake City.

CHAPTER THREE

Kit got a fresh cup of coffee and sat down at his desk. He opened the file and began to read through the contents. He kept a pen in his right hand and occasionally made small notes on the pages as he read them.

The report detailed the adoption of the baby girl by a modest income, childless Catholic family named DeSantis. The wife was unable to have children and thus the adoption of the baby girl. The DeSantise's raised the baby, naming her Charlemagne. Her adoptive father was a history teacher and was fascinated with the history of the real Charlemagne.

The girl Charlemagne grew up, did well in high school, and obtained an ROTC scholarship to a college in Ohio where she graduated with a degree in pre-med, and a minor in chemistry. After graduation, she was inducted into the United States Air Force. The Air Force sent her to several schools, and she obtained degrees and certifications as a registered nurse, a surgical nurse, and finally as a physician's assistant with the rank of major. She served on several Air Force bases in the United States and a couple overseas. She put in her retirement papers after twenty years of service while she was stationed in Cheyenne and retired from the

Air Force. The day she retired, she packed up her things, loaded up her car, left the base, and vanished into thin air.

Kit paused and took a sip of his coffee. He sat the cup down and sat back in his chair and thought about what he had just read. Then he pulled out a small note pad and began to make a list. Five minutes later he was done.

He knew a retired military member's records were protected while they were alive unless ordered by a legal subpoena. That route was unavailable to him or anyone else outside the military or Justice Department. The logical way to trace her was through the payroll records of her retirement pay. That information was privileged. She had sold her car in Cheyenne the day she retired. She took an Uber to a motel she never checked into. The motel was the last known location before she vanished. Kit was quite sure she paid the Uber driver in cash. This lady knew what she was doing, and she was smart.

Kit studied her picture. She was in uniform. She was dark haired, like her mother, but she was taller and had broader shoulders. Her features were plain and nothing about them stood out. Finding her would be like searching for a needle in a giant haystack. Then he looked at a color photo of her and realized she had piercing green eyes. At least that was something.

Kit sipped his coffee and thought. Where would she go and why? Why all the secrecy? Why did she disappear immediately after her retirement? All her actions seemed to indicate she had planned to disappear. Why?

He reread the private investigator's report. She had no close friends. She had no living relatives from her adoptive family. She belonged to no social organizations. She seemed to have no hobbies other than her work. There seemed to be almost no record of her traveling for personal reasons. She had been a true loner in every sense of the word.

Kit went to the tiny kitchen and got another cup of coffee. As he stirred in his honey and cream, a thought hit him. On the day of her retirement, she took very calculated steps to get rid of her car and took an Uber to a motel where she did not register or stay. It was a well-planned and coordinated disappearance. She disappeared because she wanted to, and she did it well. Why would she need to disappear without a trace? Was she afraid of someone or something? She had no known relatives or friends and thus no likely places to hole up if she was hiding from someone.

Swifty sauntered into Kit's office unannounced as usual. "What is the big brain working on this time?" he asked as he noticed the papers and photos spread across Kit's normally clean desktop.

"We've got a new case, and it's a real puzzle," replied Kit.

"Puzzle?"

"Yep. This one is a puzzle, and I'm not sure where to start," said Kit.

"Explain, oh wise one."

Kit ignored Swifty's digs. It was just his way. He proceeded to give Swifty a summary of his visit with Mrs. Andropolous.

When Kit finished, Swifty took a long swig of coffee and then set his cup down on Kit's desk.

"Well?" asked Kit.

"When you don't know shit, you start where the story ended," said Swifty.

"So, go to Cheyenne?"

"Yup."

"It's a long damn drive," said Kit.

"It'll give us something to do," replied Swifty. "Keep us out of trouble."

"When do we go?" asked Kit.

"I ain't doin' nothin' now," responded Swifty.

Twenty minutes later they were in Kit's truck on their way down to Interstate 80 and a long road trip to Cheyenne.

They drove to Cheyenne on I-80. When they finally reached Cheyenne, Kit punched in the address of the motel from the report, and it led them to a small motel probably built in the late fifties. The motel was old and dated, but clean and freshly painted. Kit noticed several surveillance cameras as they approached the office.

A bell rang as they entered the small office. A counter running lengthwise split the room in half. Kit could see a door at the rear of the office that undoubtedly led to the living quarters of the owner or manager. The office was empty, but the doorway to the rear of the office suddenly opened and an older lady dressed in a cowboy shirt and jeans stepped out and greeted them.

"Howdy, boys," she said. "Do you need one room or two?"

"Actually, we don't need a room," said Kit, "just some information, please."

The lady, who wore a name plate proclaiming her to be Gertie, looked disappointed, but quickly hid it. "How can I help you?" she asked.

Kit gave her the thumbnail summary of why they were there and as soon as she heard about the missing lady major from the Air Force, she said, "I wasn't here that day. I normally wouldn't remember her, but someone else stopped in and asked about her some time ago." Then she turned and yelled back through the open door, "Jimmy, come out here."

Gertie smiled at Kit and Swifty and an older gentleman appeared through the door. He was balding, short, and a tad overweight, but his eyes were bright and attentive. He looked with some puzzlement at Kit and Swifty.

"Jimmy, these men have some questions about the day the lady major was dropped off in front of the motel. I was gone that day so I thought you might be able to better answer their questions," she said. With that Gertie quickly exited through the back door and closed it behind her.

"What can I do for you gents?" asked Jimmy as he tried to size up his large visitors.

"I noticed you have a small table with some chairs out front," said Kit. "Could we possibly move out there?"

Jimmy looked at Kit, looked at Swifty, and then he turned and looked at the door behind the counter his wife had disappeared through. You could almost see the light bulb go off in his head.

"Yes, of course," said Jimmy as he led the way out of the small office and onto the front patio where the metal chairs were.

As soon as all three men were seated, Jimmy leaned forward and whispered in a low tone, "Sorry I was slow on the uptake. My wife probably has her ear to that door. She likes to snoop on the guests."

Kit looked at Swifty and both men grinned. "We understand," said a consoling Swifty.

"What is it I can help you gents with?" asked Jimmy.

"I understand you were on duty at the office when an

Uber dropped off a woman from the Air Force Base about two years ago," said Kit.

"Oh yes. Yes, I was," said Jimmy, his voice rising slightly with excitement. "Biggest damn thing ever happened here."

"I know this was almost two years ago, but I wondered if you could tell us what you saw that day?" asked Kit.

"Are you guys reporters?" asked Jimmy.

"Nope," replied Swifty.

"Are you with the FBI or the Secret Service?"

"No, we're not," replied Kit. "We're private investigators hired by the woman's family."

"Oh, I see," said Jimmy. "Well, what do you want to know?"

"Just describe what you saw and heard that day," asked Kit.

"Well, it was a Wednesday," said Jimmy. "Wednesday is a slow day at the motel."

Both Kit and Swifty nodded but did not speak. They did not want to interrupt Jimmy and understood the story might come out slowly, but it would come out.

"I had finished cleaning the rooms," said Jimmy. "We only had five rooms rented, so it didn't take me long to clean them. I was in the office and was about to eat my lunch at the desk when I heard a car pull up outside the motel. I looked out and saw this black, late model Buick four-door sedan parked in front of the motel. A lady got out. She was older, maybe forty-five to fifty, and slim. She was wearing dark slacks and a white blouse. I noticed she was wearing white tennis shoes.

I got up and opened the office door and stood there, waiting to see if I could help her with her bags. She and

24

the driver unloaded about three suitcases. Two large ones and a small one. The suitcases were blue, I think. After the suitcases were unloaded and sitting on the sidewalk, she paid the driver and he drove off."

"Did you notice if she paid with a credit card or cash?" asked Kit.

"I'm quite sure she paid in cash because the driver tried to give her change and she waved him off. The driver left, but the lady just stood out there on the curb with her suitcases. Finally, I got tired of standing at the door and went back to the desk to eat my lunch," said Jimmy.

"What happened then?" asked Kit.

"The lady stood out there on the curb and made a call on her cell phone. Then she stood there for about fifteen minutes," said Jimmy. "I finished my lunch, and she was still standing out there. It usually takes me about fifteen minutes to eat my lunch. I usually have a cheese sandwich and a bottle of water, but that day I had a peanut butter and jelly sandwich. I have a bit of a problem with high blood sugar, so I can only eat jelly about once a week."

Kit and Swifty sat silently, not commenting on Jimmy's lunch. He looked a tad flustered, and then he continued his story.

"I heard a loud engine outside. I looked out the window and an old white van pulled up next to her and stopped. An old, bearded guy wearing a battered ball cap and large sunglasses got out and he said something to the lady, and she said something back. Then he helped her put the suitcases in the back of the van and both got in the truck. Then he drove off," said Jimmy.

"What make of van was it?" asked Kit.

"I'm not sure," said Jimmy. "Those vans all look alike to me."

"Did you see the license plate?" Kit asked.

"I did, but it was covered with dried mud, and I couldn't read it other than I know it was a Wyoming plate," replied Jimmy.

Kit and Swifty sat silently, as they chewed on what they had just learned from Jimmy.

"Do you have any surveillance cameras here at the motel?" asked Swifty.

"Oh, my, yes I do," said Jimmy. "The insurance company made a big fuss about it a few years ago and I did some research and got a really cool set of cameras. They record on a disk, and you can keep the recordings forever."

"Do the cameras cover the street in front of the motel?" asked Kit.

"They most certainly do," said Jimmy. "I put one out there so I could get the license plate of any car entering or leaving our lot or parking out in front."

"Can we see the disk with the day the woman was here?" asked Kit.

"Of course," replied Jimmy. "What day was it?"

Kit was quite sure Jimmy had that disk noted and set aside, but he played along and looked up the date from his notes and gave it to Jimmy. A guy like Jimmy would hang on to anything that had made him important, even if the moment was brief.

"You gents wait here, and I'll be right back," said Jimmy. He got to his feet and went back into the motel office. Five minutes later he was back with a laptop computer. He placed the laptop on the small patio table and opened it. Then he sat down and turned it on. Jimmy pushed some keys and then motioned for Kit and Swifty to join him where they could easily see the computer screen. The optics were excellent. The recording was in color and the three men watched as the Uber car pulled up, the lady got out and she and the driver removed the luggage. Then she made a call and stood on the curb. Jimmy moved the recording ahead about fifteen minutes. Then the old white van appeared, and the old man got out. He and the lady loaded the luggage in the van, and they drove off.

"Can we get a copy of this?" asked Kit.

"Give me your email address, and I'll send it to you right now," said Jimmy.

Kit gave him his email address and two minutes later he had a copy of the surveillance tape on his phone. Kit forwarded the video to his computer and saved it on his phone.

"How much do we owe you for the video?" asked Kit.

"Didn't cost me nothing, so you owe me nothing," said Jimmy.

"It's worth more than nothing to us," said Kit, and he opened his wallet and gave Jimmy a fifty-dollar bill.

Jimmy was still standing by the table speechless when Kit and Swifty drove off.

CHAPTER FOUR

Neither man spoke as they drove down the well-shaded street in Cheyenne. After about ten minutes, Kit broke the silence.

"What did you think of that?" he asked.

"I think I'm hungry," said Swifty.

"I meant about what Jimmy told us!" said an exasperated Kit.

"I'm hungry. Let's find someplace to eat," said Swifty.

Kit started to reply with a smart remark, but then stopped himself. Arguing with Swifty when he was hungry or thirsty was a waste of time. He knew that from years of experience.

Kit drove the truck out toward Happy Jack Road and soon pulled into the gravel parking lot of the Bunkhouse Saloon & Steakhouse. Kit smiled to himself as Swifty took in the exterior of the restaurant. It was rustic to the core with a genuine old West look to it.

Kit parked the truck, and the two men entered the relative quiet of an only partially filled restaurant. The hostess led them to a booth, gave them menus and disappeared.

Swifty had his head on a swivel as they walked to their

booth. When they were seated, he turned and looked to Kit. "This is more like it," said Swifty.

They glanced at the menu and when the waitress arrived, they both ordered country fried steak. Swifty added black coffee. Kit added a Dr. Pepper and the Bunkhouse Chef Salad. The waitress left them tall glasses of ice water which both men quickly sucked down.

"I had no idea I was so thirsty," said Swifty.

"Talking is thirsty work," replied Kit.

"Then old Jimmy must be bone dry," countered Swifty.

Both men burst out laughing. Their meal arrived in a few minutes and both men dug into their food. When they were finished, they each asked the waitress for a refill of their drinks as she cleared the dishes away. After she returned with their refills, Swifty took a long sip of hot coffee and sat back in his booth seat. He produced a toothpick from his shirt pocket and proceeded to clean his teeth.

Kit grimaced at the sight of Swifty operating on his molars.

"Am I upsetting your delicate stomach by exercising dental hygiene?" snickered Swifty.

Kit ignored his partner's attempt to get under his skin and pulled out his small notebook from his shirt pocket. He spent a few moments making notes, and then he looked up at Swifty.

"I jotted down some notes from our meeting with Jimmy," said Kit. "Let me hear what you took out of our meeting with him."

Swifty looked at Kit. Then he looked up at the ceiling for a few seconds. Then he took a sip of his coffee. Finally, he looked back at Kit. "Jimmy does not wear the pants in the family. He has an interest in electronic surveillance. He's bored. He has no sense of adventure, and he may just be a closet Democrat," Swifty carefully responded.

Kit waited a few seconds and then responded. "Anything else of note?" he asked.

Swifty looked up at the ceiling again, and then took another sip of coffee. He set his coffee cup down and looked straight at Kit. "This lady doc, this Doc. She spent a lot of time and thought about getting out of the air force. She spent most of that time trying to figure out how to disappear once she stepped off that Air Force Base. Why?"

"I think you just hit on the biggest question of all," said Kit. "Why?"

"Is there anything in that pile of papers you have on her that gives some kind of clue?" asked Swifty.

"Not a damn thing," replied Kit. "She had a good, but unremarkable career in the Air Force. I think I really need to see her service record."

"I think I know someone who can help us get a copy of that record," said Swifty.

"Do you have a secret subpoena hidden under your hat," said Kit. "Because without one, we are shit out of luck."

"Legally, you are correct," said Swifty.

"You have something illegal in mind?" asked Kit with a frown on his face. Kit was very straitlaced about staying within the legal limits of the law. Swifty thought of the law as a giant rubber band that could be stretched, bent, and rolled up into a ball.

"I'll need three hundred bucks in cash," said Swifty.

"For what?" asked an exasperated Kit.

"Secrets," said Swifty in a low whisper, as he put a finger up against his lips.

"I know I'll regret this," said Kit as he pulled out his wallet and slid three one hundred-dollar bills across the table to Swifty.

"Your regret will be short-lived," said Swifty with a grin as he pocketed the money.

"How soon can you get a copy of her service record?" asked Kit.

"Probably by supper time," said Swifty. He pulled out his cell phone and sent a text message, taking his time to punch out the right keys. When he had finished, he slipped his phone back into his pants pocket.

"Are you done?" asked Kit.

"Yep," replied Swifty.

"Then let's recap what we know," said Kit. "Our missing major waited on the sidewalk in front of the motel. A van pulled up. The van was old, white, dirty, and had no signs or markings on it. The license plates were covered in mud and were unreadable. The major tossed three suitcases into the van. Two suitcases were large, the other one was smaller. The windows were tinted and there is no good picture of the driver. We know he was old, bearded, and wore a baseball cap and sunglasses. Anything I left out?"

"I don't think so," said Swifty. "The lady wanted to disappear the day she retired from the Air Force, and she did. Again, the main question is why? Let's see if we can determine the make of the van. Pass me the photo."

Kit dug out the photo and handed it to Swifty. Swifty held the photo close to his eyes. He tried looking at it from several angles. Finally, he handed it back to Kit.

"Well?" asked Kit.

"I'm pretty sure it's an old Ford Econoline van," Swifty said. "I need a magnifying glass to be sure."

"I've got one back in my suitcase," said Kit. "Let's find a place to stay for the night and move on from there."

"Works for me," said Swifty.

Kit left money on the table for the bill and a good tip, and they headed out to the parking lot. Once in the truck, Kit took out his phone and found a decent motel. He logged the address into his truck navigation system, and they drove out of the parking lot.

Fifteen minutes later they pulled into the parking lot of Little America, an old motel chain created in Wyoming by a sheepherder who got caught in a snowstorm. Twelve minutes later they were in their room unpacking their bags.

Little America was an old motel, but it was well built, had large, comfortable rooms with spacious and updated bathrooms and offered conference rooms and computer suite services that were state of the art.

Kit signed for a double room, and they toted their gear from the truck. Twenty minutes later the only noise coming from their room was snoring.

⌁

Kit was up before sunrise. He showered and shaved and got dressed. He made a cup of coffee on the little coffee maker in the room.

In minutes, Kit had plugged in his laptop and a portable printer. Then Kit logged onto the hotel internet system, and he was banging away on the keyboard. When he was satisfied with his system, he turned in his chair to face Swifty who was lounging on an overstuffed easy chair studying the photos with a small magnifying glass.

"Well, what have you found?" asked Kit.

"It's a 1974 Ford Econoline van," replied Swifty.

"So, who's driving the van?" asked Kit.

"My guess is some guy who sells used trucks and cars out of the back of his trailer," responded Swifty.

"A used car guy?" asked Kit.

"I'll bet our gal made a deal with this guy to have him pick her up at the motel, then drive her to his place. Once there, she paid for an old used Ford or Chevy four-wheel drive pickup truck in cash, and then she drove off into the sunset," said Swifty.

"Why a pickup truck? Why not a sedan or an SUV?" asked Kit.

"This is Wyoming," responded Swifty. "In this state seventy-five percent of vehicles are pickup trucks. An old used four-wheel drive pickup is one of many in the state."

"The seller or dealer would have to have paperwork to sell her the truck," said Kit.

"Just a title," replied Swifty. "If the driver of the van is what I think, he or she sells a few vehicles a month, and asks no questions. The seller takes her money and signs the title over to her. She drives off with the title. Until she registers the truck under her name, no one, including the state of Wyoming has a clue who really owns the truck. She can set up a phony sale to one or two or several buyers, also phony, on the title and hold on to the truck. Then she can register the truck to herself under an assumed name. I'm guessing she bought the truck with a phony ID and that allowed her to disappear with no trace of either her or the truck."

"What about plates?" asked Kit.

"I'll bet the seller let her keep the plates that were on the truck, and she can drive it until they expire. Then she can get new plates, likely with a fake ID," said Swifty.

"What address does she use?" asked Kit.

"Bingo, partner," said Swifty. "She needs an address to receive the renewal form from the state. My guess is a P.O. Box number under another phony name."

Kit walked over to the window and stared out at the almost empty parking lot. After few minutes he turned and looked at Swifty. "Where does that leave us?" he asked. "She did a slick job of disappearing, and we've got squat to go on."

"Maybe yes and maybe no," said Swifty.

"What the hell does that mean?" asked an annoyed Kit.

"It means I bet she bought the truck online," said Swifty.

"How does that help us?" asked Kit.

"Maybe that's what the seller does. He sells cars online. I bet he must be local. Let's get some food in me and I'll look," replied Swifty.

Kit grabbed his laptop and they headed for their truck. They drove to a small diner and found a booth in the back. A waitress brought them water and took their order. As soon as she was out of earshot, Kit opened his laptop and spooled it up. He began to search on eBay and other online selling sites like Craigs List. Kit pulled his small notebook out of his shirt pocket and produced a pen. Soon he was writing down names and phone numbers.

Their food came and while he ate, Kit began to write down names and phone numbers and email addresses. When they finished eating, Kit closed his laptop, left cash on the table for the bill and a tip, and they drove back to Little America.

Once in their room, Kit took out the photo of the van and used the small magnifying glass to study it. He saw Swifty had been correct. It was a 1974 Ford Econoline van. He pulled up photos on his laptop of old Ford vans and there was no doubt it was a 1974 Econoline. He emailed and old Friend, Sheriff Wade Nystrom in Sheridan, Wyoming. Then he waited.

Thirty-two minutes later he got a response. Kit opened the attachment and smiled. Then he woke up the printer and printed out a page of information. He pulled the page out of the printer and studied it. It was a list of nine names and addresses with phone numbers.

"What the hell is that?" said Swifty, pointing to the paper in Kit's hand.

"A list," replied Kit.

"A list of what?" asked Swifty.

"I asked Sheriff Nystrom to do a search of the motor vehicle department's records and let me know how many 1974 white Ford Econoline vans were licensed in the state of Wyoming and in Laramie County. He did a search and sent me the list," responded Kit.

"Is that legal?" asked Swifty.

"You asking if something is legal is a first for you," replied Kit with a sly grin on his face.

"What do we do with the list?" asked Swifty.

"We go prospecting," said Kit.

Kit took out his cell phone and started calling the names on the list. When he got an answer, he asked if they had a used pickup truck for sale. He got answers from four of the nine numbers on his list and none of them had any trucks for sale. He left messages on the other five numbers with his name and cell phone number.

He pulled up a map of Cheyenne online and then printed it out on his portable printer. He studied the addresses of the five phones he left a message on. When he located them on the printed map, he put a small X by the spot on the map where they were located.

"Now what are you doing?" asked Swifty.

"I'm locating where the five van owners in town are located." said Kit.

Swifty looked at the marked-up map. The five locations were spread over most of Cheyenne.

"Let's go," said Kit as he headed for the door. "Bring the map."

Swifty gave him a look of derision, picked up the map and followed Kit out the door.

CHAPTER FIVE

The first address on the list was a small, older home about a mile from the motel. It was a bungalow, not in the best repair. The yard was weedy and untended. They went to the front of the house and rang the doorbell. There was no answer. Kit rang the bell again. He could hear it almost echoing through the house. Swifty peeked through the front window and saw no lights or any sign of life.

"Strike one," said Swifty. Kit nodded his agreement, and they returned to the truck. They drove to the next address which was about three miles away. Kit noted they were now in a nice neighborhood with larger, attractive homes with well-tended lawns.

Kit found the address, and they parked in front of an attractive, brick, two-story colonial style house. There were no cars parked on the street. They walked up to the front door and rang the doorbell. No one answered the door. Kit rang it again, and they waited for a few minutes. All they heard from the house was silence. They peeked through a garage window, but the space was empty of any vehicles. They retreated to the truck and drove to the next address on the map.

The third house was in a less expensive neighborhood,

but the houses in general were well cared for. The house was an older, brick ranch house. There was an old VW Bug parked in front of it. Again, they moved to the front door and rang the doorbell. This time the door opened, and a young teenage girl stood in front of them. Loud hard rock music playing inside in the house filled the doorway with noise. Kit asked her about a car for sale. She looked at him like he was an invader from Mars. She was clueless. They retreated to the truck.

They drove to the fourth address on the map. This time the house was an old, plain bungalow and was showing its age and a lack of care by the owner. A chain link fence surrounded the house. Attached to the fence was a large sign, "Beware of Dog."

Swifty opened the gate to the yard and stood there for a minute. Nothing happened. Then he slammed the gate shut, making a loud noise in the process. Again, he waited. Again, he was met with silence.

Swifty turned and looked at Kit. "I think the dog is on strike," he said.

The two men walked up to the front door and rang the doorbell. They were met with silence. They walked over to the detached double car garage. Inside was an older Toyota sedan that had seen better days. They returned to the truck and headed for the final address. They drove to the outskirts of Cheyenne. The further they drove the more rundown the houses became. They had entered a place that was a bad neighborhood. Rundown homes, lawns full of uncut weeds, houses in need of paint, roofs lacking shingles. Their final address was for a small, run-down bungalow, with a chain link fence surrounding the property. The lot was on a corner with another driveway and a gate leading behind the house. They walked over to the gate. From there they could see a large metal building behind the house. There were four old junker vehicles parked in front of the metal building.

"I think we have a winner," said Swifty.

"We'll see," replied Kit.

"What now, Big Chief?" asked Swifty.

"We go get some food, take a nap, and come back about six tonight," said Kit.

"OK, Kemosabe," said Swift with an accompanying grunt.

They walked back to the truck and left as quietly as they had arrived.

At six P.M. they returned. An older pickup truck was in the driveway. It was old, but in good shape for a twenty-year truck.

"Nice lookin' old GMC," remarked Swifty.

"You gonna buy it?" asked Kit.

"Why the hell would I buy that rollin' piece of trash?" asked Swifty.

"With you, I'm never sure what might happen," replied Kit.

They parked the truck in front of the house and walked up to the front door. Kit rang the doorbell. They heard heavy footsteps on a wooden or stone floor. The front door opened, and they were face to face with an old white-haired, bearded man who looked to be in his seventies.

"Howdy," said the old man.

"Howdy," replied Kit. "A friend of ours said you might have a vehicle for sale."

"I might," replied the old man as he looked at Kit and Swifty with more curiosity than apprehension. "What specifically are you boys lookin' for?"

"We were led to believe you might have a 1974 Ford Econoline van for sale," said Kit.

"Yup, I sure do," said the old man. "You wanna buy it?"

"Can we have a look at it," said Kit.

"Sure can," said the old man. "Follow me to my shop in the back." He came out the door and led them around the side of the house and to the metal building behind it.

The old man, who finally introduced himself as Earl, produced a key and unlocked one of the two garage doors. Then he manually lifted the door up and out of their way. Earl stepped inside and hit a light switch. There in front of them is a white, 1974 Ford Econoline van. Kit looked at the rear license plate. It is still splattered with mud and unreadable.

Swifty walked around the van and noted the tinted windows. When he completes a full circuit of the old van, he nodded to Kit.

"Earl," said Kit. "What's your last name?"

"Pease," said Earl. "Like please but without the L."

"Mr. Pease," said Kit. "We're private investigators, and we believe both you and this van have been involved in a criminal activity."

"What?" said Earl in surprise as he began to wobble on his feet, and Swifty grabbed him by the arm to prevent him from falling over.

"I think you better sit down so we can talk," said Kit.

He and Swifty led Earl over to the side of the building where there was an old bench, and they got Earl safely seated.

Once Earl had recovered from his shock, Kit carefully explained why he and Swifty were there, and why they needed the details of his interaction with Major DeSantis. He showed Earl the photo of the white 1974 Ford Econoline van, including one with the muddy license plate.

"The license plate is muddy, and it hadn't rained in Cheyenne for almost three weeks," said Swifty. "We checked the weather reports back then. We don't believe in coincidences."

"All we want from you is what happened to Major DeSantis," said Kit. "Tell us what happened, and we'll leave and never come back. Tell us the truth, and you'll be in no trouble with the law or anyone else."

Earl looked at both Kit and Swifty. He seemed to regain his composure and then he began to talk. He told them he got hired by a woman over the phone. She hired him to pick her up in front of the old motel at a specific time on a specific date. She told him to cover his license plates, so he used mud.

"Mud's cheap," said Earl.

"She had contacted him online to buy a used truck. She bought a 1972 Ford F-250 ¾ ton pickup truck with 140,000 miles on it. It was a diesel, one of them rare 7.3-liter jobs. It can pull a damn semi-trailer truck easily," Earl said. "After I picked her up at the motel, I drove her here and she gave me cash for the truck. I signed the title over to her and gave her the keys. She had asked to leave the old license plates on it, so I did. They had about six months left on them before they expired."

"What kind of shape was the truck in?" asked Kit. "Any issues?"

"Not that I could tell," said Earl. "Course, it's an old diesel truck. That diesel is damn near bullet proof, but other stuff like wheel bearings, brakes, and electronics are always suspect when they get that old."

"Do you have a copy of the bill of sale?" asked Kit.

"Sure do," said Earl. "I'll fetch it." He got to his feet and walked over to a battered steel filing cabinet and after a couple of minutes he produced a bill of sale. Kit had him place the bill of sale on top of the filing cabinet, and he took a picture of it with his cell phone. The bill of sale reflected a sale price of $6,000, and the buyer was listed as Jane Doe. She paid Earl $200 in cash to pick her up at the motel.

"Do you have any more information on her?" asked Kit. "Like an address or a cell phone number."

"Nope," said Earl. "I don't."

Kit thanked Earl for his help, and he and Swifty walked to their truck.

"Think he's telling the truth?" Kit asked.

"He's an old man trying to make a living," said Swifty. "He's got no reason to lie to us."

Kit fired up the truck, and they drove to downtown Cheyenne. Kit parked the truck, and they walked two blocks to Wyoming's Rib and Chop House.

"Did you inherit some money?" asked Swifty as they entered the restaurant.

"What are you talking about?" asked a surprised Kit.

"Usually, you treat me to a meal at some run-down slop chute where you have to eat with your back to the wall," replied a grinning Swifty.

Kit just shook his head in amazement.

They followed the hostess as she led them to their table.

Both men ordered steak dinners and cold beers. After the waitress left, Kit looked around the dining room. It was half full and more people were coming in.

"Looks like we got here just in time," said Kit.

"As long as you're payin', any time is fine with me," responded Swifty.

The waitress returned with their drinks, and each of them took a long drink of cold beer.

"What do we do next?" asked Swifty.

"First we summarize where we are," said Kit. "We have her name. We have the make, year, model, color, and vehicle identification number of her truck. She has probably gotten new license plates since the expiration date of the old plates on the truck have long expired. She would have had to get new plates and registration for the truck, plus she has to also have at least a liability insurance policy on the truck."

"Maybe not," said Swifty. "It's possible she's someplace so remote nobody checks or cares if the plates are current," said Swifty. "This is Wyoming, after all."

"I'll email Sheriff Nystrom and send him a photo of the old plates and the information from the truck's registration," said Kit. "Maybe we'll get lucky."

"That'll be the day," said Swifty as he took another swig of his beer.

CHAPTER SIX

Once they had returned to their motel room, Kit sent a text to Sheriff Nystrom with his request for information. He added the information they had learned from old Earl.

"Now what?" asked Swifty.

"You were in the army, right?" asked Kit.

"Yeah," replied Swifty with a puzzled look on his face.

"We hurry up and wait," responded Kit with a smirk on his face.

"That's about as funny as listening to a politician make a promise," snorted Swifty.

Kit tried to do some research on his laptop and added what they had learned to his stored notes. Swifty propped himself up on one bed and watched television. After about an hour, Kit snapped his laptop shut and looked over at Swifty.

"We're missing something in this deal," said Kit.

"Other than some sleep, I don't have a clue what you're talking about," retorted Swifty.

"We know the Major planned this entire disappearance and then carried it out like clockwork on the day she retired from the Air Force," said Kit.

"So?" asked Swifty.

"We know how she disappeared, but we don't know where she disappeared to."

"What's your point?" asked Swifty.

"The big question is why did she go to all this trouble to disappear?" said Kit. "She was retiring from the Air Force with a good pension. She had no living relatives she knew of. She had no close friends we are aware of, and she was in no trouble we are aware of, so why did she go to all this planning and intrigue to try to vanish?"

The room was silent as each of them processed the information again. Swifty had turned off the television and intense quiet seemed to settle on their hotel room like a foggy blanket.

"Let's think about the obvious reasons people have done what she did," said Kit.

"Most people I am aware of who have tried to disappear were running from the law, running from creditors, or trying to ditch a wife or girlfriend they were sick of," said Swifty.

Kit pulled out a pad and wrote down each of the items Swifty had mentioned.

"Can you think of anything else?" Kit asked.

"Well, I thought of some people who have tried to disappear because they were aware someone was trying to kill them," said Swifty.

Kit wrote the new item on his list.

"Anything else you can think of?"

"People who are just plain nuts?" posed Swifty.

"Doubtful, but I'll add it to the list," said Kit.

"I'm all out of ideas," said Swifty.

"Let's go over each reason we have on the list," suggested Kit.

45

"Fire away," said a bored Swifty.

"First is running from the law," said Kit. "I'm not aware of anything she did wrong or any incident of her breaking the law that would trigger such a scheme."

"Scratch that off the list," said Swifty.

"Second is running from creditors," said Kit. He reached into the file and pulled out a sheaf of papers. "This is her latest credit report I got from our client. Her credit is spotless."

"Scratch bad credit off the list," said Swifty.

"She was never married and according to this report from the private eye our client hired, she had no on-going relationships with either men or women," noted Kit.

"Three strikes and she's out," snorted Swifty.

"That leaves running from someone who was trying to kill or hurt her," said Kit.

"Doubt that," said Swifty.

"Why?" asked Kit.

"This broad led one of the most boring lives I've ever read about. She had no close friends, no living relatives she knew of, and she never even got a traffic ticket. How much more boring can you get?" asked Swifty.

Kit sat still without moving a muscle as he analyzed what Swifty had just said.

"I think you just hit the nail on the head," said Kit.

"I did? What the hell did I hit?" asked Swifty.

"You just related how boring her life has been. Which is an absolute contradiction to her behavior in planning and carrying out her own disappearance on the day she retired from the Air Force," replied Kit.

"You just lost me," said Swifty.

"Why would you go to all this trouble to disappear from the Air Force on the day you retire unless you were afraid of something or someone?" asked Kit.

"What the hell could she have been afraid of?" asked Swifty. "The woman didn't even have friends, let alone enemies."

"Let's think about that," said Kit. "She was a medical officer in the Air Force. She was stationed for the last five years of her twenty-year enlistment on a remote Air Force base in Cheyenne, Wyoming. What could possibly happen on that base that could create a threat to her life?"

Swifty was now standing. Kit had finally aroused his curiosity. Swifty started to walk toward the door when he paused and turned to face Kit.

"She either saw something she was not supposed to see, or she has knowledge of something she is not supposed to know about," said Swifty.

"Like what?" asked Kit.

"I got no idea, but let's say someone in the Air Force decided to do something that's not lawful or not allowed by the military code of conduct and she saw it, or she found out about it. Maybe she has some kind of physical evidence to support what she saw," said a now profoundly serious Swifty. "Maybe something that happened recently, or something that happened when she first got to Warren Air Force Base. Maybe she was ordered to do something illegal and then sworn to secrecy," said Swifty.

"What kind of illegal activity?" asked Kit.

"I got no idea," said Swifty. "Whatever it was, she could be controlled while she was in the Air Force, but when she got out, that control would be lost and if what she knew was

47

truly damaging, it's quite possible there was a plan to silence her permanently with some kind of accident."

"You sure you haven't been watching too many old movies on television?" asked a skeptical Kit.

"Hey, you asked for a theory, and I just gave you one," said Swifty. "Take it or leave it, makes no difference to me."

Swifty plopped down on his bed and put his hands behind his head.

The next five minutes were filled with silence as Kit thought over what Swifty had just suggested.

"I think we're beating this part of the theory to death, and we need to move on," said Kit. "Let us agree she saw or knew something, and she was in fear of her life once she was out of the Air Force. Let us further agree she took steps to disappear from Cheyenne. What does she do then? Where does she go? How does she stay hidden?"

"I need a nap," said Swifty and he put his feet up on the bed and was soon sawing logs.

Kit tried to concentrate on his thoughts, but soon stretched out on his bed and joined Swifty in turning logs into lumber.

CHAPTER SEVEN

Kit woke up about ninety minutes later to Swifty's loud and insistent snoring. He went into the bathroom and ran cold water over a washcloth and then after squeezing the cloth relatively dry, he used the cold cloth over his face and eyes. He was immediately wide awake. He returned to the bedroom and turned on his laptop. He had a message from Sheriff Nystrom.

"Got my IT guy working on the truck angle. Might take a bit of time, but I'll get back to you. Wade."

No progress, but at least something was in motion. Some progress was better than none. Kit got undressed and slipped under the covers of his bed. He left Swifty in his chair with his feet on his bed as Swifty hit new highs or lows, depending on whether you were listening or not to his snoring.

The next morning, Swifty awoke finding himself wrapped in his own clothes and feeling like he had slept on a hard, awkward chair. Which in fact was a bed with a stiff mattress. He woke up about two in the morning in an uncomfortable chair and moved to the uncomfortable bed. He rubbed his eyes and saw Kit, obviously showered and shaved and dressed in fresh clothes, sitting at the desk working on his laptop.

Swifty slowly sat up in the bed. "Ouch," he said as he struggled to get to his feet. "I feel like I was rode hard and put away wet," he said.

Kit ignored him.

Now finally on his feet, Swifty managed to make his way to the bathroom. When he returned, he confronted Kit. "My mouth feels like the bottom of a feed lot," he muttered.

"Sorry, Swifty. I can't hear a word you're sayin' 'cause you are mumbling so much," said Kit brightly.

"Bite me," snarled Swifty. He headed to the bathroom again and didn't return for another fifteen minutes. When he did, he was clean, sober, and not a happy camper.

Kit checked them out of Little America, and they headed for the restaurant. Kit in search of breakfast and Swifty in search of lots of hot black coffee.

After Swifty had inhaled two cups of steaming hot black coffee and was starting on his third, Kit decided he was cogent enough for a brief conversation.

"It occurs to me we may be done here in Cheyenne," said Kit.

Swifty looked hard at Kit, blinked his eyes, and did not respond.

"I think we should head back to Kemmerer and come up with a plan."

Swifty grunted something unintelligible, and Kit took that for agreement. He paid the check, left a tip, and they exited the restaurant.

Fifteen minutes later they were refueled and headed west on Interstate 80.

Swifty didn't have much to say on the return trip to Kemmerer. Mainly because he slept most of the way, slouched down in his seat, with his cowboy hat pulled down over his eyes.

Kit stopped at the original Little America outpost on Interstate 80 just east of the Kemmerer exit to refuel and use the restrooms. Swifty woke up and joined Kit for the trip to relieve their bladders. As Kit paid for the gas, Swifty bought a can of cold Red Bull.

Once they were back in the cab of the truck, Kit pointed at the can and asked, "Why that?"

"I heard this crap is a good energy drink and not bad when you've got a hangover and a so-called friend who keeps wanting to talk when your brain is still in neutral," retorted Swifty.

"I see," said Kit as he started the truck and they pulled out of the Little American complex and headed to Kemmerer.

Swifty popped the top of the drink can and drained the contents in what appeared to be one swallow.

"I'd ask how it tasted, but I don't think your taste buds got a chance to register it as it roared past them," said Kit.

Swifty looked over at Kit, paused, and then emitted a loud belch. Then he smiled, slumped back in his seat and pulled his hat back over his eyes.

Forty-five minutes later they were on the outskirts of Kemmerer. Kit drove to the old bank building that served as his office and pulled into the new attached garage. The two men unloaded the truck and headed into the building.

Once inside, Kit dropped his gear at the foot of the

stairs that led to his upstairs apartment and headed for the front door.

"Where the hell are you going?" asked a surprised Swifty.

"I'm headed over to Harrison Woodley's law office," replied Kit.

"Who's suing you now?" asked Swifty.

"Nobody," replied Kit. "I just got a few questions he might be able to help me with."

"Knock yourself out," responded Swifty as he toted his gear out to his pickup truck.

Kit walked two blocks to Woody's office. When he opened the door to the law office, he was met with a surprise. Woody's old matronly legal secretary was gone. In her place was a young blonde woman he had never seen before.

She looked up at Kit and then politely asked, "May I help you, sir?"

Kit quickly overcame his confusion and replied, "I'm here to see Woody."

"Do you have an appointment?" the little blonde asked.

Kit glanced down at her desktop and saw the name plate announcing her as "Mary Fetterman." When he saw the name, he recognized the last name, but not as one he associated with anyone he knew.

"Is something wrong, sir?" Mary asked.

"No, nothing is wrong," answered Kit. "It's just a combination of surprises."

"Surprises?" she asked.

"Yes, surprises," said Kit.

"What kind of surprises?" Mary asked.

"Well, for starters, I didn't know Woody had hired a

new legal assistant," said Kit. "What happened to his old secretary?"

"She retired and Mr. Woodly hired me," replied a smiling Mary.

"Oh, I see," said a confused Kit, who obviously wasn't quite sure what he saw.

"Do you still want to see Mr. Woodly?" asked a still polite Mary.

"Yes. Yes, I do," stammered Kit. "My name is Carson, Carson Andrews, but folks call me Kit."

"Of course, Mr. Kit," replied Mary. "I'll let him know you are here." She lifted the phone, hit a button and spoke so softly into the receiver Kit couldn't hear a word she was saying.

"He said to go right in, Mr. Kit," said Mary.

"Thank you. Thank you very much," Kit managed to get out and headed past her to Woody's office.

Kit opened the office door and immediately saw Woody seated behind his large and very battered desk, which was piled high with papers and books.

"Kit, my boy," said Woody. "How are you, and what brings you to my humble office on such a nice day?"

Kit stepped forward and shook Woody's hand, then sat down in one of the two large leather chairs Woody indicated as he came from behind his desk. Once they were seated, Woody looked straight at Kit and said, "What's up?"

Kit proceeded to give Woody the bare details of his new case and new client. When he was finished, Woody said, "How can I help you?"

"I'm not real sure where this lady major physician's assistant went or why, but I need to find her to find out why.

If she just retired from the air force, what would she need to do to get licensed as a physician's assistant in Wyoming?" asked Kit.

"If she was stationed in Wyoming when she retired, not very much," said Woody. "Her military status as a PA would be enough to get a license granted promptly. She would need copies of her military medical certification and copies of her education and training certificates and a check for the required license fee."

"So, it's not like a doctor's license?" asked Kit.

"It sort of is, but it's a lot shorter and quicker," said Woody.

"But she'd still have to produce all the necessary paperwork?" asked Kit.

"Of course," said Woody.

"How long would the process take?" asked Kit.

"We're so desperate for certified medical people in Wyoming, especially in the most rural areas, the state would likely hand carry it through as fast as humanly possible," replied Woody. "As things stand today, they wouldn't want to give her time to rethink things and go to another state."

"I see," said a somewhat surprised Kit.

"Anything else?" asked Woody.

"Nope, that was it," said Kit. "Thanks, Woody."

"Anytime," said a smiling Woody.

As Kit reached the office door, Woody spoke. "What did you think?"

Kit turned at the door and looked back to Woody. "Think of what?" he asked.

"My new legal assistant," said a grinning Woody.

"She seems to be very nice," stammered out a surprised Kit.

"Actually, I thought you came in here just to check her out," said Woody.

"I didn't even know she was here," pleaded Kit.

"Right," said a grinning Woody, and he turned and walked back to his desk.

Kit shrugged his shoulders and walked out to the front door. As he passed by her desk, Mary smiled and said, "Goodbye, Mr. Kit."

Kit nodded his head and exited the law office as fast as he could.

CHAPTER EIGHT

When Kit walked into his office, he could see Swifty, sitting in Kit's chair, with his boots up on Kit's desk. When he noticed Kit, he didn't bother to remove his boots from the highly polished desk. He just swiveled in the chair to look directly at Kit.

"Where the hell have you been, Mr. Big Shot?" asked Swifty.

"What the hell are you doing in my chair?" retorted Kit.

Swifty leaned forward and stared hard at Kit. "You look a little flushed and red in the face. Did you make a fool of yourself in public again?"

Kit blushed. He tried not to, but he couldn't help himself.

"Aha, you did make a fool of yourself," crowed Swifty.

"You still haven't explained what you are doing sitting in my chair with your damned boots up on my desk," said Kit.

"Oh, that," said Swifty as he slowly removed his boots from the top of Kit's desk and sat up straight in Kit's chair. "The reason I'm in your office is we got a hit from your inquiry with Sheriff Nystrom, and I've been waiting patiently for your return so we can follow up on it."

"What's the tip?" asked Kit suspiciously.

"Oh, it's a real tip, partner, and we need to move now," replied Swifty.

"I repeat. What's the tip?" Kit asked again.

"According to Sheriff Nystrom the Ford F-250 pickup our fugitive bought in Cheyenne was sold to a young guy in Cokeville about two months after our gal disappeared from Cheyenne," said a smug Swifty.

"Cokeville?" exclaimed Kit. "That's in our damn backyard."

"Well, not exactly," said Swifty. "According to my map it's a total of 45 miles from here. That seems a little farther than my back yard."

"You got a name and address and phone number for this jasper?" asked Kit.

"Does a bear poop in the woods?" replied a grinning Swifty.

"So, why are we standing in my office jawin'?" asked Kit.

"Hey, I bin the one waitin' on you, wonder boy," said Swifty.

"Let's go," said Kit and the two men left the building, and three minutes later Kit's pickup truck was headed west out of Kemmerer.

Highway 30 took them twenty-five miles west and then turned abruptly north for nineteen miles to Cokeville. It should have taken them about forty-five minutes, but Kit managed to reach the outskirts of Cokeville in just under forty minutes. The highway was good and straight and there was almost no traffic. Cokeville was a town with a population of 506, but that probably included a few cats and dogs. It was a small ranching town right next to the Idaho border. In fact, Montpelier, Idaho was only twenty-five miles from Cokeville and as a town of about 2,800 friendly folks. It was about the same size as Kemmerer and a lot closer to Cokeville. Montpelier was famous for having their bank robbed in 1896 by Butch Cassidy and his gang. After the robbery, one of the gang had been wounded and the gang left him, with his share of the bank loot, in a cave near Kemmerer. When he first came to Kemmerer, Kit had discovered the cave by accident.

"Pull in there," said Swifty and Kit pulled into the Flying J truck stop. Kit gassed up his truck, while Swifty went inside. Kit used a credit card to pay at the pump and just as he was finishing up, Swifty came out of the truck stop.

"I think I found our boy," said Swifty.

"Where?" asked Kit.

"The gal at the cash register said he usually eats lunch at the Country Market down the street," replied Swifty.

"How in the hell would she know that?" asked Kit.

"There's only about five hundred people in this burg," said Swifty. "And they're all Mormons and go to the same church. Everybody knows everybody as well as what they're doin'."

Kit just looked at Swifty and shook his head.

The two men climbed in the truck and Kit drove to the restaurant and parked. Both men walked up to the front door.

"How do we know which one is him?" asked Kit.

"We ask the hostess or the cashier or whoever is handy," said Swifty. "In a town this size everyone knows everyone."

"I didn't see the truck in the parking lot," said Kit.

"This town is about three blocks long," said Swifty. "He probably walked here like most of the customers inside."

"How do you want to play this?" asked Kit as they hesitated before entering the restaurant.

"Let me ask around and if he's here, we'll politely introduce ourselves," said a grinning Swifty.

They entered the crowded restaurant and Swifty walked up to the lady behind the cash register. "Morning, Miss," he said. "I hate to bother you, but I was told I might find a Ned Curry having lunch in here. Do you know Mr. Curry?"

The cashier, an older lady in her sixties, smiled at Swifty and said, "Goodness gracious, I most certainly do know Ned. I've known that boy since he was in kindergarten. He's that skinny blonde boy sitting at the small table in the back of the dining room." She then pointed a long bony finger directly at the hapless Mr. Curry. Ned was sitting at a small table with another young man, both dressed in bib overalls that had seen better days and apparently had no recent contact with a washing machine.

Swifty led the way to their table. When he reached them, he stopped and addressed young Curry. "Mr. Curry, I'm Swifty Olson of Rocky Mountain Searchers in Kemmerer. I wonder if we might have a private moment with you?"

Young Ned was so surprised, he had trouble getting out an answer and finally he said, "Sure, how can I help you?"

"I just have a couple of questions and then we'll get out of your hair and let you finish your lunch," said a smiling Swifty.

"Sure," said Ned.

"I understand you bought a Ford F-250 with a 7.3-liter diesel engine," said Swifty.

"Yep, sure did," said Ned. "I bought it a while back. It's kind of old, but that big diesel can pull anything."

"Do you remember exactly when was a while back?" asked Swifty.

Ned paused and scratched on his right ear. "I think it was about fifteen or eighteen months ago, but I ain't sure," he said.

"How did you happen to hear about it being for sale?" asked Swifty.

"There was a card on the bulletin board at the truck stop," said Ned.

"Do you remember what was printed on the card?" asked Swifty.

"It listed the details on the truck. It had the price and a phone number to call," said Ned.

"So, you called the number?" asked Swifty.

"Sure did," replied Ned.

"Do you remember who you talked to on the phone?" asked Swifty.

"I ain't sure about that," said Ned. "It was a while ago."

"Was it a man or a woman?" asked Swifty.

"It was a lady, I do remember that, but I don't remember her name," responded Ned.

"Did you meet up with this lady to see the truck?" asked Swifty.

"I did," replied Ned.

"Where did you meet?" asked Swifty.

"She drove it to the truck stop here in Cokeville," replied Ned. "I believe she asked to meet me after work, which was about 5:15. We agreed on that time because I work till five at the shop."

"So, you met this lady at the truck stop," said Swifty. "Can you remember what she looked like?"

Ned paused, as if in thought. Then he looked up and said, "She was older, kind of like my mom. She was wearing jeans and cowboy boots. They were nice boots," he said.

"Do you remember her hair color, eye color, her height, her weight, anything like that?" asked Swifty.

Ned scrunched up his face as though he was trying hard to remember something lost in space. Then he shook his head and said, "No sir, I can't say as I do. I was so excited about the truck I guess I didn't pay much attention to the lady."

Swifty paused, as he was out of questions.

"How much did you pay for the truck, Ned?" asked Kit.

"I paid seven hundred dollars," said Ned.

"Was it a check or cash?" asked Kit.

"Cash, 'cause she wouldn't take no checks," replied Ned.

"Did you happen to see what kind of truck or car she got in after she sold you the truck?" asked Kit.

"No sir, I can't," said Ned. "After she signed the title and handed it over, I just couldn't wait to get in my new truck. I never paid attention to anything else, and I don't remember even seeing her after that."

"Can you remember anything else about the lady who sold you the truck?" asked Kit.

Ned thought for a minute and then shook his head. "No sir, I'm sorry, but I just don't remember," he said.

"Thanks for your time and your help, Ned," said Kit. Then he took out his wallet and gave Ned a business card and a twenty-dollar bill. "The cash is for your lunch and please keep the card and call me if you think of anything else."

"Yes, sir," replied Ned as he pocketed the twenty.

"Thanks for your help," said Swifty and he and Kit exited the restaurant and headed for their truck.

Once they were in Kit's truck, Swifty snorted in disgust and leaned back in the passenger seat. "That was a waste of time," he said.

"Yes and no," responded Kit. "We learned some things today."

"I'll bite. What did we learn, oh wise one?" said Swifty.

"We learned she sold the old Ford F-250 about a year and a half ago. We learned she sold it here in Cokeville and she came here to close the deal. We learned he bought it about a year and a half ago. We learned he bought it from an older lady. We learned she sold it for seven hundred in cash," said Kit.

"How does that help us?" asked Swifty.

Kit took the small notebook out of his shirt pocket and opened it to a blank page. Then he grabbed a pen out of the truck console and began to write. He wrote for about five minutes, and then he put the pen away and turned to face Swifty.

"First item," said Kit. "Based on when she sold the truck, it would appear she drove the truck somewhere around here and found a hiding place. She sold it shortly after we know she left Cheyenne.

Second item. She used a bulletin board in a busy truck stop in Cokeville to post the truck for sale. She didn't use the internet or a classified ad. I think she did so because

Cokeville was close to where she is living, but far enough away to be a neutral site where she is not known.

Third item. She showed up at the truck stop with the truck and sold it to the kid for seven hundred dollars in cash," said Kit.

"What's so odd about that?" asked Swifty.

"How did she leave?" asked Kit. "She had to drive the truck here. How did she get back to wherever she was hiding? She had some help. Someone came with her in another vehicle and gave her a ride back to where she came from."

"Wait," said Swifty. "Didn't she post the truck for sale on the bulletin board in the truck stop. The kid said it had her phone number on it."

"I'm pretty sure she went into the truck stop before the kid showed up and removed the ad from the bulletin board," said Kit.

"What if you're wrong?" asked Swifty.

"You're welcome to check," said Kit. With that, he fired up the engine and drove to the truck stop and parked the truck. "Help yourself," said Kit with a grin on his face.

Swifty exited the truck and walked into the truck stop. Five minutes later he came out and climbed back into the passenger seat of the truck.

"Well?" asked Kit.

"Shut up," said a disgusted Swifty.

Kit grinned and pulled his small notebook out of his pocket. "Now, where were we?" he asked. "Charlemagne sold her truck, so she had to buy transportation of some kind," said Kit. "There is no reliable public transportation in Lincoln County, unless you include the school busses."

"What would she buy and where would she buy it?" asked Swifty.

"Odds are she bought a pickup truck with four-wheel drive," replied Kit. "Where she bought it, I have no idea."

"So, what do we know now we didn't know before?" asked a puzzled looking Swifty.

Kit thought for a minute before he replied to Swifty's question.

"We know it's more than likely she lives within a hundred miles or less from Cokeville," said Kit. "She could live in Idaho or Wyoming. If it's Idaho, she likely lives in or near Montpelier. If it's Wyoming, my guess is she is living somewhere in Star Valley in Lincoln County."

"We know she has worked hard to cover her tracks since she left the Air Force base in Cheyenne. I'm betting she thinks she has done a good job of disappearing," said Kit.

"Won't get no argument from me on that point," said Swifty.

"That reminds me," said Kit, "Did you ever get any information from your secret source on where the Air Force is sending her retirement checks?"

"I did and forgot to mention it," said Swifty. "Her checks are directly deposited into a bank account at Bank of America in California."

"Does her account have a mailing address?" asked Kit.

"Nope. Her statements and correspondence go to her by email. She shows no evidence of a physical location," said Swifty.

"But wouldn't Bank of America have statements which show where she is using a debit card or using a check?" asked Kit.

"I'm sure they do, but that information is secure unless you have a court order which I'm pretty sure we ain't got," retorted Swifty.

Kit took out his phone and typed out a text and then put the phone back in his pocket.

"What was that all about?" asked Swifty.

"I texted Sheriff Nystrom to see if he had managed to get access to the state records on auto registration on the Ford F-250," said Kit. "Maybe we can unearth a name for Miss Charlemagne."

"What do we do now, oh wise leader," asked Swifty in a sarcastic tone.

"We use the process of elimination," said Kit.

"I don't think shooting people is gonna help find this Charlemagne gal," said Swifty.

"Elimination of possibilities, not people, you idiot," said Kit.

"Just testing to see if you still had a small spark of humor left in you, Kemo Sabe," said Swifty. "Where do we start this process?"

"Just for grins, let's take a ride to Montpelier, Idaho," said Kit.

"Terrific, crossing a state line for questionable purposes," said Swifty. "I think that might be illegal on some level."

"Not if we don't break any laws," said Kit as he started the truck's engine, and they pulled out of the parking area of the truck stop and headed northwest on highway 30 to Montpelier. In eleven miles they crossed over the state line dividing Wyoming and Idaho, and twenty-one miles later they were pulling into the outskirts of Montpelier, Idaho.

CHAPTER NINE

"My stomach is rumbling," said Swifty. "Let's find someplace to grab some food."

"That may be the only good idea you've had today," said Kit as he slowly drove down the main drag of the small town of Montpelier. He kept driving until he was just north of downtown. There he pulled into the Ranch Hand Trail Stop which was a fancy way of saying "Truck Stop." Kit parked the truck, and they entered the restaurant. Once inside, they grabbed a booth by a window. A middle-aged waitress promptly appeared with glasses of ice water and menus. Both men ordered lunch and sat in the booth, as they took in their surroundings. They had missed the lunch crowd, and there were only about half a dozen customers in the café.

"So here we are in scenic Montpelier, Idaho," said Swifty. "Now what?"

Kit took a drink of water and set his glass down on the table. "If you moved to a new town, what would you have to do?" he asked.

Swifty thought for a minute and replied, "I'd find a place to live."

"After you found a place to live, then what would you do?" asked Kit.

"If I was renting a furnished place, I'd be all set," said Swifty.

"Explain," said Kit.

"I have a cell phone. The cell phone doesn't care where I am. The place I rent has its own utilities covered in the rent, so I got nothing to hook up unless it was cable TV," replied Swifty.

"But, if you had been living on an Air Force Base in Cheyenne, Wyoming and you had just retired and moved to Montpelier, Idaho, what would you have to do?" asked Kit.

Swifty thought for a minute and then said, "I'd have to get a post office box or use the apartment address and notify any companies, like my credit card companies where I'm located," he said.

"If all you were going to get in the mail was bills, you could get them all in email," said Kit.

"Okay," said Swifty. "Then I'd do nothing."

"You missed something," said Kit with a slight smile.

"I sure as hell ain't registering to vote," said Swifty.

"How about your driver's license. What about the license plates on your truck?" asked Kit. "In most states you only have a couple of months before you need to get local license plates. Plus, you must notify your insurance company where you are to make sure your coverage is good," said Kit.

"Maybe Charlemagne ain't worried about being legally correct. She is trying to hide out from someone," said Swifty.

"There is an old saying," said Kit. "The best place to hide is in plain sight."

"What the hell does that mean?" asked a confused Swifty.

"You hide out where you fit in and look no different

from anyone else. You don't draw any attention to yourself, so you do what everyone else around you does," said Kit.

"And just what is it you do?" asked Swifty.

"You work at a job, you shop for groceries, you eat at restaurants and drink at bars," said Kit. "You work at blending in."

"Maybe that works in New York City, but this is Idaho and Wyoming we're talkin' about," said Swifty.

"When it comes to blending in, Montpelier and Kemmerer are no different than Chicago. You just do absolutely nothing to get yourself noticed," said Kit.

"I'm lost, what does all that crap mean?" asked Swifty.

"If Charlemagne is here, she has a job and a routine," said Kit. "By now she has a new driver's license and new plates on her vehicle. It's been over a year and a half. She has a job she works at and a pattern of how she lives."

"Where does all that mumbo jumbo leave us?" asked Swifty.

"We don't know what she is driving, but we do have a fairly recent photo of her," said Kit. "We visit the grocery store, the drug store, the post office, the beauty parlor, the restaurants, the bars, and the churches and we show the photo to folks and see if anyone recognizes her."

"Sounds like a lot of work to me," lamented Swifty.

"If we add up all those places in this small town, I doubt it exceed twenty stops," said Kit.

"Where do we start?" asked Swifty.

"We get a room for the night, and we start with the motel we stay at," said Kit. With that he started the truck and drove back into Montpelier. They checked in to the Super

8 Motel, which was the highest ranked motel according to TripAdvisor in Kit's phone.

Once they settled into their room, Kit took out his laptop and began taking notes in his small notebook. When he was finished, he had the names and addresses of all the motels, restaurants, grocery store, drug store, beauty parlors, bars, and churches in town as well as the post office.

They had supper at a Mexican restaurant named El Jaliciense. Then he pulled up the military photo of Charlemagne on his phone and sent a copy to Swifty's phone.

"When you visit the names on your list, show them the photo on your phone and ask if they know her or have seen her around," said Kit.

"Why not get your printer out and make copies?" said Swifty.

"A photo in the phone is easier, faster, and you are not accidentally leaving a photo behind that can raise questions," said Kit. "I don't want her to know we are looking for her and spook her into running."

"Seems to me she's been runnin' since she left the Air Force base in Cheyenne," said Swifty. "And she's been doin' a pretty damn good job of it. She sure as hell has been bamboozling two dumb cowboys."

Kit drove back to the motel and then used the phone book and his laptop to divide up the places they needed to visit and ask about Charlemagne. It turned out, there were 19 likely places to visit. Kit gave Swifty the four beauty shops and the 8 restaurants as there were no bars or taverns. Kit took the rest of the list. Both men turned in as it was going to be a long day starting the next morning.

CHAPTER TEN

Both men were up and dressed before the sun was up. They found breakfast at Don's Drive-in, and it wasn't bad. They finished their breakfast, paid their bill, and each got a coffee to go. Kit fired up the truck, and they drove to the end of the town's business district of town and parked. Each man had a list and they split up, Kit taking one side of the main street and Swifty the other.

Kit's first stop was Ace Hardware. He entered the store and walked up to a checkout aisle and stopped to talk to the clerk, a middle-aged lady who greeted him pleasantly and asked how she could help him. Kit explained he was with Rocky Mountain Searchers in Kemmerer, and he had been hired to find a mother's lost daughter. The clerk was immediately sympathetic and asked several questions. Kit answered each one carefully and then he pulled out his phone and showed her the picture of Charlemagne in her Air Force uniform. The lady looked carefully at the picture and said she had not seen the woman. Then, unaided by Kit, she took the phone over to the other clerk and showed to her, but she shook her head no. Kit thanked both of them and then headed to his next stop.

He walked into the Health Mart Pharmacy and repeated

his performance from Ace. He talked to three employees and showed them the photo on his phone, but none of them remembered seeing anyone like Charlemagne. He thanked them for their time and headed on to the next place on his list.

Family Dollar, a discount store, was next. There were two employees in the store and neither one remembered ever seeing Charlemagne. Again, Kit thanked them and left the store.

He stopped at both grocery stores, Broulin's Supermarket, and Jenson's AG Market, but after showing the photo to a total of nine employees in both stores, he still struck out. He bought a coke at Jenson's and after leaving the store, he found a bench in front of a law office and sat down to take a break and drink his coke. When he finished his drink, he tossed the can into nearby garbage can and headed to the Presbyterian Church.

The church was small, and he figured the attendance did not fill the building in an almost all Mormon town. The church was locked, and he could see no nearby parsonage, so he headed for the Mormon church. There the door was open, and he stopped the first person he saw, and they directed him to the office. This church was a Stake House in Mormon terms and he soon found himself in a well-lit office with several people working. Kit introduced himself and then showed his photo to each of them. They all crowded around to look, but none of them recognized Charlemagne. Kit thanked them and left the church.

He walked back toward the business district, but he saw no sign of Swifty. He found himself in front of the library and got an idea. He remembered libraries rented out personal computer time and allowed copies of things to be printed out on the library printer for a fee. He went into the library and walked up to the checkout desk. He introduced himself to a pleasant young lady and explained what he was looking for. He asked her if she ever had strangers come into the library and ask to use the computers?

The young woman, whose name tag indicated her name was Sharon, wasn't sure, because she didn't usually handle the computer rentals. Sharon excused herself and within a few minutes she reappeared with an older, grey-haired woman who introduced herself as Madeline. Kit explained his reason for asking about strangers wanting to rent computer time and then showed the phone picture to Madeline.

Madeline looked at the phone, then held out her hand. "May I?" she asked.

"Of course," said Kit and handed the phone to her. She took it over to the desk, sat down and turned on a desk lamp to give her better light. She turned the photo back and forth and then she shut off the lamp, stood up, and handed the phone back to Kit, who looked at her quizzically.

"Have you seen her?" asked Kit.

"Yes, yes, I have," replied Madeline.

"Once or more than once?" asked Kit.

"Twice, I believe," said Madeline.

"Do you remember when she was in the library?" asked Kit.

"I'm not exactly sure," said Madeline. Then she paused as if she were trying to recollect something.

Kit wisely remained silent and waited.

After almost five minutes, Madeline snapped her fingers and said, "I remember!"

"What do you remember?" asked Kit.

"I remember she came in here twice to use the computer," said Madeline. "I believe the first time was almost a year and a half ago and the last time was almost a year ago. The reason I remember was her posture. She was dressed like most folks in town, but she stood ramrod straight and she was polite, but she came across as firm, almost demanding."

"Like a military officer?" asked Kit.

"That's it!" said Madeline. "That's it. It reminded me of my uncle who was a career army officer."

"Do you remember how she paid for the use of the computer?" asked Kit.

"I'm not sure, but I can look it up," said Madeline.

"Do you remember the name she gave you?" asked Kit.

"I do," said Madeline. "Using her name is how I can look it up."

"What name did she give?" Asked Kit.

"When I asked her for a name, she said 'Doc Charlie'," replied Madeline.

Kit took out his notepad from his shirt pocket and quickly made a notation and replaced the pad while Madeline was doing her search.

Madeline looked up from her computer search with a triumphant smile on her face. "She paid cash, both times," she said.

"Thank you," said Kit. "Thank you very much. You've been a huge help, and this is going to make her mother extremely happy."

Both Madeline and Sharon smiled, pleased they had been able to help Kit.

"I have another question," said Kit.

"Yes?' said Madeline.

"Do you have security cameras here in the library?" he asked.

"No, no we do not," replied Madeline. "They are so expensive, and we've never had any kind of problem here that would warrant such an expense."

"Thank you again," said Kit.

Kit was smiling to himself as he exited the twin library doors and walked down the stone steps to the sidewalk. He walked back to the parked truck and got in the driver's seat. He rolled down the windows and sat back to wait for his errant partner. Luckily Swifty had no bars or taverns to visit, but he did have beauty parlors and restaurants. Knowing it could be a while, Kit sat back in the truck seat, pulled his cowboy hat down over his face and closed his eyes. It could take a while for Swifty to make his way back to the truck.

CHAPTER ELEVEN

It was another two hours before the noise of Swifty pulling open the passenger door of the truck woke Kit up. Swifty swung into the passenger's seat and closed the door.

"Any luck?" asked Kit.

"If it weren't for bad luck, I'd have no luck at all," snorted Swifty. "Huge waste of time."

"I take it you didn't run into any willing females during your survey," said Kit sarcastically.

"If I saw a woman under the age of seventy, it was an accident," said Swifty. "You ever see an eighty-year-old woman with her hair up in curlers?" asked Swifty. "It was enough to get me to swear off women for at least a week."

Kit looked at his friend and just shook his head and grinned.

"All right, maybe not a week, but at least for a couple of days," countered Swifty.

"So, you struck out of finding anyone who recognized the photo?" asked Kit.

"Haven't you been listening?" responded Swifty. "If I'd found someone who knew our gal, I'd a lead with that when I got in the truck. And after all that palaver, I need a drink."

Kit sat quietly and waited for the rest.

"Did you know there ain't a damn bar in this entire Mormon town?" snarled Swifty.

"Mormons don't drink," said Kit. "I thought you knew that."

"Hell, I know that, but there's always a Jack Mormon in every town and they got to get their booze somewhere," said Swifty.

"Apparently not in Montpelier, Idaho," replied Kit.

"Well, what are you waiting for?" asked Swifty. "Let's haul ass out of this two-bit no booze town and find us a tavern for cowboys."

"Aren't you going to ask me how I did?" asked Kit.

Swifty looked at Kit like he had grown two heads. "What?" he asked.

"Thank you for inquiring," said Kit. "I struck out as well until I thought to go to the library."

"The library?" said a surprised Swifty.

"Yep, the library. I got to thinking and remembered today you can go into a library in almost any town and rent the use of a computer for a small fee," said Kit.

"You're kidding?" asked Swifty.

"Nope, I'm not," replied Kit. "I went in and showed the photo and found out our fugitive daughter was in the library twice in the last eighteen months. She used a computer each time and she paid cash. She gave her name to the clerk as 'Doc Charlie'."

"How in the hell did they remember her after all this time?" asked a now interested Swifty.

"She had a very military bearing, from her posture to her voice and how she phrased things when she spoke," said Kit.

"Do you think she's still around here?" asked Swifty.

"I don't think so," said Kit. "First of all, no one else we talked to has seen or talked to her and second, I think she chose to come here to use the library computer and for no other reason. That means she had no computer, and she wanted to use one not near where she was actually living."

"Where the hell is she living?" asked Swifty.

"Well, it ain't in Montpelier, Idaho, and it ain't in Cokeville, Wyoming, but it's somewhere close," replied Kit. "And I think I might have a good idea just where she is hiding out."

"Where?" demanded Swifty.

"I can't say for sure until I do some checking, but I promise you, you'll be the first to know after I do," said Kit.

Kit started the truck and pulled out into traffic.

"Where are we headed?" asked Swifty.

"Back to Kemmerer," replied Kit. "I got some heavy-duty computer work to do, and I need my setup back at the office."

"Wake me when we get there," said Swifty. "All this interviewing crap has plumb wore me out." He settled back in his seat, pulled his cowboy hat over his eyes and was sound asleep before Kit drove past the Montpelier city limits.

CHAPTER TWELVE

Swifty's nap lasted about an hour when the truck came to a stop, and Kit flipped Swifty's cowboy hat up above his eyes.

"We're home, cowboy. Rise and shine," said Kit sarcastically.

Swifty mumbled something obscene that Kit chose to ignore and the two of them unpacked the truck and headed into the old bank building that housed the offices of Rocky Mountain Searchers.

After unloading the truck, Kit headed into his office and Swifty went to his locker in search of a semi-forgotten bottle of bourbon. Kit was busy on his computer when Swifty arrived in his office, a glass of bourbon in his hand. Swifty plopped down in one of the chairs in front of Kit's desk and took a long sip of his whisky.

After a less than proper interval of waiting for Kit to acknowledge him, Swifty finally spoke. "Just what in the hell are you doin' beside beating that poor defenseless machine to death?" he asked.

Kit typed for a few more seconds and then paused and sat back in his office chair. "I have a theory and I'm trying to find out how good it is," said Kit.

"What's the theory?" asked Swifty. "Tryin' to prove up is different than down?"

"Nope," said Kit. "I'm homing in on the name Charlemagne used at the library."

"What name?" asked Swifty.

"She used, 'Doc Charlie', and I think there's a reason," said Kit.

"Doc Charlie could be short for Doc Charlemagne," said Swifty.

"It could be, but I don't think she's using her real name," said Kit.

"Why wouldn't she?" asked Swifty.

"If she went to all that trouble to disappear the day she got out of the Air Force, why would she start using her real name and announce to the world where she was?" said Kit.

"You could be right," said Swifty. "I'm not sayin' you're right, but you could be."

Kit went back to the keyboard and punched in some more keys. When he finished, he looked up at Swifty.

"Well?" asked Swifty.

"I need more verification and some copies of records, but I think I know what she did and how she did it," said Kit.

"Other than retire from the Air Force and then disappear, except to reappear twice in eighteen months at the library in Montpelier, Idaho, what the hell are you talkin' about?" asked Swifty.

Kit leaned back in his office chair and looked up at the ceiling of his office. "We know her service records are sealed unless we have a court order which we don't and can't get," said Kit. "We know she is getting retirement pay from the Air Force, and it's likely going straight to a bank account in her name in California. And we know she has remained hidden for over a year and a half since she retired. We also know she is around here fairly close, but not in Montpelier or Cokeville."

"All that adds up to not much," said Swifty.

"True, but she bought a truck, licensed it, got insurance for it, and made a home someplace. If she were using her real name, it would have popped up somewhere in Wyoming, but it hasn't," said Kit.

"I'm lost," said Swifty.

"I got this idea when we were in Montpelier," said Kit. "What if she is using the name of someone she worked with at the base in Cheyenne?"

"Seems to me that would start alarm bells ringing wherever this other person was," said Swifty.

"You are correct," said Kit. "But what if she made a deal with a friend who got out of the Air Force before Charlemagne did. Someone of her same rank and position. What if that person were getting married when she got out and then would have a different last name and what if that person were no longer going to be working in the medical field?"

"That's a hell of a lot of what ifs," said Swifty.

"Maybe and maybe not," said Kit. "By this time tomorrow, or maybe even sooner, I will know if my hunch is right."

"Based on what?" asked Swifty.

"I've been doing some digging electronically and I've made a few phone calls," said Kit. "It turns out one of Charlemagne's few friends in the Air Force was another major at the base in Cheyenne. She too was a physician's assistant. She retired from the Air Force a year before Charlemagne did. When she retired, she immediately got married and moved to Nova Scotia in Canada. She has no medical license in Canada of record."

"All that is interesting, but so what?" asked Swifty.

"I left out the best part," said Kit.

"What's that?" asked Swifty.

"Her name," said Kit.

"Her name was also Charlemagne?" asked Swifty.

"Nope. Her name was Charlotte, Charlotte Hennings. Her nickname was Doc Charlie in the Air Force," said Kit.

"So, what are you waiting for if you have all this?" asked Swifty as he took another long sip of whiskey.

"I'm waiting for verification and physical records to back up what I was told over the phone," said Kit. "All I have so far is scuttlebutt and conjecture. I'm waiting for some physical records to back up what I think I know."

"So, our gal is using this Charlotte Hennings broad's name as her ID here in Wyoming?" asked Swifty.

"I believe so," said Kit. "I think she applied for a PA license in Wyoming using Hennings military medical status and from talking to folks in Cheyenne, it would just be a formality. They were likely thrilled to get a license application for an Air Force Physician's Assistant to practice privately in Wyoming."

"So, Doc Charlie is really Charlemagne, pretending to be Charlotte?" asked Swifty.

"Yep. That's what I think," said Kit.

"And people say I'm devious," muttered Swifty as he took another swig from his glass.

"They don't say it, they know it," said Kit with a grin.

"Screw them," said Swifty. "What next?"

"I can't get records from the military, but I can get copies of the records of anyone applying for a medical license in Wyoming, including one for a physician's assistant license," said Kit. "That's what I'm waiting for."

"Will you get it today or tomorrow?" asked Swifty.

"Hopefully today, but more likely tomorrow," said Kit.

"Then what?" asked Swifty.

"We find out exactly where physician's assistant Charlotte Hennings office is located and we go pay her a visit," said Kit.

"Works for me," said Swifty. He rose from his chair, drank the remains of the bourbon in his glass and headed for the door. "I'm headed to my office for a nap and some medicinal whiskey. Wake me when you find out where this Doc Charlie is holed up."

"Will do, but it might not be until tomorrow," said Kit.

"Until then," said Swifty. "I got more than one bottle of whiskey," and he disappeared into the building.

CHAPTER THIRTEEN

Kit didn't receive the information until eleven o'clock the next morning. When he received an email with an attachment, he pulled up the attachment, read it, and then printed it out.

He took the four pages from the printer and carried them to the break room. There he poured himself a fresh cup of coffee and added cream and honey. He took a sip. Satisfied, he took the pages and the coffee into his office. He sat in his big chair, sipped his coffee, and slowly and carefully read every line of every page. When he had finished, he took out a pen and made some notes in the margins of the pages.

When he was finished, he reread what he had written and then put the pages in a folder and placed it on his desk. He got up and checked on Swifty. He was dead to the world. Kit quietly left the room and returned to his office. There he picked up his phone and called a well-remembered number.

"Hello!" came out of the tiny speaker like fifty pounds of potatoes trying to get out of a ten- pound sack all at once.

"Is this Big Dave?" asked Kit.

"Who the hell else would be answering this phone?" came the rough answer.

"It's Kit, Dave. Got time for lunch?" Kit asked politely.

"I've always got time to eat, especially when you're buyin'," snorted Big Dave in reply.

"El Jalicience OK with you?" asked Kit.

"Hell yes," replied Big Dave. "Them Mexican sombitches know how to cook."

The next sound Kit heard was Big Dave shutting his phone off. Kit grinned to himself and headed out the front door of the office. By the time he got to the restaurant, Big Dave was already seated and chatting with the waitress. Big Dave never passed up a chance to talk to the ladies. Young, old, big, small, skinny, fat, it didn't matter with Big Dave. And the women loved him for it.

Kit slid into the booth seat opposite Big Dave who barely noticed him as he chatted with the somewhat chunky waitress. Kit sat quietly in his seat, looking over the menu, even though he knew it by heart. Finally, Big Dave got done chatting and he turned his attention to Kit.

"I ain't heard from you in a coon's age," said Big Dave. "What the hell have you been up to, you sumbitch?"

Kit grinned and marveled at the larger-than-life character that was Big Dave Carlson. Ever since Big Dave had pulled his sorry ass out of a snowbank down by Interstate 80, he had been both Kit's friend and mentor. He had taught Kit almost all he knew about Wyoming, the West, and surviving and hunting in the mountains. Meeting Big Dave was like meeting the characters John Wayne had portrayed in the movies. He was one of those people who was truly larger than life. He also rarely ever uttered a sentence without some form of cuss word in it.

"I caught a strange case about a missing woman," said Kit.

"In a state where there are about four men for every woman, that seems hard to figure that one of them women could get herself lost," said Big Dave.

The waitress appeared with cups of coffee and then took their orders. As soon as she was out of earshot, Big Dave took a sip of his coffee and leaned forward on the small Formica tabletop.

"Tell me about the case," Big Dave said in a much softer and quieter tone.

Kit began by telling him about the visit of Mrs. Andropolous to his office. He explained what she had done trying to find her daughter she had given up for adoption as a baby, and her lack of success and why she had come to Kit.

"Was this Mrs. Andropolous hot?" asked Big Dave.

"She's in her sixties!" exclaimed Kit.

"It's always a better story if the women in it are hot," said Big Dave.

"Good lord," muttered Kit.

"Go on with your story," said Big Dave.

Kit went on to tell him about the trip to Cheyenne, what happened there, and then their trip to Cokeville and then to Montpelier, Idaho.

"Montpelier," said Big Dave. "I used to use a veterinarian out of there for years. I think the old boy is dead now."

Kit rolled his eyes and continued with his story. He explained about his trip to the library and then his checking with the State of Wyoming medical licensing board in Cheyenne.

"How the hell did you figure out this here Charlemagne gal had switched identities with another gal she worked with who had left the Air Force, got married, and moved to Canada?" asked Big Dave.

"It didn't make sense Charlemagne would go to all that trouble to disappear and then start working in Wyoming using her real name," said Kit. "To do that she had to have a way to get a license using someone else she knew, so it wouldn't come back to bite her later," said Kit.

"I guess that does make sense, but goddamnit why in the hell would this Charlemagne go to all this trouble just to set up and work in some backwater in Wyoming in some other gal's name," asked Big Dave.

"That is the sixty-four-dollar question," replied Kit. "She has to have some pretty darn serious reason to retire from the Air Force and then stay hidden like this. The question is why and who is she hiding from?"

"I don't envy you none on this case," said Big Dave.

The waitress appeared with their orders and each man dug into their food like they hadn't eaten in a week.

When they were finished, the waitress cleared the table and refilled their coffee cups, leaving the bill on the table. Kit grabbed the bill, pulled out his wallet and pulled out several bills and left them and the bill on the side of the table.

Big Dave took a sip of coffee and set his coffee cup down on the table. "So why are you having lunch with me?" he asked. "I don't think you just wanted to bring me up to date on your latest damn shenanigans."

"You're right," said Kit. "I need some advice on what to do next."

"Explain," said Big Dave.

"I got information from Cheyenne today on the medical

license they issued to Charlemagne. Only it's issued in the name of Charlotte Hennings, her friend who retired from the Air Force a year before Charlemagne did," said Kit.

"Damn sneaky if you ask me," said Big Dave.

"Actually, pretty clever of her," said Kit. "The reason we're having lunch is I need your advice, and I may need your help on this one."

"Why is that?" asked Big Dave.

"Here's the location where this Doc Charlie is working out of," said Kit, as he shoved one of the printed pages from the report across the table to Big Dave.

"This here location is an old building in Freedom, Wyoming. That's a tiny burg over in Star Valley at the north end of the county," said Big Dave.

"Yep, and it's a 100% Mormon up there," said Kit.

"And you ain't a Mormon," said a grinning Big Dave.

"Nope, I'm not, but you are," said Kit.

"I'm a damned Jack Mormon," said Big Dave.

"You're still a Mormon," said Kit. "And neither Swifty nor I am."

"So, what do you need from me?" asked Big Dave.

"I'd like you to go up to Freedom with Swifty and me and pay this Doc Charlie a little visit," said Kit.

Big Dave paused for a moment, then grinned and said, "Hell yes I'll go with you boys. I just remembered I actually got a good reason to head up to Freedom."

"I don't remember you having any relatives up in Star Valley," said Kit. "I thought you were the black sheep of your Mormon family."

"I am, and damn proud of it," said Big Dave. "But I still

got a good reason to make a trip up to Freedom. You ever been there?"

"Can't say that I have," said Kit. "What's in Freedom?"

"Mormons, same as in the rest of the damn Star Valley," laughed Big Dave.

"Can we leave tomorrow morning, right after breakfast," asked Kit.

"I'll be on your doorstep around seven," said Big Dave. "You bringin' that damned Swifty?"

"Sure am," said Kit.

"That boy has the damnedest knack for gettin' in trouble I ever did see," said Big Dave.

Both men rose from their chairs, shook hands, and Kit and Big Dave exited the café, Kit heading toward his office and Big Dave headed somewhere unknown except to him.

CHAPTER FOURTEEN

Kit was up early the next morning. By six-thirty he was finished with breakfast and was packing a few items for the trip to Freedom, Wyoming. He heard the front door open, and slam shut. He stepped out into the hallway from the conference room just in time to see Big Dave rumbling down the hall. Big Dave came up short when he saw Kit standing there and lurched to a halt.

"Where the hell is the godamneded coffee?" Big Dave demanded.

Kit grinned and said, "Go have a seat in my office. I'll bring you a cup."

Big Dave was seated on the small couch in Kit's office when Kit entered carrying two steaming hot cups of coffee. He handed one to Big Dave and turned to go to his desk.

"Black?" asked Big Dave.

"Been black ever since you showed me how to make cowboy coffee right after you hired me as a sheepherder years ago," Kit shot back at him.

"You were a pitiful sheepherder. Pitiful!" snorted Big Dave. He took a sip of coffee. "Not bad coffee for a greenhorn," said Big Dave. "Ten more years and you might learn how to brew a decent cup of coffee."

"I'll keep working on it," replied a smiling Kit.

"Where's that no-account partner of yours?" asked Big Dave.

"You told me to be ready at seven A.M.," said Kit. "Knowing Swifty, he'll show up about 6:55 A.M."

Big Dave grunted something Kit couldn't understand, and so he just ignored it as he drank his coffee and completed packing his small duffel bag.

"What in the hell do you have in that damn bag?" asked Big Dave.

"We're doing an investigation," said Kit. "I packed a few things we might need since I have no idea how far behind the twenty-first century Star Valley and Freedom might be."

"If they aint' got it, they don't need it," snorted Big Dave.

"They ain't me," said Kit firmly.

"Thank God for that!" exclaimed Big Dave.

Big Dave took another swig of his coffee, looked around Kit's office, and then said, "You got an address for this here lady doctor?"

"Yes, I've got the address she gave the state boys in Cheyenne, and I took a look at it on Google Earth," said Kit.

"Google what?" said Big Dave.

Kit paused, thinking of the best way to explain Google Earth.

"You've heard of satellites up in the sky?" asked Kit.

"Yeah, I heard of them. Never seen one of the bastards though," said Big Dave.

"Well, those satellites can take pictures of almost everything on the planet earth," said Kit. "They store those pictures and make them available on the internet. You type in an address or a longitude and latitude and up comes a picture of that location."

"Can't be much of a damn picture taken from that far away," said Big Dave dismissively.

"They can take a pretty good picture of your face from way up there," said Kit. "The military satellites can take a good picture of your driver's license if you were holding it in your hand standing out in front of this building."

"Bullshit," snorted Big Dave.

Kit grinned and swiveled his chair around to face his computer. He fired it up and punched some keys. Almost immediately a picture appeared of the sidewalk in front of the old bank building they were having coffee in. Kit swiveled the computer screen so Big Dave could get a good look.

"Well, I'll be damneded," stammered Big Dave. After he thought about it for a couple of minutes, he said, "We need one of them damn satellites to use next time we go elk huntin'."

"I kinda doubt that will happen," said a smiling Kit.

The door to his office swung open and there stood Swifty, holding a steaming hot cup of coffee. "It's damn near seven o'clock in the damn morning. You boys get your asses movin' so we can get this show on the road. I got places to go and people to see and you boys are holdin' me up," said Swifty.

Both Big Dave and Kit quickly finished their coffee. Kit grabbed his small bag, and all three of them trooped out of the building to Kit's parked pickup truck. Kit and Swifty got in front, and Big Dave took up a comfortable position in the back seat.

Big Dave got himself situated where he felt good and said, "You boys wake me up when we get to the edge of Star Valley, and I'll do my best to hold off them bloodthirsty Mormons," he said. Then he pulled his cowboy hat over his eyes and settled back into the big rear seat.

Kit looked over at Swifty, but he too had his hat down over his eyes and was slumped down in his seat. Kit was on his own for this trip.

Kit drove until he passed Sage. Sage was nothing but a whistlestop for the railroad. There were no buildings, no animals, and certainly no people. All there was to Sage was an old, battered metal sign.

At Sage, Highway 30 turned abruptly north and nineteen miles later Kit passed through Cokeville. Just before Highway 30 turned toward Montpelier and crossed the state line, Kit took Highway 39 north. The highway briefly slid inside the Idaho state line, but then turned northeast back into Wyoming. Twenty-three miles later Kit drove into Smoot.

Kit was admiring the green scenery when a voice from the back seat jolted him.

"Kinda looks like them pictures you see of Switzerland, don't it?" said Big Dave.

The countryside was dotted with small dairy farms and lush pastures and surrounded by snowcapped mountain peaks. Big Dave was right. Kit had never been to Switzerland, but in his mind, this was what he imagined it might look like.

Smoot was home to about one hundred eighty-four folks, mostly Mormons and a scattering of about fifty homes and buildings. They passed through without encountering a single person. Soon they were back in a flat, grassy valley, dotted with small farms. After about eight miles, they came to Afton, one the of largest towns in Star Valley with about nineteen hundred residents and a thriving business district. Kit counted no less than three banks, which seemed ridiculous in a town this small. He pulled into a Burger King, and he and Big Dave got coffees to go. Then they were back on the road, heading north.

They quickly passed through Grover, population one hundred and forty-seven and then drove into Thayne, home to three hundred and sixty-six hardy folks. Thayne had a small business district which included a bank. About four miles north of Thayne, Kit took a left on highway 34. After a couple of miles, they were entering the hamlet of Freedom, Wyoming, not to be confused with Freedom, Idaho. The town population of two hundred and fourteen was split by the north-south state line dividing Idaho and Wyoming. Highway 89 runs north and south and divides the town in half.

"This place has been here a long time," said Big Dave.

"How long?' asked Kit.

"It was established in 1879 and is the oldest settlement in Star Valley," said Big Dave. It was settled as a border town by Mormon polygamists in order to escape arrest for polygamy."

"Polygamy?" asked Kit.

"Old guys with lots of wives, including some really young ones," said Big Dave. "Originally they built homes right on the border between Idaho and Wyoming. That way if the law in Idaho came to their house, they just moved to the east side of the house which was in Wyoming where they were safe. Years ago, they built Highway 89 right down the state line and got rid of the border crossing houses. They named it freedom because it gave the original settlers freedom from the law of Idaho."

"I assume the end of polygamy had something to do with that?" asked Kit.

"I got no idea, but back then, Freedom was a pretty big deal," said Big Dave. "Freedom used to be the largest settlement in Star Valley. They had a general store, gas station, billiard hall and other stores. Some of the old buildings are still standing, but few are in use. They still use the post office and the old baseball field, and the LDS Church. The church was built in 1889. The only real business in town is Freedom Arms."

"Freedom Arms? What's that?" asked Kit.

"It's where we're headed before we go look up this missing gal doctor of yours," said Big Dave. "I ordered a pistol from them, and It's been ready for a couple of weeks. I agreed to tag along with you and Swifty so I could pick it up."

"What kind of pistol?" asked Kit.

"They make a great big pistol you could take a grizzly bear down with," said a grinning Big Dave. "It's a five-shot revolver chambered in .454 Casul."

"I never heard of that caliber," said Kit.

"Turn east at the next corner, and I'll show you," said Big Dave.

Kit turned right and after a block, saw a large metal building with a parking lot on his right.

"Turn in that lot," said Big Dave.

Kit turned in the lot and parked his truck. As the two

men exited the truck, Swifty woke up and looked around like he expected to be surrounded by wild Indians. "Where the hell are we?" he demanded.

"Freedom Arms," responded Big Dave.

"Freedom Arms? Cool," said Swifty, and he joined Big Dave and Kit as they headed for the front door of the building.

As they walked to the entrance, Big Dave gave them a brief history of the place. "Two guys named Baker and Casul started this place in 1978. They made different handguns but settled on the .454 Casul five shot pistol. I think they recently added a smaller pistol in .357 Magnum and a few other calibers, but I ain't real sure. I ordered the .454 Casul in Premier Grade which is a little nicer than the Field Grade model," said Big Dave.

They walked into a small showroom with a couple of offices on one side and what was obviously a doorway to the factory beyond. A middle-aged bearded man approached them.

"Can I help you boys?" he asked.

"I'm Dave Carlson from Kemmerer," said Big Dave. "I'm here to pick up the Premier .454 Casul I ordered. You folks called and said it was ready."

"Yes, sir, Mr. Carlson, I've been expecting you to show up," said the clerk. "I'll go get it for you." He walked over to a steel cabinet with a combination lock. He worked the combination and then popped the door open and took out a long, flat box with Big Dave's name written on it.

He removed the box and took it over to a display counter and placed it on the countertop. He opened the box and pushed the open box toward Big Dave.

Big Dave carefully picked the large revolver out of the box and turned it over a couple of times. Then he held the pistol in front of him pointing toward the wall, holding it in both his large hands. He flipped open the cartridge cover and spun the cylinder. Satisfied, he closed the cover and placed the gun back in the box.

"What do I owe you?" asked Big Dave.

"You paid in advance, Mr. Carlson, so you owe nothing. The gun is all yours," said the clerk.

"You got any ammo for this gun?" asked Big Dave.

"We have a limited amount of .454 Casul ammo, Mr. Carlson, but since you are picking the gun up here at the factory, we'd be happy to make you a gift of a box of .454 Casul ammo," said the clerk.

"Works for me," said Big Dave.

The clerk grinned and turned away from the counter and pulled out a lower drawer. When he turned back to the counter, he had a box of ammo in his hand which he gave to Big Dave.

Big Dave pocketed the box of ammo and picked up the gun box. Then he led Kit and Swifty toward the entrance of the gun shop.

"Pleasure doing business with you, Mr. Carlson. If you have any problems at all, please bring the gun back and we'll make it right," said the clerk.

"Thanks, son," said Big Dave, and the three men left the gun shop and walked back to the truck.

Once they were in the truck, Swifty looked back at Big Dave. "Can I handle the new pistol?" he asked.

"You got twenty-five hundred in cash on you?" asked Big Dave.

"No," said a puzzled Swifty.

"Then no, you can't handle it," said Big Dave. "You want to handle a gun like this, you get the cash together and buy one for yourself."

"I just might do that," said a chastened Swifty.

Kit grinned to himself and started the pickup truck's engine.

CHAPTER FIFTEEN

"Where to?" asked Kit as he stared at Big Dave's face in the truck's rear-view mirror.

"Nowhere," said Big Dave.

"Nowhere?" asked a puzzled Kit.

"We ain't goin' no place till we get us a plan," said Big Dave.

"A plan?" asked Swifty.

"I know this small town looks like it's almost dead and gone, but it ain't," said Big Dave. "If this here lady you come to see is working as a Doc and helping folks here in Star Valley, she's gonna be protected by them. Bargin' into her office and pissing a lot of people off won't end well for any of us, including the Doc."

"What do you suggest?' asked Kit.

"We need to be open and honest," said Big Dave. "We don't wish this lady doc no harm, and we need to make that clear. From what you told me, she's here helping people and likely doin' it for free or not much. It's likely she's takin' stuff in trade for her help, and I don't mean hard cash."

"So, what should we do?" asked Kit.

"Just Kit goes in, and he tells them who he is and asks

to see the Doc for fifteen minutes and gives them his card and a hundred-dollar bill," said Big Dave.

"Why a hundred?" asked Swifty.

"If you were told someone wanted to talk to you for fifteen minutes and offered their card and a hundred bucks, would you turn it down?" asked Big Dave.

"I get your point," said Kit. He pulled out of their parking space, and they drove to the ancient, wooden one-story building. Kit pulled into the dirt parking lot and parked the truck. He opened the driver's side door and stepped out onto the dusty parking area.

Kit walked up to the cheap wooden front door and paused. "Here goes nothing," he said to himself and opened the door and stepped inside.

As soon as Kit disappeared inside, Big Dave turned to Swifty. "Get your ass out of the truck and set up behind the building where you can cover the rear door."

"Me? Why?" asked Swifty.

"Just in case the lady decides to hightail it outta her office to avoid talkin' to Kit," said Big Dave. "I'll cover the front."

Swifty slipped out the truck door and quickly and quietly made his way to the rear of the old wooden one-story building that served as the doc's office. He reached the rear of the building and took up position behind an old pine tree about fifteen yards from the back door of the office.

Once he was inside the old building, Kit was in what must have been a parlor when the house was originally built. It was a large room with windows on both sides and an old, scarred, but clean and polished oak floor. An older woman was behind an ancient, battered metal desk, talking on an old phone. Kit noticed the phone had buttons along the bottom of the unit, but only three of the buttons were marked and one was lit up, likely the line she was talking on.

Kit glanced around the small waiting room. There was a mishmash of old chairs, none matching and all in sad shape. Three of the chairs were occupied. Two by an old couple dressed in denims that had seen better days and the other by a young girl dressed in a plain and likely homemade dress.

The lady behind the desk was old, her face lined with years of hard work, hard times, and the kind of experiences not often shared with others.

She hung up the phone and looked up at Kit. "Can I help you?" she asked politely as her eyes carefully checked Kit out. Her tone was polite, but suspicious at the same time.

"Good morning, ma'am," said Kit. "My name is Carson Andrews. I'm from Rocky Mountain Searchers in Kemmerer. I'm here to see Doc Charlie on a personal matter. I only need fifteen minutes of her time, and I'm willing to pay for it."

With that said, Kit handed her his card and a folded up one-hundred-dollar bill.

Surprise covered the woman's face. She recovered quickly and stood up from her chair. She reached out and took the card and the cash and looked at Kit.

"Excuse me for a moment, Mr. Andrews," she said. Then she turned and walked down a narrow hallway and knocked on a door. Kit heard muffled voices. Then the lady opened the door and stepped through the doorway, closing the door behind her.

After a few minutes had passed, she reappeared and walked up to her desk. She looked at Kit, puzzlement filling her face. "The doctor will see you now, Mr. Andrews. She wishes me to tell you she only has a few minutes available," she said.

"Thank you," said Kit. He slowly walked down the narrow hallway to the doorway. The door was open, and he stepped into a small office crammed full of medical books, files, three ring binders stuffed with pages and a tiny desk with a single wooden chair in front of it. Behind the desk was a middle-aged woman in a white coat that had seen better days.

The woman was the spitting image of her mother. She was thinner but looked fit and her eyes were bright and piercing, their green color reminding Kit of the Wyoming plains he saw in the spring.

She noted Kit's reaction and looked at him carefully. "Is something wrong, Mr. Andrews?"

"No, ma'am," replied Kit. "I was just surprised. You are the spitting image of your mother."

"My mother?" asked Doc Charlie. "My mother died of cancer almost seven years ago. How could you have possibly known her?"

"Not your adopted mother, your birth mother, Miss Desantis," said Kit.

"My birthmother? You must be joking," said Doc Charlie. "I never met my birthmother. I don't even know her name."

"Your birth mother is Marie Andropolous. Andropolous is her married name," said Kit.

"Neither she nor her name mean anything to me," said Doc Charlie.

"You meant a lot to her," said Kit. "Would you like to hear why?"

Doc Charlie kept her facial expression hard, but she did not object.

"She had you when she was in high school. She gave you up for adoption. She was seventeen and the father disappeared when he heard she was pregnant," said Kit. "She went to college, met a good man and got married. She had two children with him, a boy and a girl, your half-brother and half-sister," said Kit.

Doc Charlie said nothing, but her eyes told Kit she was hanging on to every word Kit uttered.

"Her husband was successful. Her children grew up and left home to get married and have families of their own. Several years ago, her husband died of cancer and left her well off," said Kit. "A couple of years ago, she became curious about what happened to the child she abandoned to adoption when she was so young. She began searching for you. She hired a private detective and he tracked you down to the Air Force Base in Cheyenne. But, by the time he arrived there, you were gone. You had retired from the Air Force and on the day, you retired, you magically disappeared," said Kit.

Kit paused and searched Doc Charlie's face for a reaction. Her expression was unchanged, but now tears had formed in the corners of her bright green eyes.

"May I continue," asked Kit.

Doc Charlie said nothing, but she nodded her head in assent, the tears now running down her cheeks.

"The private detective gave up on finding you and sent your mother his report. She took his good advice and contacted me. She flew out to Salt Lake City, rented a car and drove up to Kemmerer to meet me. After hearing her story, I took the job of finding you for her," said Kit.

"You found me," Doc Charlie said softly, the tears flowing hard now.

Kit pulled out his clean handkerchief and handed it to her. She took it and wiped her eyes as she openly struggled to gain her self-composure.

Kit remained silent, waiting for her to speak.

"What do you want from me?" Doc Charlie said softly.

"Nothing," said Kit. "Your mother hired me to find you and determine what had happened to you. When she hired me, she told me if I managed to find you, she wasn't sure she wanted to meet you and would make that decision when I found you," said Kit.

"She was ashamed of me?" asked Doc Charlie, her expression changing from hard to hurt.

"No," said Kit, "She was ashamed of herself, that she never tried to find you, never helped you and never offered you a mother's love," said Kit.

Doc Charlie began to sob and then cry harder.

Moments like this were always unsettling to Kit. Nothing in his life had prepared him for a sad, crying female. He was starting to wish he had brought along another clean handkerchief.

Doc Charlie turned to her desk and grabbed a couple of tissues from a box and dabbed at her face and eyes until she managed to get herself under some semblance of emotional control.

Kit did what he did best under these circumstances. He

sat in his chair and kept his mouth shut until Doc Charlie was ready to continue the conversation.

It wasn't his best moment, but it was a long way from his worst.

CHAPTER SIXTEEN

When Doc Charlie had regained her composure, she sat in the old chair behind her desk and handed the handkerchief back to Kit.

"Please tell me about my mother," said Doc Charlie.

Kit paused and thought before he answered her question. He didn't really know her mother that well, but he decided to go with what he did know.

"I can only tell you what I know and that's not a great deal," said Kit.

"I want to hear about her," insisted Doc Charlie.

"I'll try," said Kid. "Your mother is an attractive older woman. She presents herself well and she is not shy. She was nervous meeting with me, but she quickly got over it and told me she wanted nothing more than to find where you were and how you were doing. She was unsure if she wanted to meet you, not because of anything about you, but because she was ashamed for not searching for you years ago instead of waiting until just recently. She came to me as a last resort to find you. I believed her when she told me how important it was to her to find you and learn what had happened to you. I believed her and that's why I took the case, I found your mother to be a strong woman who feels she failed you and is trying to find a way to bridge the gap between both of you. To be honest, Doc Charlie, I wish she were my mother."

Kit had run out of words, and he stopped talking. The silent seconds that followed seemed like an eternity to him as he sat there, hoping he had said the right words.

Doc Charlie grabbed another tissue and dabbed at her eyes. Then she looked straight at Kit, her eyes bright and her gaze firm.

"I want to thank you for finding me. I never thought I would ever say that to anyone," said Doc Charlie. "I planned my retirement with the added burden of knowing I would need to disappear where I could not be found. Your presence here today tells me I didn't do nearly as good a job of disappearing as I thought I did."

"You did a pretty good job," said Kit. "Finding you was not easy."

"But, not good enough," said Doc Charlie. "Here we are, and I'm the one who is surprised, not you. I worried I might be found, and the result would be devastating for me."

"Devastating is a pretty strong word," said Kit. "What are you talking about?"

Again, Doc Charlie paused and looked up at the ceiling as if seeking guidance or sign from some higher power only she could see. Her silence was interrupted by a knock at the door.

"Excuse me," she said and walked to the door and opened it.

The older lady from the receptionist desk was standing in the doorway. "Excuse me, Doc," she said. "But we have patients waiting and more due in shortly."

"You're right," said Doc Charlie. "I got so swept up in our talk, I totally forgot the time."

She turned to Kit. "I'm so sorry, but my patients must come first."

"I understand," said Kit.

"I still want to continue our discussion," said Doc Charlie. "Can we meet for dinner somewhere?"

"Of course," said Kit. "What time should I pick you up?"

"Pick me up?" asked Doc Charlie. Then she looked directly at Kit. "I trust you. Pick me up at seven here at the office."

"I'll be here at seven," said Kit. With that, he rose from his chair and walked to the door. There he paused and turned around to face Doc Charlie. "Thank you for your time and I look forward to talking to you again." Kit touched the brim of his cowboy hat with a finger and was gone out the door.

CHAPTER SEVENTEEN

As Kit walked back to his truck he was joined by Big Dave. He noticed the truck was empty when they got closer. "Where's Swifty?" Kit asked.

"I told him to watch the back door of the place in case you scared the crap out of her, and she tried to squirt out the back door," replied Big Dave.

Both men got in the truck and Kit slammed the door shut. That was enough to startle Swifty and he quickly appeared at the side of the small, old medical building and strode toward the parked truck. After he pulled himself into the passenger seat, he turned and looked at Kit.

"Well?" Swifty asked.

"She's our gal," said Kit.

"That's all? No details. No exciting play by play?" asked Swifty.

"Big Dave thinks we need a drink and I agree," said Kit. "We'll talk then." He started the truck and headed toward Alpine, a small town about twelve miles north which was likely to have a bar, even in this thickly Mormon populated part of the county. It was on the way to Jackson and lots of resort workers lived there.

When they reached Alpine, Kit pulled into the parking

lot of the Bull Moose Lodge and Saloon. "Looks good to me," said Swifty.

"A hog house with a six-pack would look good to you," said Big Dave.

"I'll stop in the office and get us some rooms and I'll meet you guys in the saloon," said Kit.

"Works for me," said Swifty.

Big Dave just looked at Swifty and silently shook his head. He followed Swifty to the saloon entrance, while Kit headed to the office.

Both Big Dave and Swifty were seated at the bar in the Bull Moose Saloon when Kit came through the front door. He walked to a table up against the wall, sat in the chair against the wall and motioned for Big Dave and Swifty to join him.

Both men grabbed their drinks and joined Kit at the table.

"Still choosing the Wild Bill Hickok seat in a saloon," said a grinning Swifty.

"As I recall, he got shot in the head in a Deadwood, South Dakota saloon while he was playing poker," remarked Big Dave.

"He got shot in the head because he did not sit in a chair with his back to the wall," said Kit. "Do you history buffs remember what cards he had in his hand when he got killed?" asked Kit.

"A pair of aces and a pair of eights," said Big Dave.

"Forever known to history as a dead man's hand," added Swifty.

"You two are an absolute fountain of historical

knowledge," said Kit. "Next thing I know you will be telling me when the government created the federal income tax."

"Who the hell gives a crap about that?" said Swifty.

"Not their best year," said Big Dave.

Kit just shook his head. Then he tossed Swifty and Big Dave each a room key. "If you lose the damn key, don't come to my room expecting to flop there for the night," said Kit.

Big Dave just looked at Kit and grinned.

"You ain't drinkin'?" asked Swifty as he nodded toward the empty space on the table in front of Kit.

"I wasn't planning on it, but after dealing with you two, I think I need something stronger than water," replied Kit.

He rose from his chair and walked to the bar. When he returned to the table, he was carrying a small tray with three large mugs of beer. He placed the tray on the table and sat down.

"You gonna drink all three of those?" asked Swifty.

"Nope," replied Kit. "I got one for me and while I was up there, I got another round for you two. I knew it was only a matter of time before you would be asking me to go get you another beer, so I saved myself a trip."

Two hours and several beers later, Kit excused himself and went to the motel room he had rented to take a nap. When he was in his room, he fired up his laptop and sat there, looking for answers in a silent electronic screen.

He had found Doc Charlie, but he still didn't know why she tried to disappear on the day she retired from the Air Force. He didn't know who she was trying to disappear from, or why. No answers magically appeared on the blank screen, so he shut the laptop off and laid down on the bed and tried to get some sleep.

He was awakened by a pounding on his door. He got off the bed, rubbed his eyes, and walked over and opened the door. There in the doorway, stood Swifty and Big Dave.

"Sorry to interrupt your beauty rest, but it's a bit after six," said Big Dave. "Ain't we supposed to pick up Doc at her place at seven?"

"You're right," said Kit. "Thanks for waking me up." He turned and walked back into his room and picked up his laptop.

"Whatcha' doin'?" asked Big Dave.

"Thought it'd be a good idea to make a reservation for dinner, so we don't have to wait around," responded Kit.

"Already done," said Big Dave with a slight smirk on his face.

"Good Lord," said Kit. "Please tell me you got a reservation someplace where they regularly pass the health inspection."

"Me and Swifty looked it up on his phone," said Big Dave. "Supposed to be one of the best in Alpine."

"What's the name of the place?" asked Kit, suspiciously.

"Brenthoven's Restaurant," replied Big Dave.

"Never heard of it," said Kit.

"Check out the reviews," said Swifty, holding out his phone.

Kit glanced at the phone and after about a minute's review of the site, he sighed, and said, "All right. The Brenthoven's Restaurant it is."

Kit ushered his friends out of his room and then took a quick shower and changed clothes. When he was finished, he walked outside and found Swifty and Big Dave leaning against his truck.

"Saddle up, boys," said Kit.

All three men climbed into their seats and Kit fired up the engine and they were soon on their way south to Freedom to pick up Doc Charlie for dinner.

CHAPTER EIGHTEEN

They arrived at Doc Charlie's place about ten minutes before seven. Kit got out of the truck and walked up to the front door and knocked. The door opened and Doc Charlie stepped outside, dressed in black slacks and a white blouse. She closed and locked the front door and then followed Kit to the truck. Kit held open the door to the back seat for her and she got in the truck next to Big Dave.

As Kit was getting into the driver's side, both Big Dave and Swifty introduced themselves. Doc Charlie did not seem at all surprised she was having dinner with three men rather than just one. If she did, she gave no indication Kit could discern.

On the drive to Alpine, Big Dave kept Doc Charlie entertained with his stories of his experiences in Star Valley. Kit heard Doc Charlie laugh for the first time. She had a nice laugh. It sounded soft and natural, not at all forced.

"So, you're a Mormon," said Doc Charlie.

"Kinda," said Big Dave.

"Kinda?" asked Doc Charlie. "What's a kinda' Mormon?"

"I'm what's known as a Jack Mormon," replied Big Dave.

"What's a Jack Mormon?" asked Doc Charlie. "That's a term I don't think I've heard before."

"A Jack Mormon is someone born and baptized a Mormon, but instead of being true to all the rules of the church, he kinda picks and chooses the rules he thinks are OK to follow," said Big Dave.

Doc Charlie laughed.

Kit smiled to himself. He was starting to like Doc Charlie.

After another fifteen minutes, he pulled into the parking lot of the Brenthoven Restaurant in Alpine. Kit got out of the driver's side and quickly moved to the rear door. He opened the door and held it open as Doc Charlie gracefully slid out of her seat and stepped away from the door. Kit closed the door and led the way to the entrance of the restaurant. Kit walked straight to the stand manned by a pretty young hostess. Kit gave her his name and reservation time. She smiled and gathered up four menus and led them to a table in the back of the restaurant. Kit noted with satisfaction the table was against the back wall, which would give him a clear view of anyone entering or exiting. It was an old habit Big Dave had taught him. He remembered Big Dave's words. "I ain't never been snuck up on, and I damn sure don't plan to start now."

The waitress came, and they ordered dinner and drinks. Dinner was pleasant and both Swifty and Big Dave managed to entertain Doc Charlie with tales of their exploits. Some true, some not so true, and some outright lies.

When they left the restaurant, Kit drove to their motel. He had rented a small conference room there. It would allow them to talk in private and away from any prying eyes. The room was bigger than they needed, but they all took a seat at a round table.

Kit broke the initial awkward silence. "Doc Charlie, I hope you understand that my job was to find you for your birth mother, then let her know so she can decide what she might do next. Neither I nor my two friends will speak a word of finding you, who you really are, or where you are. Is that clear?" he asked.

"Perfectly clear," said Doc Charlie. "I would like you to tell my mother. I'd really like to meet her."

"I plan to do just that," said Kit.

"Thank you," said Doc Charlie.

"Now that we have that part settled, I do have some questions," said Kit. "I understand you have no obligation to answer any of them, but I plan to ask anyway."

"Fire away," said a smiling Doc Charlie.

"All during my search for you, I had a nagging question in the back of my mind," said Kit.

"And that was?" asked Doc Charlie.

"Why did you plan your exit from the Air Force so you would seemingly disappear on the day you retired, leaving little or no trace of where you had gone?" asked Kit.

Doc Charlie paused for a couple of minutes. It seemed she was both preparing herself and reviewing what she felt free to say to Kit and his two friends.

"I guess it is always best to begin at the beginning. When I think of what's happened to me, it seems like a bad dream that I keep hoping I will wake up from," said Doc Charlie.

Kit remained silent and used his eyes to ensure Swifty and Big Dave did the same.

"I was transferred to Warren Air Force base in Cheyenne after I had served sixteen years in the military," said Doc Charlie. "I had a good, not great, career and I thoroughly enjoyed my job as a physician's assistant. Sometimes you worked for doctors who were professional assholes, and sometimes you got lucky and worked for doctors who were both good and professional. At Warren, I was fortunate and worked for good doctors. I enjoyed my time at Warren Air Force base both professionally and personally. During my military career that was not always the case." Then Doc Charlie paused, as though what she wanted to say next was likely to be painful.

Again, Kit kept his mouth shut and looked at both Swifty and Big Dave. They both understood this was a time to listen.

Doc Charlie took a deep breath and then began to speak in a softer, lower voice. "About two years before I would reach twenty years of service and be eligible to retire, something happened."

Again, she paused and looked up at the ceiling, her face grim. Then she seemed to relax and looked directly at Kit.

"It was about 1:30 in the morning. I was asleep in my quarters when my phone rang. As a physician's assistant, it was not an unusual occurrence. At least twice a week I received a call at odd hours to report to the emergency medical area because of a fight, an accident, or altercation, either on or off the base. In this case, I was ordered to get dressed, grab my medical bag, and wait in front of my quarters."

Doc Charlie paused, as if unnerved by the mention of that night.

"Was that normal?" asked Kit.

"No, it was not normal," replied Doc Charlie. "In a medical emergency I would report to the emergency medical area. I had never before been ordered to stand in front of my quarters and wait."

Kit nodded and kept his mouth shut, indicating Doc Charlie should continue with her story.

"I was no sooner out in front of my quarters when a Humvee pulled up and a man I had never seen before, exited the Humvee and grabbed my bag, and told me to get in the Humvee," said Doc Charlie.

"This man you had never seen before, was he Air Police?" asked Kit.

"No, he wasn't," said Doc Charlie. "Normally an airman would come to fetch me during the day, but at night, I just made my way to the emergency center after I was called."

"How was this man dressed?" asked Kit.

"It's odd you mention how he was dressed," said Doc Charlie. "He was dressed in all black, not in regular fatigues."

"Was that unusual?" asked Kit.

"I'd never seen anyone in all black, not in fatigues nor any other combat or formal uniform," replied Doc Charlie.

"Go on," said Kit.

"Another man dressed in all black was in the driver's seat. I got in the passenger seat and the other man with my bag slid into the jump seat in the back of the Humvee," said Doc Charlie. "He didn't drive to the emergency center. Instead, he drove to what I thought was an unused hanger."

"Had you ever been to the hanger before?" asked Kit.

"No, I had not," said Doc Charlie. "I had this feeling something wasn't quite right, but it was in the middle of the night. I was still a bit sleep groggy and I was on an Air Force base, so I tried to remember if I had everything current in my medical bag."

"Did you?" asked Kit.

"Yes, I did," said Doc Charlie. "I never put the bag away after I use it without resupplying it with anything I had used in the call."

"What happened when you got to the hangar?" asked Kit.

"The Humvee stopped and the guy in back jumped out with my bag, and he headed for the door in the side of the hanger. I got out of the Humvee and followed him into the hanger," said Doc Charlie. "Inside the hanger was one of the strangest sights I'd ever seen."

"Strange?" asked Kit.

"Yes, strange," said Doc Charlie. "Only the overhead lights at the end of the hanger were on. There was this large Baker tent erected at the back of the hanger. The man in black carrying my bag opened the tent flap and motioned for me to enter. I did, and inside the tent I was almost blinded by the bright lights."

"Bright lights?" asked Kit.

"Yes, bright lights. Very bright lights," said Doc Charlie. "Inside the tent it was like high noon in the desert."

"What did you see in the tent?" asked Kit.

"I saw a metal portable operating table with a naked man strapped to it," said a grim-faced Doc Charlie. "There were three or four men standing around the table. They were all dressed in surgical operating clothes with surgical masks over their faces and surgical caps over their heads. When they saw me, they all stopped talking and faced me."

"Did you recognize any of them?" asked Kit.

Doc Charlie cracked a small smile. "You've never been in surgery before?" she asked.

"I have, but I was unconscious," said Kit.

"In surgery, everyone looks basically the same, and they are covered head to toe with surgical gear," said Doc Charlie. "When you're part of a surgical team you get used to the gear and you know exactly who everyone else is. But, to any outsider, they all look the same, except for things like height, size, and eye color."

"Were any of them familiar to you?" asked Kit.

"I'm almost positive I'd never seen any of them before in my military career," said Doc Charlie.

"You didn't recognize anything about any of them that was familiar to you?" asked Kit.

"No, I didn't," replied Doc Charlie.

"Then what happened?" asked Kit.

"One of the men dressed in surgical scrubs took me by the arm and led me away from the man on the operating table and out of the tent," said Doc Charlie.

"He told me what I was seeing was a top-secret government operation. They were interrogating a Muslim terrorist who was part of a plot to plant a nuclear device in a major city in the United States and detonate it during a visit to the city by the President of the United States. The man was severely injured, and they feared he might be dying before he talked," said Doc Charlie.

"What did they want with you?" asked Kit.

"They wanted me to save the man," said a stone-faced Doc Charlie.

"Why you and not one of the doctors on base?" asked Kit.

"I have no idea," said Doc Charlie. "Maybe because I was available, maybe because I was just a physician's assistant and could be easily intimidated. I don't know."

"What did you do?" asked Kit.

"I went back into the tent, grabbed my bag from the man dressed in black, and then took the patient's vital signs. They were not good. His pulse was weak, his breathing irregular," she said.

"Was he injured?" asked Kit.

"You could say that," said Doc Charlie cynically. "He had been beaten. His face was bloody and pulpy. His chest was covered with lacerations and there was blood smeared all over his upper body. His upper torso was covered with burn marks, likely made with something like a cattle prod. I opened his mouth and several of his teeth had been broken off. The inside of his mouth was a mess."

"What did you do?" asked Kit.

"I attempted to restore his breathing. Then I gave him an injection of adrenaline to help his heart. Nothing I did seemed to help. I was losing the patient, and I was helpless to stop it," said Doc Charlie.

Kit wisely remained silent and motioned for Doc Charlie to continue her story.

She paused and looked up at the ceiling. When she looked back at Kit, her face was taut, rife with her emotion. "I failed," said Doc Charlie. "The patient died, and my attempts to revive him were unsuccessful."

"The patient died?" asked Kit.

"Yes, the patient died," said Doc Charlie. "It was all I could do to keep from bursting into tears. I didn't even know this poor man, and I was thrust into the role of saving his life when it was clearly way too late for me to be of any help to him."

Doc Charlie paused, tears forming in her eyes.

"I have had other patients die," she said. "But each time I was pretty sure I had done all I could and saving the patient was beyond medical science available to me at the time."

"This was different?" asked Kit.

"Yes, this was different. This was like being rushed to a fire of a house fully engulfed in flames and given a teaspoon of water and being told to save the house," she said. "I didn't even know the patient's name."

"What happened then?" asked Kit.

"I told the men who were there the patient was gone and there was nothing more I could do," she said.

"How did they react to the news?" asked Kit.

"They were angry, like they felt it was my fault the man died," said Doc Charlie. "I was both puzzled and surprised. This guy didn't die from injuries he got in a car wreck. He died from being tortured to death. And this happened in some secret area in a United States Air Force Base in Cheyenne, Wyoming. Those bozos acted like it was my fault the poor guy was dead."

"Did they accuse you of being responsible for his death?" asked a surprised Kit.

"More or less," said Doc Charlie. "They were angry and one of them called me a stupid bitch. I was upset, angry and more than a little frightened. Nothing like this had ever happened to me before, and I had no idea what would happen next."

"What did happen next?" asked Kit.

"One of them took me outside the tent and had me get in the Humvee," said Doc Charlie. "The driver and another man with an M4 rifle drove me to a building I was not familiar with. I'm not sure I could have found it in the daylight, let alone at three in the morning."

"What happened there?" asked Kit.

"The armed guard took me inside the building and led me to a small conference room. The room was poorly lit and had a long conference table in it surrounded by chairs. He motioned for me to sit at one end of the table. The room was empty. I was frightened. Then I gathered myself and tried to think of what to do. I got a thought and took out my new Apple iPhone and punched in some buttons to record and put the phone in the pocket of my uniform blouse. A man in an Air Force uniform entered the room and sat at the other end of the table. I had never seen him before. He wore emblems with the rank of colonel. The name on his nametag was Kane. The guard then stood by the door, his rifle at port arms. I was unsure of what to do, so I just sat there, waiting for this Kane guy to speak," said Doc Charlie.

"Did he speak?" asked Kit.

"He waited for quite some time. He kept looking at me and tapping his finger on a folder laying on the table in front of him. I knew he was trying to intimidate me, and he was doing a damn good job of it. I was as afraid as I had ever been in my entire life."

"Did he introduce himself?" asked Kit.

"No, he did not. He was silent for at least five minutes. I kept glancing down at the watch on my arm so that's how I knew how long he waited to speak," said Doc Charlie.

"Then he spoke in the deep, very authoritative voice. It only added to my fear."

"What did he say?" asked Kit.

"He told the guard to wait outside. The guard promptly left the room," said Doc Charlie.

Doc Charlie paused. "Could I have a drink of water?" she asked.

Swifty produced a cold bottle of water and took off the cap for her.

"Thank you," said Doc Charlie, as she accepted the bottle and took two long swigs from it. She put the bottle down on the table and looked up at the three men listening to her story.

"He told me I had witnessed a top-secret military operation, and I was never to speak of it again. Not to anyone, at any time, in any circumstance," said Doc Charlie. "I was told I needed to sign a nondisclosure agreement that would guarantee my silence about this event forever. If I refused to sign, I would be tried as a traitor under the Uniform Code of Military Justice and sentenced to life imprisonment at Leavenworth Military Prison. He told me he was there under orders from General Ventura. He said the general had ordered him to have me sign the nondisclosure agreement. He produced the agreement and I signed it. I was absolutely terrified."

"Did you know this General Ventura?" asked Kit.

"I had heard of him, but never met him," replied Doc Charlie.

"I'm so sorry you went through this," said Kit. "What happened next?"

"He took out his phone and photographed me holding

up the agreement. Then he told me if I ever violated the terms of the nondisclosure agreement, I would be thrown out of the Air Force, stripped of my rank and denied all military benefits, including my military pension. Then he called the guard in, and the guard returned me to my quarters," said Doc Charlie. "I undressed and threw my clothes into a laundry bag and took a long hot shower. When I finally felt somewhat clean, I went to bed and tried to sleep."

"Did you replay the recording on your phone?" asked Kit.

"I was so upset and frightened, I forgot about the phone until I woke up hours later," said Doc Charlie. "When I tried to find and play the recording, I couldn't find it. I must have screwed up when I tried to set it on record."

Disappointment showed in Kit's face. The recording would have been invaluable. "Did the man give you a copy of the agreement?' asked Kit.

"He did not," replied Doc Charlie.

"What happened the next day?" asked Kit.

"Nothing. Absolutely nothing. It was like the night had never happened," said Doc Charlie.

"The man in the colonel's uniform with the Kane nametag. Did you recognize him?" asked Kit.

"I'd never seen him before, nor did I ever see him again," said Doc Charlie.

"Did you report this to your superior officer on the base?" asked Kit.

"I was specifically forbidden in the agreement to ever mention the affair to anyone, ever," said Doc Charlie.

"So, you told no one?" asked Kit.

"I never breathed a word of what happened in the tent until tonight," said Doc Charlie.

"Why did you try to disappear when you retired from the Air Force?" asked Kit.

"Over the final two years of my enlistment at Warren Air Force base, I had some strange incidents," said Doc Charlie.

"Incidents?" asked Kit.

"Every now and then I felt like I was being spied on. It would turn out to be Air Force personnel I didn't know watching me or being near where I worked or lived. I even had incidents of strangers show up when I was working or in the chow line at mess," said Doc Charlie. "On an air base, personnel come and go. Some are attending classes, and some are changing deployment, so I kept telling myself I was imagining things," said Doc Charlie.

"Were you?" asked Kit.

"I think someone was keeping tabs on me," said Doc Charlie. "I knew I could be watched as long as I was in the Air Force, but when I retired, things might change."

"How so?" asked Kit.

"Once out of the Air Force, what I did could be quite unpredictable and it would be harder to keep tabs on me. I also worried that I had made some subtle inquiries about what happened that night and no one seemed to know what I was talking about. I figured once I was out of the Air Force, it might be convenient for me to just disappear," said Doc Charlie. "So, I made a plan to disappear on the day I retired. I thought the plan was pretty good until today when you walked into my clinic."

Kit did not speak. He sat back in his chair and stared

at the ceiling for a few minutes. Then he looked directly at Doc Charlie.

"I like to think Swifty and I are pretty good at what we do," said Kit. "But the truth is, if we can find you, someone high up in the Air Force with a lot more assets at his disposal can surely find you as well. In fact, as I think about it, we were searching for a lost child for a concerned mother. This was one of the least sinister cases we've ever had."

"You look worried," said Doc Charlie. "Should I be worried too?"

"I'm worried that in our search for you, we didn't hide who we were nor what we were looking for and we talked to several people in the process of hunting you down," said Kit. "We may have made it easier for someone else to follow on our coattails and learn what we found out."

"You think someone was following you?" asked Doc Charlie.

"Maybe not right behind us," said Kit. "But we left a pretty clear trail of where we went and what we were doing. It wouldn't take a genius to follow our path and wind up at your office in Freedom. If what you have told me is accurate, and someone was keeping tabs on you, they would likely have panicked when you disappeared.

"So, what should I do?" asked an obviously shaken Doc Charlie.

"Let me go to my room and make a couple of phone calls," said Kit. "Swifty and Big Dave will entertain you while I'm gone."

"How long will you be gone?" asked Doc Charlie more than a little anxiously.

"Half an hour at the most," said Kit.

Kit rose from his chair and turned to Swifty and Big Dave. "You two keep Doc company and make sure she's safe and sound," he said.

Kit left the room and heard Swifty slip the lock on the door behind him. Kit smiled to himself and walked to his room.

In slightly less than thirty minutes Kit returned to the conference room and rapped on the now locked door. The door opened just a crack and then it opened wide. Swifty was putting his pistol away while Kit was coming through the door and into the room.

He took a seat and then took out his small notebook. He glanced at it and then looked up at Doc Charlie and his two expectant friends.

"I did some research on this General Ventura," said Kit.

"What did you learn?" asked Doc Charlie.

"It seems General Ventura may have a new and more urgent reason to find our where you disappeared to," said Kit grimly.

"What do you mean?" asked Doc Charlie.

"The general is apparently up for an appointment to the Joint Chiefs of Staff," replied Kit.

"Oh God," said Doc Charlie.

"What does this appointment mean to the Doc?" asked Big Dave.

"It means the price of poker just went up through the roof," said Kit. "Anyone in the military up for that type of post is going to have every nook and cranny of their background thoroughly investigated." Said Kit.

"So, the good general is gonna want to do some very thorough house cleanin' to make sure no one knows about any of the bad stuff he's done," said Swifty with a smirk on his face.

"Housecleanin' like having someone like Doc Charlie disappear into thin air?' asked Big Dave.

"You are a lot smarter than you look," said Swifty.

"Watch your mouth, boy," snarled Big Dave.

"I think I have a plan," said Kit.

"Let's hear it," said a now solemn Big Dave.

"I think we need to take Doc Charlie back to her office tonight. She can pack what she needs, and we'll load it into my truck. She'll write a note to her help and tell them she has been called away on a medical emergency and she will call them when she is able. In the note she will tell her help to cancel any appointments she has for the next week," said Kit.

"Questions?" asked Kit.

"Where the hell are we takin' the Doc?" asked Big Dave.

"I'll tell you on the way," said Kit. "I now am suspicious of anything and everything and there is a remote chance this room is bugged. So, the less said the better. Understood?"

Both Big Dave and Swifty nodded their assent in silence. Then the four of them left the conference room. Each of them went to their rooms, gathered their gear and headed to the truck. Kit stopped at the office and paid the bill in cash. Twenty minutes later, after stopping at Doc's office, Kit was driving his truck south toward Cokeville, heading to Kemmerer.

CHAPTER NINETEEN

By the time Kit drove into Kemmerer, Doc Charlie was fast asleep in the back seat of the truck. After pulling into the garage next to the old bank building that served as the office for Rocky Mountain Searchers, Big Dave gently shook Doc Charlie, and she woke up with a start. Initially she was confused by her surroundings and then Big Dave patted her on the head and said, "There, there. Don't worry, Doc. You're in good hands here."

Doc blinked her eyes several times, as if to make sure her surroundings were real and not part of a dream. Then she smiled and sat up.

"Where are we?" she asked.

"Someplace safe and private," said Big Dave.

Kit was listening carefully to the conversation behind him. He was constantly amazed at Big Dave. No one he knew was rougher or tougher. But Big Dave had the ability to be as polite and charming as an English gentleman when the occasional called for it. He really had the ability to charm and to comfort people when he chose to.

Kit opened the driver's door and stepped into the large garage attached to the old bank building. The interior of the garage was now well lit, but there were no windows to betray their presence to any passerby who might notice the light flooding out into the evening's darkness.

Doc Charlie stepped out of the truck and Big Dave took her elbow in his hand and led her to the side door to the main building. Kit led the way and Swifty brought up the rear, carrying Doc Charlie's bags. They went down a short hallway and stopped after entering a sizeable conference room.

"Have a seat, Doc," said Kit.

Doc Charlie sat and the other three men joined her.

"I know you have lots of questions, Doc, but I don't have many answers yet," said Kit.

"Why are we here?" asked Doc Charlie. "And where is here?"

Kit paused to gather his thoughts before answering her. He glanced at Big Dave and Swifty. They were quiet, but they were listening intently, as they had no clue what the next step might be.

"I'm going to ask you some more questions," said Kit. "But first, I'll answer yours. You are here in my office in Kemmerer because I believe it is a safe place for you. I'm sorry if the questions seem annoying, but I need to make sure I have all the facts straight. Then we need to make a plan to keep you safe."

"Safe from what?" asked Doc Charlie.

"I have no idea," said Kit. "But I think your instincts have been correct. You saw something you weren't supposed to see and were made to sign an agreement to keep silent about it under penalty of imprisonment or worse. I don't think you went to all that trouble to disappear when you retired just for fun. I think you did it because you are a very smart woman, and you knew the day you were no longer in the Air Force you were in possible danger for what you witnessed that night."

Kit paused again, as if to make sure he was not missing any information about that night in Doc Charlie's past.

"If what you told us is accurate, and I have no reason to believe it isn't, you may be in serious danger," said Kit. "Someone in authority may even want you dead."

Doc Charlie was silent for a minute and then she put her hands on the conference table and looked directly at Kit. "I have good instincts, Mr. Andrews. I served in a field hospital in both Afghanistan and Iraq. I saw things I do not wish to ever see again. I also saw intense human suffering and misery. But I also saw uncommon bravery. I learned war doesn't care if you are brave or a coward. To war, you are just another victim," she said.

Then she paused. "May I have some water, please?" she asked.

Both Big Dave and Swifty rose from their chairs and actually bumped into each other in their haste to rush to the tiny break room to get her a bottle of water. If the moment were not so serious, it would have been quite funny.

Swifty won the race and handed Doc Charlie a bottle of water.

"Thank you," she said, taking the bottle from Swifty's hand.

She opened the bottle and took a couple of long swigs of the cold water. Then she replaced the cap and set the bottle on the table in front of her.

"I've thought about that night a great deal," she said. "Someone pretty high up in the Air Force brought that man to the base in Cheyenne. I think they chose Warren Air Force Base because it's remote. They could fly onto the base with their prisoner, set up the interrogation tent I saw in the hanger, and conduct a secret interrogation in secure privacy and without a chance of discovery. Who ordered all that is a mystery. No one I saw that night was familiar to me. Not even the creep who tried to intimidate me and made me sign that non-disclosure agreement. I never saw any of them again after that night. When their interrogation methods went too far and the prisoner began to fail, they panicked. I think they picked me because I was available, I was a woman, and I was a physician's assistant, not a doctor. I think they figured I would be easy to intimidate and scare.

Doc Charlie paused for a moment and looked up at the ceiling. When she regained her composure, she looked directly at Kit.

"They succeeded. They scared the crap out of me, and I'm not proud of that," said Doc Charlie. "I decided to retire after my twenty years in the Air Force, and to disappear on the day I left the base for the last time. I thought I had planned it pretty well until you boys showed up at my office. Now, I'm worried that I may have lulled myself into a false sense of security working out of my little office in Freedom and using my friend's identity."

Doc Charlie paused, and put her folded hands down on the table in front of her. She stared at her hands for a couple of minutes and then she looked up.

"I'm scared and I admit it," said Doc Charlie. "I don't like admitting it, but I know that if you could find me, so could people who don't have good intentions. I guess I should be thankful you found me first."

"Then you should thank your mother," said Kit, softly. "She's the one who hired us to find out where you were and what had happened to you."

"Does she know you've found me?" asked Doc Charlie.

"She will in about fifteen minutes," said Kit with a smile. "I'm sure she'll be thrilled to know we found you. Can you think of anything else from that night? Something that you haven't told us about before?"

Doc Charlie shook her head no. Then she excused herself to go to the restroom. Kit told her where the main bathroom was and watched as she left the conference room.

As soon as they heard the door to the restroom open and close, Big Dave turned to Kit.

"What now?" he asked.

"We take her to my dad's place west of here," said Kit. "He's on a cruise with his girlfriend from Santa Fe. The cruise still has eight days to go and then he told me he plans to spend a week in Santa Fe. The house is available, and it's very private."

"I remember that place," said Swifty. "Three guys could hold off a small army from it."

"It'd have to be a pretty small army," said Kit with a grin. "But it is private. It is defensible, and we need to keep her whereabouts secret except to us."

"We're gonna need some more manpower to protect her," said Big Dave.

"You're right on that score," said Kit. "Got any suggestions?"

"I got spare time," said Big Dave. "So does my son, Thor."

"Count me in," said Swifty. "And don't forget your

half-brother up in Sheridan. This sounds like his kind of deal to me."

"Don't forget the honorable Harrison Woodly," said Big Dave. "That old fart would be damn pissed if we didn't include him on this deal."

"I forgot about Woody," said Kit. "Can he still handle a gun?" he asked.

"Does a bear shit in the woods?" responded Big Dave. "That old bastard was born with a gun in his hand instead of a rattle."

"That makes six of us," said Kit.

"We can make it seven," said Swifty.

"Who do you have in mind?" asked Kit.

"My grandfather, Bushrod," said Swifty. "He might even drag some of his old green beret pals along with him."

"Just what we need," snorted Big Dave. "The over-the-hill gang who are likely to shoot first and ask questions later."

"Actually, I'd love to have them," said Swifty. "Those old geezers are tough as leather, and they know how to melt into the background."

"Those old boys were pretty damn tough as I recall," said Kit.

Kit took a few notes on the small pad he kept in his shirt pocket. When he was done, he looked at both Big Dave and Swifty.

"When Doc comes back, I'll take her to my dad's place. You two need to get on the phone and do some recruiting," said Kit.

"How long do we tell them this operation will last?" asked Swifty.

"Till it's over," replied Kit. "In the meantime, you too get on your phones and see if you can get some commitments from our list to help protect the Doc."

Both men nodded their agreement to the idea.

Kit pointed at Swifty. "When you're done making your calls, get your butt out to my dad's place and we can assess what needs to be done to shore up any potential weak points in the defensive perimeter."

"Will do," said Swifty. "Is the code for the main gate still the same?" he asked.

"Still the same," said Kit.

"What's the code?" asked Big Dave.

"I'd just as soon keep it secret until we get everyone on the same page," said Kit. "Not that I don't trust you, Big Dave, but I'd prefer having to keep Dad's place secure until we have a plan."

"Lot of bullshit if you ask me, but O.K.," said Big Dave.

"One last thing," said Kit. "We tell no one about the doc. And I mean no one. Is that clear?"

"What about the guys we are asking to help out?" asked Swifty.

"Same thing goes for them. There's plenty of time to fill them in when they get here," said Kit.

"If they come," said Swifty.

"I'm betting no one we ask says no," said Kit.

"As soon as Doc comes back in, I'll get her stuff together and take her out to Dad's place. Any questions?" Kit asked.

There were none.

CHAPTER TWENTY

Ten minutes later, Kit was driving west out of Kemmerer with Doc Charlie in the passenger seat of his truck.

"Did you contact my mother?" asked Doc Charlie.

"I thought I'd do that when we get to where we're going, and you can talk to her directly," said Kit.

Doc Charlie was quiet for a couple of minutes. Then she spoke in a low voice.

"I don't know what to say to her," she said with concern in her voice.

"I have a feeling your mother will do plenty of talking, and you'll figure out what to say pretty naturally," said a smiling Kit.

Doc Charlie had no response. Kit glanced over at her. She seemed deep in thought. He decided the best thing to do was nothing. He kept quiet for the rest of the trip.

Just before he entered Nugget Canyon, Kit took an inconspicuous dirt road to his left and slowly made his way uphill. The dirt, sand, and boulders soon gave way to lodge pole pine trees and quaking aspen. The road became rougher with more potholes as he made his way through a couple of sharp switchback turns. As they came out of the switchbacks, the trees abruptly ended. In front of them appeared a one-story rambling log cabin nestled up against the sheer rock wall of a tall butte. Next to the cabin was a large metal barn that resembled a small airplane hangar. Attached to the barn and running down the slope from the butte was a sizeable empty corral of solid looking wood fencing. The posts looked like what they were, recycled railroad ties.

Kit stopped the truck and turned to Doc Charlie. "Turn and look back. Tell me what you see," he said.

Doc Charlie turned and looked back the way they had come. She looked back and forth a couple of times before she spoke. "I see nothing but pine trees and aspen," she said.

"Good," said Kit. "That's what you're supposed to see. From down on the road, you can see nothing through the tree cover."

Kit drove on up toward the log cabin. The road suddenly became well graded with a stone surface. Kit parked the truck in front of the cabin and got out. He motioned for Doc Charlie to do the same and she did.

When she joined Kit in front of the truck, he turned and faced the way they had come up the butte. "You can see we're on this small plateau that comes out of the butte like a shelf. The plateau slopes slightly downward and is all meadow until it reaches the pine trees. The trees shield us from the highway and vice-versa."

Doc followed his gaze. The meadow was fenced and surrounded on three sides by the pine and aspen forest. The meadow led up to the cabin and the butte, which rose about five hundred feet above the cabin. Kit then led her back to the truck and motioned for her to get back in. As soon as she was seated, Kit pulled a small device from the sun visor and pressed a button on it. A large door at their end of the barn began to rise and continued until the door was completely open. Kit started the truck and drove it into the barn. As soon as they were inside, he hit the device button again and the door began to descend. Overhead lights in the barn automatically came on and they exited the truck.

Doc Charlie looked around at the inside of the barn. It looked large enough to hold about twelve vehicles. Currently it held only two. One was a relatively new Lexus GX SUV, and the other was a like new John Deere Gator with an enclosed cab and seating for two.

"It's surprisingly large inside," said Kit. "It'll hold about a dozen vehicles, depending on size. The doors are reinforced steel, made to look like old wood. The sides are also reinforced steel. On the west side are stalls for horses, a tack room, supply room, and a shop. You get to them through that door," he said pointing to a Dutch-door painted bright red. "The stalls open out to the corral," he said pointing to a large steel door behind the stalls. "The end of the barn is up against the rock wall of the butte."

On the steel wall against the butte was a large steel reinforced door. Kit went to a small metal box mounted on the wall. He opened the box with a key, and it revealed a small panel with pushbuttons on it. He pressed a series of buttons, and they heard a loud click. Kit pulled down on a steel bar handle and the steel door opened easily.

Kit led the way as they went through the door and entered a small hallway. They found themselves at the end of a small shooting range with targets at the far end and two shooting stands at their end. Each stand had a small control panel. Kit went to one panel and flipped a switch and the panel lit up. He pressed a button and the target at the far end moved on a cable back to where they were standing.

"This allows the shooter to mount and then change targets and check how they did," he said with a grin.

"How far away is the target?" Doc Charlie asked.

"This is roughly a twenty-five-yard range," replied Kit.

Kit pointed to a bench against the wall and next to the door. "This serves as a mini-shop for repairs or reloading," he said. Next to the bench was an old steel safe door set in the wall with a combination lock on the front of the safe. The safe was a bit dusty and the faded gold letters on the door spelled out, "DIEBOLD."

"What's in the vault?" asked Doc Charlie.

"Let's see," said Kit. He spun the combination lock counterclockwise several times and then dialed in a combination from memory. Then he turned the lever and the safe door popped open. The door led to a small room blasted out of the butte's natural rock. Inside the vault room were several tall heavy gauge steel lockers, each with quality looking padlocks. On both sides of the room were sturdy wooden racks holding shotguns, rifles, and pistols. Below the racks were shelves filled with boxes of ammunition of various calibers.

Doc Charlie was no stranger to guns, having spent twenty years in the Air Force and having spent several tours of duty in Afghanistan and Iraq, but she was staggered at the display in front of her.

"These are all yours?" she asked.

"Nope," replied Kit. "They belong to my father. This is his place. All my weapons are back at my place."

Doc Charlie's face was filled with surprise. She seemed

to want to say something, but she was having trouble coming up with something coherent. She swallowed her surprise and kept her mouth shut.

Kit shut things up and led the way back into the barn. Then he closed the big steel door and tapped a code into the control box. A noticeable click filled the air. Kit led the way out of the barn through a steel side door that was also controlled by a combination locking system. Kit checked the door and then led the way toward the cabin.

The front of the cabin faced slightly northeast and had a roofed porch that wrapped around the front and both sides of the cabin. They entered the massive wooden front door after Kit utilized another push button combination lock system. The front door was heavy steel made to look like wood.

Once inside, they found themselves in a mudroom. A rough wooden bench ran against one wall, with storage spaces under the bench. Above it was wooden pegs fitted into a thick wooden board. Two jackets hung from pegs. The floor was slate. Kit led the way through a door at the end of the mud room and they were in a large kitchen. The kitchen had a slate floor, and the backsplash was painted southwestern tiles. The countertops were granite, and the cabinets were cherry wood. All the stainless-steel appliances appeared to be new. The kitchen was well lit.

Doc Charlie looked around in awe. "Do you keep the lights on all the time?" she asked, pointing to the overhead lighting.

Kit laughed. "No, we don't. The lights are motion activated and came on when we entered the room," he said.

Kit gave her a tour of the "cabin," which consisted of

about three thousand square feet of living space. The cabin was decorated like a southwestern ranch house. The furniture was mostly massive in wood and leather and looked and felt amazingly comfortable. One wall of the great room was solid bookshelves filled with books and photos. The ten-foot-high walls were stucco painted an off-white. The floors were slate with Navajo throw rugs. The ceiling had exposed wood beams, and the walls held paintings of western art. Each room had indirect lighting, and motion sensors turned on the lights wherever they entered a room. The great room, a combination living room and family room was spacious.

The great room was at the north end of the house and had floor to ceiling plate glass windows with views of the mountains and Nugget Canyon.

As they left the great room and started down a short hallway, Kit stopped and turned to face Doc Charlie. "There are four bedrooms, each with its own bath. My dad's room is kept locked. You can have your pick of the other three," said Kit.

Doc Charlie nodded her understanding, and they continued on down the hall. As they entered the first available bedroom, Doc Charlie noticed there was a fireplace in the corner.

"I think I like this one," she said with a smile.

"Because of the fireplace?" asked Kit.

"Yes," answered Doc Charlie.

"You noticed the big stone fireplace in the great room?" he asked.

"Yes, I did," replied Doc Charlie.

Kit smiled. "There is a fireplace in the great room and one in each of the four bedrooms," he said.

"Then let's see the rest of them," replied a smiling Doc Charlie.

They toured the other two bedrooms and she stuck with her first choice. Kit brought her bags into the bedroom and put them on folding stands.

"There's a phone on the desk. Feel free to use it at any time," said Kit. Then he pulled out his small notebook and a pen and wrote on the page then tore off the page and handed it to Doc Charlie.

"This is your mother's phone number," said Kit. "I'll leave you alone so you can unpack and call her in private."

Kit handed her the page and walked out of the bedroom, carefully closing the door behind him. Then he went into the kitchen and checked the stocks in the refrigerator, freezer, and pantry. He noted some items and wrote them down on the small notebook and returned it to his pocket. Then he proceeded to make a pot of coffee. While the coffee was brewing, he got out coffee mugs, cream, sugar, and a jar of honey. When the coffee was done, he poured himself a cup and went into the room that served as a small office and fired up the computer. He sent some messages and did some inquiries and then made a list and printed it out. When he was finished, he shut off the computer and took the list back to the kitchen, where he refilled his coffee mug.

There was no sign of Doc Charlie, so he took his coffee into the great room and sat in one of the big comfortable leather chairs. About ten minutes later, Doc Charlie appeared.

"Did you get to talk to your mother?" asked Kit.

"I did, and thank you for connecting me with her," said Doc Charlie. "It was a bit awkward at first, but pretty soon we were talking like good friends, and I found myself crying while I talked. I hate crying. I always think it's a sign of a woman's weakness, but this time it actually felt good."

"I'm glad it went well," said Kit. "Would you like some coffee?"

"Absolutely," said Doc Charlie. "Is it in the kitchen?"

"Yes, it is," replied Kit.

"I'll get my own cup," she said. "I may be a woman, but I'm not helpless. You don't need to wait on me hand and foot. All I need is answers to where stuff is or how to work it."

She returned with a mug of coffee and took a seat in a big chair facing Kit.

"My mother wanted to fly out here to see me as soon as she could get a flight," said Doc Charlie.

"I don't think that's a good idea until we have a better idea of what we might be dealing with," said Kit.

"I understand. That's pretty much what I told her. She was not happy, but she agreed. I have some questions," said Doc Charlie.

"I'm sure you do," said Kit.

"When we drove up here, I didn't see any power poles," she said.

"Good observation," said Kit. "There is a power company riser down by the entrance to the road. The meter is on the riser and the power line is buried up to the ranch house as is the phone line. In addition, we have a standby generator powered by a propane tank that also provides fuel for the furnace and the hot water heater. There are three buried propane tanks down at the end of the meadow by the road. There are also two hidden water wells that supply us with fresh water. At the top of the butte is a spring fed pond. We have a hidden pipe from the pond running down to the water tank in the corral."

Kit paused to see if Doc Charlie had any questions. When she didn't, he continued.

"There is a buried five-hundred-gallon gasoline tank by the barn. We have satellite television and internet service. This place was designed and built by my dad to be private and difficult to find. The cabin has a surveillance system with cameras covering almost 100% of the property. There are also motion sensors surrounding the property," said Kit.

"What about all the chimneys you have?" asked Doc Charlie. "Couldn't someone see the smoke from the chimneys?"

Kit smiled. "All the chimneys are designed to diffuse the smoke. And the chimneys and exhaust pipes are disguised to look like rocks on the top of the butte," he said.

Kit got to his feet. "Let me show you one more thing," he said.

Kit led her to a control panel in the cabin and explained how to work the heating and cooling system. He also explained how to work the generator and the security system. He took her into a small room which contained the monitors for the security system and had controls for the generator as well. Then he reached into his pocket and produced a small key on a keyring.

He walked out to the great room and pulled a picture on the wall away from the wall. The picture was on a hinge. Behind the picture was a small metal locked door. He used the key to open the door. Inside were labeled keys hanging from small stubs. On the back of the door was a diagram listing what each numbered key was for. Kit explained what each key was used for. Then he closed the box, locked it, shut the picture flat against the wall, and gave Doc Charlie the key.

"Any questions?" asked Kit.

"Not now, but I'm kind of overwhelmed with information," said Doc Charlie. "I'll make a list as I think of things so I can ask all of my questions at once, instead of bothering you every ten minutes with a new one."

Kit laughed. "Don't worry. You'll get used to this place soon enough. There's a television in each bedroom, plus the one in the great room. The satellite television system is DISH and there is a controller with each television set. Are you familiar with DISH?"

"Yes, I am," replied Doc Charlie.

"Good," said Kit. "Now, I have a suggestion for you."

"Fire away," said Doc Charlie.

"Check out the kitchen, particularly the refrigerator, the freezer, and the pantry," said Kit. "Please make a list of things you like to eat that are not in any of those places and I'll see to it we get this place properly restocked."

"Are you serious?" asked Doc Charlie.

"Of course, I'm serious," said Kit. "I have no idea how long we'll need to stay here, and I assure you any food in this place will get eaten. Especially if Swifty stays here for any length of time."

CHAPTER TWENTY-ONE

While Doc Charlie did an inventory of the kitchen, Kit checked the surveillance system and then verified the amounts in the gasoline tank, the propane tanks, and the condition of the water pumps. When he was finished, he retrieved his laptop from his truck and returned to the ranch house.

Once inside, he fired up his laptop and checked his messages. He had several emails. One was from his half-brother, Billy McMaster in Sheridan. Kit looked at the message.

"Got update from Big Dave. Am packing now. Will leave for Kemmerer in one hour."

Kit smiled. His half-brother was a lot different than Kit. But, at his core, they were one and the same. If it took Billy an hour to pack, God knows what he was bringing with him. In an hour, Billy could pack an entire arsenal. He was glad Billy was coming. The former Marine top sniper would be a welcome addition to his tiny force.

Next was a text from Woody the attorney. "Talked to Big Dave. Will be there in an hour."

Another old timer who could be counted on. Woody was no soldier, but he was a good shot and a very smart man and an experienced big game hunter. His presence would be more than welcome.

Kit sat back in his chair and thought. With himself, Swifty, Big Dave, Woody, and Billy, their tiny defense team now numbered five. He was fairly sure about Big Dave's son, Thor. If Thor was able to get time off from the mine, he would be another welcome addition. Thor was a slightly smaller version of Big Dave and every bit as tough. That would make them a six-man team.

As Kit continued to check and reply to emails, he was interrupted when Doc Charlie came into the great room. She walked up to where he was seated and handed him a hand-written list.

"Is this your final list?" asked Kit.

"More or less," replied Doc Charlie. "I may think of something I forgot, but I think the list is pretty complete."

Kit scanned the list. He was quite sure everything on the list was available at the grocery store in Kemmerer. He could pick up all the items on the list when he went into town. But that would have to wait until he had some more armed bodies here at his dad's place.

It was almost four hours later when a soft bell alarm rang in the house. It rang twice like two soft strokes of a clapper in a bell.

"What's that?" said Doc Charlie with a note of alarm in her voice as she looked quickly from side to side as she tried to determine the source of the sound.

"It's just the road alarm," said Kit. "Whenever any thing comes up the road down by the power box, the alarm is triggered to let us know we have guests."

"Guests?" asked Doc Charlie.

"Yes, guests," said Kit. "Sometimes they are invited guests and sometimes they are not. Either way, we know they are coming and can get ready to properly receive them."

Doc Charlie finally stood still in the middle of the great room with a puzzled look on her face.

"Relax," said Kit. "We are expecting guests and if you want to check on them, go back to the security room and look at the monitors."

Doc Charlie looked at Kit, then at the door to the security room and then back at Kit. Curiosity got the better of her, and she quickly strode to the security room and disappeared inside. Two minutes later, she came back out and returned to her seat on the large leather chair.

"What did you see on the monitors?" asked Kit.

"A big black pickup truck with Mr. Swifty driving it," replied Doc.

"Was anyone else in the truck?"

"Not that I could see. Just Mr. Swifty," said Doc.

"For God's sake, please don't call him Mr. Swifty to his face," said Kit with a grin on his face. "He's hard enough to handle now, let alone allowing someone to call him Mr. Swifty," said Kit.

"I'll keep that in mind," said a non-smiling Doc.

Ten minutes later Swifty was coming through the front door of the cabin. He had two armfuls of groceries and he carried them to the kitchen and set them on the counter. Then he turned to go back outside.

"Don't just sit there like a bump on a log, Tenderfoot," said Swifty. "Lend a working man a hand. There's more stuff in the truck."

Kit got up and joined Swifty going out to the truck. It

took two more trips to haul the balance of the groceries into the cabin. Kit started to put things away, and Doc came into the kitchen and began helping. Soon, they had all the groceries stowed away. Perhaps just as important, Doc now knew where everything was. After Kit left to join Swifty in the great room, Doc continued to open cabinets and drawers as she familiarized herself with where things were stored in the kitchen.

"After seeing all this, I think I need to redo the list I made," said Doc Charlie.

Swifty went out to his now empty truck and pulled it into the barn. As he exited the barn, he hit a button and the large garage door started rumbling down to close off the building.

CHAPTER TWENTY-TWO

Swifty and Kit began to make a list of things they felt necessary for the defense of Kit's dad's cabin site. Next to each item on the list, they noted whether they had it in hand or needed to obtain it. By the time the list was completed and thoroughly discussed between the two friends, over three hours had passed.

As Kit was gathering up the paper sheets, they had written their list on, he looked up to see Doc staring at them with a questionable look on her face.

"Is something wrong?" asked Kit.

"I spent twenty years in the Air Force," said Doc. "I was in the medical branch, but I saw some hostile action in Iraq and Afghanistan. I got shot at and I managed to shoot back," she said. "I can think of a couple of things you may have omitted in your list I think would come in pretty handy in defending a place like this."

"We're all ears," said Kit as he sat back down and motioned for Doc to join them.

Doc sat on the end of the couch and looked straight at both men. "I've been listening to you discuss putting items on your list," Doc said. "And I heard you discuss how many men you hope to have available and how you plan to deploy them. In all your discussions, I never heard my name mentioned as one of the defenders. These unknown people may come here with the intent to kill me. I understand that. But I'm trained military. I can shoot. I can fight. And I've been trained by some of the best on how to do both. I'm not your sister or your mother. I'm a trained soldier."

"You have our undivided attention," said Kit.

"You need to engage the enemy when they are out in the open or on the edge of your defenses. That requires a couple of things I didn't see on your list," she said.

"What things?" asked a puzzled Swifty.

"Based on what I've seen of this property, you need an observation post on top of the rock ridge behind this cabin. It's the highest point on the property," she said. "And you need communication links between that post and the rest of the defenders."

"What else?" asked Kit who was taking notes.

"I would place at least three rings of surprise defenses between the road and the cabin," she said.

"What kind of surprise defenses?" asked Kit.

"Booby traps that use both trip wires and remote controls," Doc replied.

"You mean something like claymore mines?" asked Kit.

"Exactly," replied Doc. "Using three rows of them slows them down, announces to us they are out there, and creates wounded and dead issues for the rest of the attacking force."

"What else?" asked Kit.

"You have no artillery, so I propose the next best thing," said Doc.

"Artillery?" asked a surprised Swifty.

"Grenade launchers," said Doc. "They're light, mobile, and damned accurate and very devastating."

"Sounds great, but where the hell would we get those things?" asked Kit.

"Actually, I think I know just where I can get my hands on both of those items," said Swifty.

"Where?" asked a surprised Kit.

"You remember my grandfather, Bushrod?" asked Swifty.

"Sure. I remember you telling me all about him. So what?" asked Kit.

"He has both claymores and grenade launchers plus plenty of frag grenades up at his place in the mountains," said Kit.

"Where the hell did he get stuff like that? And how old are those things? Did he bring them back from Vietnam?" asked Kit.

"Actually, they are like new," said Swifty.

"How do you know that for sure?" asked Kit.

"Because I obtained them for him last summer when we were trying to figure out who killed my old man," replied Swifty.

"Oh," said Kit.

Silence engulfed the room as all three people tried to digest what they had just learned from each other.

"Can you get in touch with Bushrod?" asked Kit.

"I already did," said Swifty. "He's agreed to join us here for our little welcome party and he's trying to locate a couple of his old green beret pals to join him."

A surprised Kit paused for a minute and then said, "That'd be a plus."

"I think so too," said Swifty. "Bushrod carried a M-203 grenade launcher attached to his M-16 on every mission he went out on in Vietnam. He's really accurate with one."

Kit looked over at Doc. "Anything else you think we should have on hand?" he asked.

Doc smiled and shook her head no.

Kit stood up. "Those are damn good ideas. We've got some work to do and calls to make," he said.

Doc held up her hand, like a second grader in school.

Kit looked at her and then said," Yes?"

"I think we could use a good-sized map of your dad's property and the land around it so we can tape it on a wall and note where everything is placed," Doc said.

"Good idea," said Kit. "When I go to town, I'll stop by the BLM office and pick up a map which should include land contours as well.

"Anything to add?" he asked and looked right at Swifty.

"Let's get ready to rock 'n roll," said Swifty.

"I was born ready," replied Kit.

Doc just smiled.

CHAPTER TWENTY-THREE

About an hour and a half later, Kit, Swifty, and Doc were eating frozen sandwiches they had nuked in the microwave when the road alarm went off.

Kit and Swifty threw down their sandwiches and ran to the equipment room. Doc ran to the window. Once in the equipment room, Kit and Swifty looked at the camera monitors. They could see clearly in the monitor a big GMC Pickup truck. Big Dave was driving and his son, Thor, was in the passenger seat. Both men were giving the camera the finger, laughing as they drove by.

A few minutes later, the truck pulled up in front of the cabin. Kit and Swifty went out to greet Big Dave. Doc Charlie followed them out of the cabin and stood back to the side of the rowdy welcome.

Big Dave noticed her and stepped over and took her gently by the arm.

"Doc, I'd like you to meet my son, Thor. Thor, this is Doc Charlie, the lady I been tellin' you about."

Thor was a younger, but only slightly smaller version of Big Dave. He smiled and extended his hand. Doc Charlie took it and found his grip firm, but gentle, for such a huge hand on a big man.

"Nice to meet you, ma'am," said Thor.

"Good to meet you, Thor," said Doc.

"I swear," said Swifty. "That's the most words in one sentence I think I ever heard old Thor utter in public."

Everyone laughed and Thor blushed, looking like a giant who got his hand caught in the cookie jar.

"Where do you want this stuff stored?" asked Big Dave as he extended his arm and pointed to the bed of the truck which was covered with a canvas tarp.

"Put the truck in the barn and unload it there," said Kit. "There's plenty of room for all your gear. Sort it out while you're in there and then come up to the cabin."

"Where do you want me to put the truck?" asked Big Dave.

"Leave it in the barn," replied Kit. He had thought about the vehicles and decided keeping them out of sight was a good idea. The less obvious their presence at the cabin the better for the time being.

Big Dave climbed into the cab of the truck and started the engine. He drove it over to the barn, and Kit opened the door for him. As soon as the truck was inside, the four men and Doc all helped unload it and stow the contents in the spacious barn. When they were finished, Kit closed the barn door and the group headed up to the cabin. As they walked to the cabin, all four men were carrying rifles, pistols, and ammunition.

Once they were inside the cabin, they stowed the ammo, but kept the rifles and pistols within easy reach. Kit had all five of them sit at the dining room table, and he showed them his map of the property and the surrounding area. He explained where the cameras were located and the approximate location of all the sensors on the property. Then he had Doc explain her idea of booby traps set in three layers. Everyone agreed with her idea. When she brought up the idea of grenade launchers, both Big Dave and Swifty were enthusiastic in their support of her idea.

When he had finished with his overview of the defense plan, Kit paused and looked over his audience. He saw faces that were grim, businesslike, and determined.

"Anyone got any questions or thoughts?" asked Kit.

"Time to rock n' roll," said Swifty. Big Dave and Thor nodded their heads in agreement.

The meeting broke up and Swifty took Big Dave, Thor, and Doc on a ground tour of the property. Doc brought along a hand-held electronic map and each time they picked a site for a claymore mine she made an electronic waypoint on her map.

While they were gone, Kit opened his laptop and began to type an after-action report on what Doc had told them about her fateful night at Warren Air Force base in Cheyenne. He typed it as a written report on the incident as told by Doc. He reread the report, made a few changes and then printed it out after saving it to the laptop's memory. Then he went out to the kitchen and got a cup of coffee. After adding some honey and cream, he stirred the coffee and went into the great room. He sat in an easy chair and read the printed statement one more time.

CHAPTER TWENTY-FOUR

When Doc and the rest returned to the cabin, Kit motioned for her to take a seat in the chair next to him. Once she was seated, Kit handed her the printout he had made. He sipped his coffee, as she carefully read what he had handed her.

"Is it accurate?" asked Kit.

"It sounds almost exactly the way I remember it," replied Doc.

"Should there be any changes?" asked Kit.

"No, I don't think so," answered Doc. "It sounds just as I remember that night. Why did you write this up?" she asked.

"As private citizens, we have lots of freedoms, but we don't have the connections, communications, and information that government agencies have access to," said Kit. "I plan on sending a copy of this to two friends of mine in Law Enforcement in Wyoming."

"What friends?" asked Doc.

"One is Detective Bob Parcell in the Laramie Police Department. The other is Sheriff Wade Nystrom of Sheridan County," said Kit.

"Why them?" asked Doc.

"I know them, and I trust them," said Kit. "I plan to

ask them to let me know if they get any inquiries from any outside government agencies about you."

"And if they do?" asked Doc.

"I'm going to ask to let me know, off the record, unofficially, and secretly," said Kit.

"Is that legal" asked Doc.

"Probably not, but it won't be the first time I've bent over the line from legal to illegal," said Kit.

Doc smiled.

"It's a bad habit I picked up from hanging around Swifty too much," muttered Kit.

"It works for me," said Doc.

Kit handed her the last page of the printout. "Please sign where indicated at the bottom of the page," he said.

Doc signed the paper and handed it back to Kit.

Kit took the paper and added it to the bottom of the pages he had typed up. "I'm going to scan these and send them as attachments to emails to Parcell and Nystrom," he said.

"Won't they get in trouble for doing this?" asked Doc.

"They would if they got caught," said Kit. "Those two wily old bastards are experts at not getting caught."

Doc laughed.

"Do you want a copy of this printout?" asked Kit.

"No thank you. That night is burned into my brain," retorted Doc.

Kit excused himself and went back to his bedroom and used his equipment to scan the pages of the document. Then he originated emails, attached the document scanned, and sent them off into cyberspace, a process that still amazed him.

They rest of the day passed by quickly and just before supper time, Harrison "Woody" Woodley showed up. He was driving a Mercedes SUV and parked it outside the cabin. He extracted a leather suitcase and a garment bag along with two long rifles in cases, a metal ammo box and something extremely long in a case.

Big Dave and the others came out to help him pack his gear into the cabin. Big Dave hefted the long case. "We aint goin' fishin', Woody," he said.

"That's not a fly rod, you thick skulled Sheep Herder," retorted Woody. He stepped forward and retrieved the case from Big Dave. He quickly opened the case and extracted a long and strange looking rifle.

"What the hell is that?" asked Thor.

"It's a Sharps buffalo rifle," replied Woody.

"Ain't it a little old for a shootout with bad guys," replied Thor.

"It was manufactured in 1880, one year before the company was dissolved," replied Woody. He opened his ammo box and retrieved a cardboard box. From it he extracted an exceptionally large cartridge. "This is a 45-70 cartridge. The rifle is bored for this particular bullet."

"It ain't got no scope, just open sights," commented Thor.

"Even with open sights, this gun is extremely accurate up to 1,000 yards," replied Woody. "At the battle of Adobe Walls in Texas, a buffalo hunter killed a Comanches warrior with his Sharps rifle just like this one at a range of one mile. Open sights, indeed," sniffed Woody.

Woody passed the rifle around and each man and Doc took their turn examining the old rifle and pulling it up to their shoulders to get a sense of what it would be like to fire it.

"Are those old black powder cartridges?" asked Swifty.

"No, they are modern smokeless powder cartridges," replied Woody.

"Won't they hurt the barrel?" asked Swifty.

"In previous tests, the barrel of the Sharps has not been affected in the least," said Woody.

"Hells bells," said Big Dave. "We're looking to defend a cabin against bad guys where one hundred yards will be a long shot in this here terrain. A long-distance cannon ain't likely to be very damn useful."

"But if it is," said Woody. "I'm ready."

"Hell, that'll be a first," said Big Dave. He slapped Woody on the back and the group, and their baggage made their way into the cabin.

CHAPTER TWENTY-FIVE

Kit drew up a schedule so one person was on guard duty in the camera room and a second person was stationed by the front of the cabin. They all agreed to three hour shifts with Doc demanding to take her turn as well. She made it clear she would be pulling her own weight, even if she was the target of an attack.

After the group broke up, Doc stayed behind to talk to Kit. He waited until the room was clear and then motioned for her to take a seat next to him.

"What's on your mind?" asked Kit. "You look like you need to say something."

"As an officer in the United States Air Force, and a veteran of Iraq and Afghanistan, I'm no stranger to violence and combat conditions," Doc said. "With that said, it's been a long time since basic training and a long time since I've shot a weapon with any regularity."

Then Doc paused, as if not certain if she'd said too much or not enough.

"Are you asking me for some shooting instruction and practice on our little indoor range?" asked Kit.

"I am," said a grim and resolute looking Doc.

"I'll give you a choice of two of our best shots and gun handlers," said Kit.

"Who are they?" asked Doc, somewhat timidly.

"Big Dave and Swifty are our best shots. Swifty is the most up to date on weaponry and has done lots of training while he was in the army," replied Kit.

"I think Swifty would probably be the best choice, but I'm inclined to ask for Big Dave," said Doc.

"Big Dave is tough on the outside and a big teddy bear on the inside," laughed Kit. "But for what we might be facing, you are probably better off with Swifty as an instructor. Do you have a problem with him?" asked Kit.

"No, no, I don't," responded Doc. "You're probably right about having Swifty as an instructor."

"When would you like to start?" asked Kit.

"Whenever is convenient," said Doc.

"When you are faced with getting shot at, there is no such thing as a convenient time to learn about shooting a gun," said Kit. "I'll grab Swifty and the two of you can start right now. Is that all right with you?"

Doc looked like she was relieved to have taken a heavy load off her back. "Now is fine with me," she said.

Fifteen minutes later, Swifty and Doc were entering the small indoor shooting range carved into the butte behind the ranch house. Swifty turned on the lights and the ventilation system. Then he reached into a shelf and pulled out two pairs of shooting safety glasses and earmuffs.

He motioned to two wooden stools next to the work bench. "Have a seat and let's find out what you know and don't know about shooting," said Kit.

Doc sat on a chair opposite Swifty and smiled.

"I assume you had basic training in the Air Force, so I hope we can skip the basics of firearm instruction," said Swifty.

"I did learn about and fire guns in basic training," said Doc.

"What kind of weapons have you fired?" asked Swifty.

"I fired the M-16, and the M9 Beretta 9mm semi-auto pistol," replied Doc.

"Were you any good with any of them?" asked Swifty.

"I was fairly good with the M-16. Not so much with the pistol," replied Doc. "But I haven't had to qualify with a weapon in years so I'm probably a bit rusty."

"How about we go to the indoor range and shoot a few rounds," said Swifty.

"Fine by me," said Doc.

He placed a 9mm semi-auto pistol on the table in front of her.

"Are you familiar with this weapon?" asked Swifty.

"Yes, I am," said Doc. "It's a 9mm semi-automatic pistol."

"Pick up the pistol, please," said Swifty.

Doc reached down and picked up the pistol by the grips, being careful to keep the muzzle pointed away from Swifty. Then she pressed the magazine release button, catching the magazine as it fell. She used one hand to slightly pull the slide back to peek and check no bullet was in the chamber and ready to fire. She checked the magazine, and then reloaded it into the pistol.

"Very good," said Swifty. "It may have been a while, but you remembered all the basics of handling a pistol." Then he produced an AR-15 and laid it on the table. "Pick up the rifle, please," he said.

Doc picked up the rifle, again keeping the muzzle pointed in a safe direction. She checked the chamber and found a bullet properly lodged. The rifle was ready to fire. She pushed the button to eject the magazine and then pulled back on the charging handle to eject the bullet in the chamber. The bullet shot up into the air, and she retrieved the bullet from the floor.

"You remember your basics well, Doc," said Swifty. "The pistol has a loaded magazine, but no bullet in the chamber and the safety is on. Please pick it up and let's walk over to the firing position on the range."

Doc laid the rifle on the bench and picked up the pistol. She walked to the firing position, being careful to keep the gun muzzle pointed down range. When she was standing in the firing position and holding the pistol in front of her, Swifty had her stop.

"Bring up the pistol as if you were going to fire it at the target," said Swifty.

Doc did as he instructed and smoothly brought the pistol up with one hand and joined her second hand on the pistol grip as she brought the gun up to eye level. Swifty worked with her on her grip and had her draw the weapon several times to make sure she was getting the grip correctly each time.

"Ready for some live fire?" asked Swifty.

"Ready as I'll ever be," replied Doc.

Swifty handed her safety glasses and earmuffs and put on his own.

"Put the pistol in front of you and pull back the slide to chamber a round," said Swifty.

Doc did as she was instructed. When she had chambered a round, she flipped the safety in place.

Swifty noticed. "Good move, Doc," he said.

Swifty pushed a button on the side of the firing position and a life-size target on a cable at the end of the target range moved on a wire back to their position. Swifty pointed to the center of the man-sized target's chest.

"I want two rounds, center mass when I say fire," said Swifity.

Swifty pressed the button and the target returned to the end of the range, twenty-five yards away.

"Bring your weapon up, engage the target and fire when I give the command," said Swifty.

Doc nodded her head that she understood.

Swifty waited for over a minute, knowing the time added strain and tension to the shooter.

"Fire," said Swifty in a loud voice.

Doc brought her weapon up to her eyes, flipped off the safety, acquired the target and fired two rapid shots. Then she slipped the safety on and brought the weapon down, so the muzzle was facing the floor.

"Let's see how you did," said Swifty. He pressed the button on the side of the firing position and the target on the wire slid back to them. When it was directly in front of them, Swifty released the button and the target stopped.

Swifty pointed to the two holes in the target. They were about six inches apart and seemed to bracket the center of the target's chest.

"Not bad for the first try," said Swifty. "You must have

jerked your hand slightly to cause the separation of hits on the target. We can fix that with practice." He turned to Doc. "How do you feel?"

"It felt good," said Doc. "Actually, it felt very good."

"You handled the gun very well," said Swifty. "How you handle the weapon has a lot to do with how well you react and how smoothly you manage to draw and fire the weapon. Let's try this again." Swifty made two circles around the bullet holes on the target with a red pen. Then he sent the target back down range.

CHAPTER TWENTY-SIX

After over an hour of shooting, Swifty showed Doc a quick way to disassemble and clean the pistol. Then he had her do it several times until she felt comfortable taking the pistol apart and putting it back together again. When the cleaning lesson was complete, Doc helped Swifty put the guns, ammo, and the cleaning materials away.

As they left the shooting range, Swifty locked things up, and they made their way back to the cabin.

"Can I ask a question?" asked Doc.

"Of course, I expect questions," replied Swifty.

"How often can I practice on the range?" asked Doc.

"I thought we might try to practice for an hour and a half in the morning and repeat the plan in the afternoon after lunch," said Swifty. "Does that work for you?"

"Absolutely," said Doc. "And Swifty."

"What?" he responded.

"Thanks for helping me with my shooting," said Doc.

"You're welcome," said Swifty. "We may need all hands-on deck, and those hands need to have guns in them."

Doc smiled to herself and following Swifty into the back door of the cabin.

"What's for supper?" yelled out Swifty as he entered the cabin.

＝⁀

Two more days passed and Doc and Swifty spent sessions in the small shooting range every morning and every afternoon. When suppertime rolled around on the second day, Big Dave was busy in the kitchen. Rough and tough as he might be, Big Dave was one hell of a camp cook and no one ever complained about his food, not even Swifty.

Supper consisted of grilled T-bone steaks, fried potatoes, green peas, and home-made sourdough biscuits with butter and jam. The others found a seat at the big dining table, and Thor helped Big Dave bring the platters out to the table.

As everyone dug into the food, an unusual quiet fell over the cabin. People were too hungry and too busy eating to chat.

When supper had been pretty much demolished by five hungry men and one woman, Kit had everyone take their plates and utensils to the kitchen sink. Then he asked everyone to grab a fresh cup of coffee and sit back down at the dining table.

When everyone was seated, Kit looked at each of them in the face and then he pulled out a couple of sheets of typed paper.

"Two days ago, I typed up what Doc Charlie described as having happened to her that night at the Air Force base in Cheyenne. You've all heard her story by now. I typed up the story like an incident report and had her sign it as accurate," said Kit. "Then I scanned the report and sent It to two friends of mine in Wyoming law enforcement.

One went to Sheriff Wade Nystrom in Sheridan, and the other went to Detective Bob Parcell in Laramie. I asked each of them to read the report and get back to me with any questions. I've talked to both. They made some quiet inquiries to people they know and trust, and there is no record of what Doc Charlie saw and heard that night, either official or unofficial."

Kit paused to let his words sink in.

"I believe there is a good chance someone high up in the Air Force wants Doc Charlie silenced forever. We are here to make sure that does not happen," said Kit.

He paused again and looked at his audience. Every person at the table was giving Kit their undivided attention.

"Then I asked them to do some quiet snooping in their own areas. I wanted to know if there had been any inquires to their departments, either official or unofficial, as to Doc Charlie's whereabouts. They told me this would take a couple of days. I expect to hear from them in the next day or two. If they have heard anything, they'll let me know. I'm using them as a form of scout because they can go where we can't and ask what we can't," said Kit.

Kit again scanned his audience. All he saw was their full attention.

"Does anyone have any questions?" asked Kit.

"What do we do next?" asked Big Dave.

"We wait to hear from Nystrom and Parcell," said Kit. "Either they've heard nothing, and we may be making a mountain out of a mole hill, or they have heard evidence some folks are out there trying to find Doc Charlie. Until we know one way or the other, we sit tight and wait."

"This so reminds me of my time in the army," said

Swifty. "I spent half of my career practicing hurry up and wait."

Everyone at the table laughed, and it broke the tension.

As the group got up from the table to leave, Kit motioned for Big Dave and Thor to stay seated. When they were alone, he addressed the father and son.

"I have no idea what might happen next," said Kit. "Nor do I know how long we might be staying here. That said, I think you two should go back to Kemmerer."

"Why in the hell would we do that?" snorted Big Dave.

"I think you can do more for me in town than waiting around here for something to happen, which might not," answered Kit.

"What do you have in mind?" inquired Big Dave.

"If someone in the Air Force is looking for Doc, they'd likely start with an electronic search. In this day and age, it is a remote possibility a person can stay hidden," said Kit. "But, if the person they are looking for has actually disappeared, then they are going to have to use boots on the ground."

"Spies," said Thor in an excited tone of voice.

"Maybe not spies, but some kind of scouts," said Kit. "I remember when I ended up in Kemmerer and the Chicago Mob was trying to find me, they ended up sending two different teams of scouts to Kemmerer. The first scouts failed, and the second group was larger, smarter, and better equipped."

"I remember the first two bozos," said Big Dave with a chuckle. "Me and Woody ambushed them buzzards in a parking lot. They never heard us and never saw us coming."

"What happened to them?" asked a curious Thor.

"We stripped them fools of their clothes and used rope to tie them spread eagle to the walls of a cattle truck headed for Mexico," chortled Big Dave.

"But the mob sent more killers to Kemmerer," said a grim Kit.

"And you think we'll be getting' some snoopers in Kemmerer?" asked Big Dave.

"If they are looking for Doc, I'm sure of it," said Kit. "Someone high up in the Air Force has a lot of resources at their disposal, and they aren't afraid to use them."

"But that would be illegal," said Thor.

"People high up in the military don't give a shit about legal," snorted Big Dave.

Kit smiled at Big Dave's remarks. He wished they weren't true, but he knew they could be from past experience.

"Humor me," he said. "Go back to Kemmerer and keep your eyes and ears open. Strangers in Kemmerer should stick out like a polar bear on the Kemmerer Triangle Park."

Big Dave looked hard at Kit. He seemed to be weighing what Kit had said.

"All right," he said. "We'll head back to Kemmerer. But, if something happens, you damn well better get on a horn and let us know so we can high tail it back out here."

"I promise," said Kit with a wry smile.

"Go grab your shit, Thor, and we'll head out," said Big Dave.

Ten minutes later, Big Dave's truck was loaded, and the father and son were roaring out of the area in front of the barn. Within seconds, nothing was left but a cloud of dust.

CHAPTER TWENTY-SEVEN

The rest of the day went quickly at the log cabin. Kit worked out a surveillance plan for the property. Two of them would be on alert at a time. One in the camera room and one of them up on top of the bluff. The bluff sentry would be dressed in camo and would have binoculars, a sniper rifle, a pistol, and a couple of flash bang grenades, as well as a walkie talkie set to the same frequency as the base radio in the camera room.

The sentry shifts were to last six hours, starting at seven P.M., running to one A.M., then from one A.M. to seven A.M. Kit and Woody would take the first shift and Swifty and the doc would take the second shift.

The audible alarms in the cabin would be initiated by the motion cameras surrounding the cabin property.

At a few minutes after four that afternoon, the alarm by the road entrance chimed and Kit dashed to the camera room and what he saw brought a smile to his face. Driving up the road to the ranch house was his half-brother, Billy McMaster, in his big ¾ ton jet black Dodge pickup truck.

By the time Kit alerted everyone else and stepped out the front door of the log cabin, Billy was roaring into the area between the barn and the log cabin. He pulled up to the front of the log cabin and stopped the truck. He quickly stepped out of the truck, and he and Kit hugged like the brothers they were.

"A little late to the party, Billy," said Kit with a grin.

"You know what they say, better late than never," retorted Billy. "But I do have a good excuse for being a bit late."

"I'm waiting with baited-breath," said Kit.

"It took me a bit of time to coordinate with Bushrod and to get all the items I felt would be useful together," replied Billy.

"What kind of items?" asked Kit.

"Let's take a look," said Billy with a grin on his face.

Kit followed Billy to the back of Billy's pickup truck. The bed of the truck was covered with one of those expanding canvas covers. Billy released the catch and the cover retreated to the back of the truck's cab.

"Ahhh," said Kit admiringly. "I see why you were a bit late."

Inside the bed were three rifles in cases, several boxes of ammunition, trip flares, boxes of claymore mines, three M-203 grenade launchers, and several boxes of grenades, as well as other boxes Kit could not identify.

"How did you get your hands on this stuff?" asked Kit.

"It's actually Swifty's stuff," said Billy. "He had gathered up most of this stuff back when he was dealing with who murdered his dad and he never had to use it. It was all stored up at his grandfather's place. He and I packed it up in the truck and here we are."

"How is Swifty's grandfather?" asked Kit.

"He's fine," replied Billy. "In fact, he and one of his old

green beret buddies should be joining us soon. As soon as I explained what was going on, he insisted he be included in our little defense post. I believe his exact words were, 'I'd love the chance to kick the crap out of some of those Air Force pukes.'"

"Let's get this stuff unloaded," said Kit.

"Where do you want it?" asked Billy.

"What do you suggest?" asked Kit. "You're the weapons expert."

"Let's take the rifles and ammunition up to the house and then deposit the rest of the stuff in your barn," replied Billy.

"Works for me," said Kit.

Woody and Doc moved the guns and ammo up to the cabin and Billy, Kit, and Swifty lugged the rest of the material into the barn. At Swifty's suggestion, they stored the material in two of the empty stalls. When they were finished, Swifty said, "This is thirsty work. I move we have a beer break."

"Second the motion," said Billy with a grin on his face.

"I'll just vote yes," said Kit. "But I do have a suggestion."

"Fire away, oh learned one," said Swifty.

"I think we should take the M-203 grenade launchers and the cases of grenades up to the cabin. It's possible we might need them before we have a chance to place the trip flares and the claymore mines out on the ranch property," said Kit.

"An amazingly good idea for a doofus who never served," said a grinning Swifty. "I agree."

"No argument from me," said Billy.

The three men shouldered the weapons and then

returned on a second trip to haul the boxes of grenades up to the cabin.

At Billy's direction, they set one M-203 by the front door, one by the back door and the third one was left leaning against the wall in the living room. A crate of grenades was placed with each launcher.

When they were finished, Swifty turned to his two companions. "Now can we have a beer?" he asked with a hint of disgust at being side-tracked from his original suggestion.

"Now works for me," said Billy. Kit just grinned and shook his head at his old friend.

Five minutes later, the three of them were seated on rustic chairs outside the front of the cabin. Each man held a cold beer in his hand, and Billy out a sniper rifle and it leaned against the wall of the cabin, within easy reach of his chair.

"Expecting company?" asked Kit as he sat his beer down and pointed at Billy's rifle.

"Nope, I'm not," said Billy. "And I learned a long time ago that's usually the best time to have a good sniper rifle within easy reach."

"Truer words were never spoken," said Swifty between gulps of cold beer.

"So, who is the opposition on this caper," asked Billy.

"At this point in time, we don't actually know for sure we have any opposition," replied Kit. "But based on what we heard from Doc Charlie, I think and feel it's more than likely someone in the Air Force wants her silenced for good."

"Why would someone in the Air Force want her dead?" asked Billy.

Kit proceeded to give Billy the story of what happened to Doc Charlie that night on the Air Force base in Cheyenne and what had happened to her since. He also related the story of how he and Swifty had gotten involved when they were hired by Doc Charlie's mother.

"Sounds to me like your instincts are spot on in this deal," said Billy. "Could be some asshat in the Air Force is up for a significant promotion and he's worried what he did illegally a few years ago to some political prisoner could surface and blow back on his career. It sure as hell wouldn't be the first time that's happened in our armed forces."

"And it likely won't be the last," echoed Swifty.

"So, do we have a plan?" asked Billy.

"Our plan is to hole up here with the Doc and wait to see what happens," replied Kit.

"Not much of a plan," said Billy. "I'm not much good at sitting still, fat, dumb, and happy, waiting for some assholes to put unwanted holes in me. Got anything else?"

"I've got two good friends in law enforcement, one in Laramie and one is Sheridan. I've talked to both. They are alerted to catch any unusual inquires to their offices for information of any kind about Doc Charlie. If they hear anything, they'll pass it on to us," said Kit.

"I also have Big Dave and his son Thor in Kemmerer alerted to keep their eyes and ears open as they go about their regular business. If they sniff anything suspicious, they'll pass it on to us. Plus, they're available as additional guns if we need them," said Kit.

"Does the opposition have any idea we have Doc Charlie hidden out up here in Dad's place?" asked Billy.

"I have no idea," replied Kit. "I think we were careful,

but we had no idea Doc Charlie might be in danger. It's more than likely we left crumbs for anyone skilled to follow."

"That might lead them to your office in Kemmerer, but how about here at Dad's ranch?" asked Billy.

"I have to assume if they track Doc to Kemmerer, they'll be smart enough to figure out she might be here," said Kit. "I chose dad's place because it is unknown to most people, and it's a very defensible location."

"Unless they show up with helicopters with Hellfire missiles," said Swifty.

"Using Hellfire missiles and helicopters in Wyoming might be hard to explain away, even for some high-ranking Air Force puke," said Billy.

"I'd guess they want to get rid of Doc Charlie as quietly and with as little muss and fuss as possible," said Kit.

"It wouldn't be the first time some government pukes had staged an accident to take out someone the government wanted to get rid of," said Swifty.

"It probably wouldn't," said Billy. "But, in my career I never ran into a situation like this one. I don't like not knowing who the enemy is."

"I think we can count on anyone who shows up here armed, either in the open or in the dark, as someone who doesn't have our best interests at heart," said Swifty.

"Do we shoot first if we feel threatened?" asked Billy.

"If you're asking me for the rules of engagement, I'm not sure," replied Kit. "I think we need to consider setting up some kind of ambush, so we can take any attackers alive and then figure out what to do with them after we've tried to get information out of them."

"It will all depend on who the opposition is," said Billy.

"If it's real elite troops who've been given bullshit orders, it's one thing. If it's hired mercenaries or thugs, it's another."

"I thought the military could not be ordered to assault civilians in this country," said Kit.

"Even in this country, there's a lot of things going around in the dark beside Santa Claus," said Billy. "We could find ourselves up against some anti-terrorist outfit. That could get very unpleasant for us."

"I don't think so, Billy," said Swifty. "In my outfit we did a lot of stuff that was off the books, but it still went through lots of channels. I doubt an Air Force puke, no matter how high up, could get inter-service cooperation for a gig like this."

"Not to mention I think this cat needs to keep this operation quiet, secret and off any official books," said Kit. "The opposition has limited options, and I think we're capable of dealing with them."

"All this high-level bullshit is boring me and making me thirsty," said Swifty. He rose from his chair. "Who's ready for another beer?"

CHAPTER TWENTY-EIGHT

Early the next morning Swifty, Kit, and Billy were up, dressed, fed, and after grabbing selected items, they were out the door of the cabin. They quickly made their way up the narrow trail to the top of the butte the cabin nestled up against.

Once they reached the summit, they dropped their loads and scouted the top of the butte. Although the portion of the butte facing the north was a sheer drop, the western and southern portion of the butte was a more gradual drop-off. The trail was located on the western side of the butte.

In the middle of the butte was a small, spring-fed pond. Bushes grew up around the perimeter of the pond and hid its presence until you were right on top of it.

"This is the pond and spring that feeds the water trough in the corral," said Kit.

"Does it ever dry up?" asked Billy.

"It never has in the years dad has owned it," replied Kit.

Swifty knelt by the spring and cupped his hands to catch some cold, fresh spring water. He raised his hands to his mouth and took a quick drink.

"If he keels over, the water is not very damn good," said Billy.

"If he keels over, I get his truck and his guns," said Kit.

"Screw you two. This is damn good spring water. Got a few minerals in it, but it tastes better than some of that bottled, recycled crap you buy at the store," sputtered Swifty.

"Enough bullshit let's get to work," said Billy.

He pulled open the sacks and cartons they had lugged up the butte and began sorting things out. He pulled out an interesting looking tripod and set it up.

"What's that for?" asked Swifty.

"It holds these little beauties," said Billy as he produced two sets of high-powered binoculars. "One's for daytime and the other is heat detecting night vision binoculars," he said. Then he pulled out a small collapsible chair and set it up behind the tripod.

"We keep one person up here, day and night. They can sit on this stool and look right through the binoculars. They can be set to the height of the watcher and switched from day to night in about three seconds," said Billy.

Billy set the day binoculars on the tripod and sat on the stool. He adjusted the tripod height slightly and then peered through the binoculars. Satisfied, he got off the stool and faced his two companions.

"Give it a try," said Billy.

Kit and Swifty each took a turn viewing through the binoculars. They moved on a swivel, so panning the landscape around and below them was easy.

Billy then took out a small communications pack and opened it. He took out the satellite phone and set it on the ground in front of him. Then he removed a small battery pack with a folded up solar panel. He set up the solar panel, securely anchored it, and connected it to the battery pack.

"There are two sets of batteries. One in the phone and one in the charger. The sun used the solar panel to charge the spare battery. Everything is waterproof and secure," said Billy.

The three men walked around the top of the butte and compared what they were looking at to a small plastic map Billy produced.

"The map is specifically for just this area. Orient the map to true north on your compass and you know exactly what you are looking at," said Billy. He put the map back in a small pack and set it on the ground. Inside the pack is a Kimber 1911 .45 ACP pistol and five magazines of hollow point ammo. "I suggest the three of us rotate the duty up here," said Billy. "We three are probably the best shots in the group. When on duty, each of us will bring our own rifle. Also, I want to keep one of the grenade launchers along with a dozen grenades in a box up here. Anyone disagree?"

"Sounds good to me," said Swifty.

Kit thought for a moment and then spoke.

"How about bringing up a few rounds of smoke?" he suggested.

"Smoke grenades?" asked Swifty. "Why smoke grenades?"

"Smoke can provide cover for us," said Kit. "It can also create confusion for any attackers."

"He's got a good point," said Billy. "Think about a night attack. Smoke plays havoc with night vision googles, which I would expect any unwelcome visitors to come provided with. Smoke grenades it is. I just happen to have a box of them in the barn."

After walking the perimeter of the butte once again and

going over Billy's checklist, the three men made their way down the narrow trail on the west side of the butte.

Once they were back in the cabin, they, Doc, and Woody grabbed a cup of coffee, and all sat at the dining room table. Billy explained what they had done at the top of the butte and answered any questions from Woody and Doc. Once he was sure everyone understood the plan and was on board, he laid out the strategy.

"We do not know if or when the enemy could come. Nor do we know how many or how well armed they might be. Our plan is to wait. Maybe no one will come. But from the evidence Kit has gathered, it appears more than likely someone high up in the Air Force has a reason to have Doc disappear from the face of the earth," said Billy.

"May I speak?" asked Doc.

"You have more right to speak than anyone else at this table," replied Billy. "Go ahead."

"I admit I don't have hard proof of a plot to kill me, but a combination of small events that have occurred and my own innate sense of fear tells me I saw something that could be trouble for some officer who ranks far above me," said Doc. "I suspect it is some general who is up for a big promotion. He could be concerned that my knowledge of what happened on the base in Cheyenne that evening could become public and destroy his chances. I'm not sure who that general is, but I am quite sure they are at the top of the heap in the Air Force."

While Doc was talking, Woody had been thumping on his iPad and when she was finished, he raised his hand.

"Yes, Woody," said Billy.

"I think I just found the missing piece to our little puzzle," said Woody.

"What is it?" asked Kit.

"According to my immediate research, a major general in the Air Force is up for appointment to the Joint Chiefs of Staff. I just read his bio and it looks like this might be our boy," said Woody.

"May I see the screen?" asked Billy.

"Certainly," replied Woody and he passed the iPad to Billy.

Billy studied the iPad and then passed it on to Kit.

"Based on my quick read of the report on Woody's iPad, I tend to agree with his assessment. Woody, can you get that story printed out on our printer here?" asked Billy.

"Consider it done," replied Woody and he got to his feet and headed to the security room.

"I think we should forward that information along with our suspicions to Big Dave, Thor, Sheriff Nystrom, and Detective Parcell," said Kit.

"I agree. Get it done," said Billy.

The group spent the next ten minutes working out a schedule for sentry duty on top of the butte and for manning the security room with the monitors. When they had finished the schedule, the meeting broke up.

Kit had drawn the first shift on the butte, and he grabbed his sniper rifle, one of the grenade launchers and a knapsack filled with twelve rounds of grenades. He slipped a headlamp band around his head and headed up the trail to the top of the butte.

Once on top of the butte, he placed the day binocular on the tripod, made some final height adjustments to the tripod, and put the satellite radio and his rifle and the grenade launcher close to his seated location. He also brought a jacket and a pair of shooting gloves.

The temperature at his dad's ranch usually dropped about forty degrees every twenty-four hours. It could get cold at night, and he was a good two hundred feet above the cabin. Kit glanced at the sky. A few clouds, but mostly clear. He settled in for his six-hour shift.

CHAPTER TWENTY-NINE

The sun came up east of the cabin. Swifty was on duty up on the butte and Doc was manning the security room. Kit woke up to the smell of fresh coffee and bacon frying on the stove. He showered, dressed and went to the kitchen to join Billy and Woody. Woody was manning the stove and Billy handed him a cup of hot black coffee. Kit looked at the coffee and went in search of cream and honey. Billy watched him as he doctored his cup of coffee and just shook his head.

"Ain't no damn milk cows or honeybees in Iraq," said Billy. "I was damn glad to get real coffee, the blacker and hotter the better."

"Look outside," said Kit. "This is Wyoming, not some damned camel farm."

"Just sayin'" said Billy with a grin on his face.

Kit ignored his half-brother and sat on a stool, drinking his coffee from a mug.

Woody announced, "Breakfast is ready. Eat it or I'll throw it out."

"Temperamental cook," said Billy.

"First time I ever saw him cook," said Kit. "Check for critters in your food," he added with a grin.

185

Kit, Billy, Woody, and Doc sat down at the table after helping Woody put the food containers on it. Each container had a big spoon or fork in it. The four of them passed containers around the table and when the containers hit the table again, they were empty.

Doc and Billy cleared the table as Woody, and Kit had another cup of coffee. Doc filled the dishwasher and Billy scrubbed the cookware and then washed them by hand. Doc dried them and put them away in the cupboards.

When they were finished, they joined Kit and Woody for coffee in the great room.

"What about Swifty?' asked Doc.

"Swifty has stolen more food than most men have ever eaten," replied Kit.

"Trust me, that boy won't starve," said Billy. "My guess is he managed to smuggle an entire cooked ham up to the top of the ridge and is over halfway through it by now."

Doc just smiled.

"When does he get over his shift?" she asked.

Kit looked at his watch. "He'll be getting relieved by Billy in about an hour," he said. "Why the interest in that reprobate's activities?"

Doc didn't blush or act embarrassed in response to Kit's question. "He's been giving me shooting lessons on the range, and he said we'd shoot for half an hour when he got off ridge duty," she said.

"I've got to give that army brat his due," said Billy. "He's a pretty good shot, especially with a pistol. I'd beat his ass like a drum on a rifle and a shotgun, but he's damn deadly with a handgun."

Woody was about to add an insult of his own when Kit's cell phone rang.

"Hello," said Kit.

The others were silent as Kit listened to his phone. He said nothing and continued to listen for about two minutes. Then he spoke. "Thanks. I'll call you back." He ended the call and returned the cell phone to his pocket. Then he looked up at his expectant audience.

"That was Big Dave. When I asked Sheriff Nystrom and Detective Parcell to be alert to any inquiries about Doc's whereabouts, I requested they call Big Dave and have him relay the information to me," said Kit.

"Why?" asked Woody.

"Makes it harder to trace us," replied Kit.

"Oh," said Woody.

"Big Dave says he got a call from Sheriff Nystrom about an hour ago. Then he got a call from Detective Parcell just ten minutes ago. Both calls indicate someone representing himself to be from the Air Police at the Air Force Base in Cheyenne. Each call was requesting any information on the whereabouts of Charlemagne," said Kit.

"What happens next?" asked Woody.

"The caller will get squat from either Nystrom or Parcell, but someone else they contact will point them to us and Kemmerer," said Kit.

"How will we know when they arrive in Kemmerer?" asked Woody.

"Either Big Dave or Thor will see or hear about them and let us know," replied Kit. "Whoever shows up will not be in uniform nor will they likely be real Air Police. In a small town like Kemmerer, they'll stand out like a whore in church."

"So, what do we do until then?" asked Woody.

"We train, we practice, we watch, and we wait," said Kit.

CHAPTER THIRTY

Everyone was sitting around the table talking about what they thought they should do or shouldn't do, when Swifty came in the door after being relieved by Billy.

"I've got a little good news," said Swifty.

"Let's hear it," said Kit.

"I got an email from my grandpa. He and one of his old Green Beret team should be here in about two hours," replied Swifty.

"That is good news," said Kit. "We can use the manpower in our defensive plan."

"We got a defensive plan?" asked Woody. "That's news to me."

Everyone broke out in laughter.

"What's going on?" asked a puzzled Swifty.

"I just got a call from Big Dave," said Kit. "He got calls from Parcell and Nystrom. Both their departments got inquiries from someone alleging to be Air Police from the Air Force base in Cheyenne."

"What were they asking for?" asked Swifty.

"They were asking about the possible whereabouts of Doc Charlie," replied Kit.

"Did they give a reason for the request?" asked Swifty.

"They said, and I quote, 'Possible criminal investigation of a dangerous fugitive,'" replied Kit.

"The game is afoot!" said Woody.

"What the hell are you yapping about?" asked Swifty.

"Sorry. My remark was the product of a classical education," replied Woody.

"What game? What foot?" asked Swifty, now more curious than before.

"Arthur Conan Doyle," replied Woody.

"Was he some football player?" asked Swifty.

"No, not at all," replied Woody. "Arthur Conan Doyle was the author and creator of the famous fictional detective Sherlock Holmes."

"Sherlock Holmes? What the hell has he got to do with games and feet?" asked Swifty.

"'The game is afoot' is a famous Sherlock Holmes saying in Doyle's books he used when the plot began to unfold," said Woody.

"What plot?" asked Swifty.

"As educational as this may be, we have work to do," interrupted Kit.

Woody shut up and Swifty sat back in his chair and kept silent, but his face was filled with frustration.

Kit turned to Swifty. "When do you expect Bushrod and his pal?" he asked.

"He should be here around before suppertime, if I know my grandpa," said Swifty, his mouth twisted into a wry grin. "Those old green berets are big on mealtime. Especially when someone else is doin' the cookin' or footin' the bill."

"Here's the plan for the day," said Kit. He handed out sheets of printed paper. "These are copies of maps of the property. I found the original maps in my dad's desk and made copies. Saves me a trip to the ranger station. I've made stars on the locations where I want the claymore mines planted and where I want the triggers placed. As soon as Swifty is done with his target practice with Doc, he and I will go out and place the claymores. Doc and Woody will man the camera room while we have Billy up on the ridge. Any questions?"

Woody put up his hand.

"Yes, Woody?" said Kit.

"Who's in charge of making supper?" he asked.

"You asked, so you're in charge," replied Kit.

Everyone laughed.

When Swifty returned to the cabin, he and Doc left for the small firing range. Kit got on his computer and did some research on current news in the Air Force, hoping to get some idea of who they might be dealing with.

After an hour, Swifty and Doc returned from the range and Doc went see if she could help Woody with getting supper ready.

Kit and Swifty went out to the barn and loaded the claymores onto the bed of the John Deere Gator. Then they climbed into the small cab and Kit drove. Swifty used the copy of the property map to direct him to each of the proposed claymore locations.

At each location they took time to observe the area around them and pick the best spot to locate the claymore and conceal it. The triggers were carefully placed where they could only be seen and found by someone looking out to the perimeter of the property and easily accessed. Swifty was familiar with the claymore, and he did all the placement and wiring.

They worked hard and patiently and after about three hours, they had placed all the claymore mines at the map's designated positions. When they were done, they loaded up their trash in the back of the Gator and then Kit drove them back up to the barn. There they pulled into the barn, parked the Gator, and dumped the trash into a steel barrel.

No sooner had they finished dumping the trash when the big barn door started moving up. When the door was high enough to see, Kit and Swifty got a clear view of the smiling face of Swifty's grandfather Bushrod and the stern countenance of Chief, the full-blooded Comanche green beret.

"OK if we put our stuff in here?" asked Bushrod.

"Help yourself," said Swifty.

"Head up to the cabin when you're unloaded," said Kit. "Supper should be ready soon, but I have no idea as to its quality, but there should be plenty of it."

"Good," was the one-word response from Chief.

"We'll be up shortly," said a grinning Bushrod.

CHAPTER THIRTY-ONE

Twenty minutes later, Bushrod and Chief pushed open the cabin's front door and stepped into the great room.

Chief sniffed the air and the aromas floating in from the kitchen. "Good," he announced.

"How does he know the foods any good?" whispered Kit to Swifty.

"Obviously, you have never seen a big Indian eat," replied Swifty. "If its edible, and there is lots of it, it's good."

Swifty introduced his grandfather and Chief to everyone, and Woody handed the two men hot cups of black coffee. Pretty soon everyone was seated around the great room.

After a few minutes of polite conversation, Bushrod looked around the room and said, "So, can we get a sitrep?"

Kit took a deep breath and then began telling Bushrod and Chief how things had progressed from being hired to find a long-lost child for a mother to defending that now grown child from a possible threat.

During the lengthy explanation of the current situation, Bushrod and Chief remained silent.

When he was finally finished, Kit looked at the two old Green Berets and asked, "Do you have any questions?"

"What's the opposition like?" asked Bushrod.

"I have no idea," said Kit. "We don't really know if there really is any opposition."

"I see a but, in your eyes, Kit," said Bushrod.

"You are correct. There is a but," said Kit. "Today I learned someone alleging to be with the Air Police in Cheyenne called two law enforcement locations in Wyoming inquiring about the possible whereabouts of Doc Charlie."

He went on to explain that Big Dave and Thor were in Kemmerer keeping watch because Kit was sure whoever was looking for Doc Charlie would trace her to Kit's office.

"Why wouldn't they know about this place then?" asked Bushrod.

"It's my dad's place, and he used to work for the CIA," replied Kit. "Pretty much everything about this place is off the books."

"Are you expecting real Air Force types or hired guns?" asked Bushrod.

"I expect hired help," said Kit. "If I were a general in the Air Force and I needed to get rid of someone who could hurt my career, I don't think I'd run the risk of it getting out in public by using real troops. I suspect our opposition will be hired mercenaries of some kind."

"That's too bad," said Bushrod.

"Why's that bad?" asked Kit.

"I always wanted a chance to shoot one of those pompous Air Force brass hats, who put their own careers over the welfare of their men," replied Bushrod.

"Can't say I disagree with that," said Swifty.

"What's the defensive set up here?" asked Bushrod.

Kit got to his feet and left the room briefly. When he returned, he had a paper map of the property. He laid it out on a coffee table, and everyone pulled their chairs up around it. Kit pointed out the features of the property on the map after he oriented the map to the true north south directions where they were located.

Kit pointed out the observation post on top of the ridge, and the locations he and Swifty had placed claymore mines. Then he gave them a review of the camera locations and told them about the control room.

"The road is the only one into the ranch?" asked Bushrod.

"Yep," said Kit.

"So, the only other way here is on foot?" asked Bushrod.

"That's correct," said Kit. "They could come overland by moto-cross bikes or ATVs, but it would be awkward, noisy, and they have to come across a lot of open ground to get here."

"I'd like to walk the ground with the Chief if that's O.K.," said Bushrod.

"I'll take you and Chief for a tour right after we eat," said Swifty.

"Sounds good to me," said Bushrod.

"Come and get it," said Woody as he banged a wooden spoon on a metal pot for emphasis.

There was a quick rush to the dining room table.

CHAPTER THIRTY-TWO

After dinner was over, Swifty, Bushrod, and Chief went out to walk the property. Swifty carried a sidearm, and Bushrod and Chief stopped at the barn and armed themselves with AR-15 rifles.

Kit helped Woody and Doc to clear the table, do the dishes, and clean up the kitchen. Kit saw Doc with a covered tray and said, "What's that?"

"Dinner for Billy," she replied. "I'm putting foil on it and setting it on the counter. All he has to do is heat it up when he gets in from the butte."

"That's nice of you," said Kit.

"I don't know about nice, but a man coming in from sentry duty is usually, tired, bored, and very hungry," replied Doc.

"I think you just described my half-brother perfectly," said a smiling Kit.

Doc smiled back and returned to policing up the kitchen. Kit headed to his room to check his computer for messages.

***

The next morning Doc and Woody were in charge of breakfast and the dining room table was crowded with others not on sentry or comms duty. The group had just finished eating and Bushrod and Chief were helping Doc and Woody clean up and do the dishes. Kit and Billy were drinking coffee out in the great room.

Kit had filled Billy in with what he had heard from Parcell and Nystrom.

"Do you think these guys will show up in Kemmerer?" asked Billy.

"No doubt in my mind," replied Kit. "We left a pretty wide trail in our search for Doc and were not secretive or quiet about who we were. My guess is they are headed for Kemmerer even as we speak."

"If they do arrive in Kemmerer, we should find out from Big Dave or Thor?" asked Billy.

"If a stranger stops in Kemmerer and gets gas or lunch and moves on, no. But if a stranger starts asking questions, especially about me or Swifty, then everyone in town will know about it in less than half an hour," said Kit.

Billy laughed.

Two minutes later, Kit's cell phone rang.

"Hello?" he said. Then he was silent for about a minute and a half. Then he said "Thanks. I'll call you back," and he shut off the call.

"News?" asked Billy.

"That was Big Dave. Thor spotted some guys checking out our office. Three guys, all very fit. All with beards and longish hair. None of them locals," said Kit.

"What happens now?" asked Billy.

"Thor will tail them, find their vehicle, get the plate number and call Sheriff Nystrom and have him find out who the owner is. Then Big Dave will forward the information to us," said Kit.

"What do you plan to do about them?" asked Billy.

"If they head on out of town, nothing," replied Kit. "If they get rooms and stick around, then we need to set up a plan."

"Sometimes it's a good idea to have a plan in place for several alternatives, just in case," said Billy.

Kit grinned at his half-brother. "You think just like our old man," said Kit. "Do you have an idea of what we might do?" he asked.

"Do you remember you telling me that story about when you first came to Kemmerer and those mobsters in Chicago sent a couple of goons here to find and eliminate you?" asked Billy.

"Yep," replied Kit.

"I really liked that idea," said Billy with a grim looking grin on his face.

"That's when Big Dave and his friends surprised the goons out at Bon Rico and the two hired guns woke up naked and taped to the inside walls of a livestock truck headed to Mexico," said Kit.

"That's the story I remember," said Billy.

"Not original, but it could work fine in this case," said Kit.

"I'm thinking of sending them north, not south," said Billy.

"To Canada?" asked a surprised Kit.

"I wasn't thinking of dropping them off in Montana," said Billy.

"Even now it'd be damn chilly at the Canadian border,"

said Kit. "Especially when they're traveling light with no clothes."

"Plenty of heat coming off all that livestock," said Billy. "And if their butts get a bit frosty, what's so bad about that?"

"Brother, you have a wicked mind. Remind me to never piss you off," said a grinning Kit.

"I'll drink to that," said Billy.

The two brothers clinked coffee mugs and drank to Billy's plan.

An hour later Kit got a call from Big Dave.

"Them three yahoos took rooms at the Antler Inn. They been in the Stock Exchange Bar and two other local saloons asking about you and Swifty," said Big Dave.

"Do you have the room numbers?" asked Kit.

"Does a bear shit in the woods?" asked Big Dave.

Kit gave Big Dave the outline of Billy's plan.

"That sounds goddamn good to me," said Big Dave. "But, since I know the plan so well, I need to lead the team on this one."

"You're in charge," said Kit. "I'll send Billy, Swifty, and Chief to help you. I assume you'll have plenty of heavy-duty packing tape."

"If I don't, I will have by the time they get here," replied Big Dave.

"Don't take any silly chances," cautioned Kit.

"Hells bells, when have I ever done that?" asked Big Dave.

"Almost every day I've known you," replied Kit, and he ended the call.

CHAPTER THIRTY-THREE

Kit got Billy, Swifty, Chief, and Bushrod out on the front porch. He explained the plan to them and told them Big Dave would be in charge, and he was sending Swifty, Billy and Chief to help Big Dave. Bushrod was pissed because he was not included, but Kit put his hand on Bushrod's shoulder.

"There are only three of them. We need to take them down with a minimum of noise and fuss. Big Dave has done this before, and Swifty and Billy are trained in this stuff. Too many of us would just draw unwanted attention. We need the thing to go down quickly, quietly, and smoothly."

"Dadgum it, I hate missing out on all the fun," said Bushrod.

"I need you here," said Kit. "We know about the three in Kemmerer, but there could be more. The three could be a diversion."

"You're right," said Bushrod reluctantly.

"When do we go?" asked Billy.

"I suggest you gear up and go now. Swifty will coordinate with Big Dave and direct you as to where to go and when to show up where he wants you. He's done this before. Trust him and things will go fine," said Kit.

"Works for me," said Billy.

Billy, Swifty, and the Chief left to gear up and take Billy's truck into town. The other vehicles were well known in Kemmerer, but Billy's was not.

Fifteen minutes later Billy's truck pulled out onto the highway and headed for Kemmerer. It was starting to get dark when they reached the outskirts of the small mountain town. Billy drove slowly into town, staying well below the local speed limit. Just before they reached the vicinity of the Antler Inn, Swifty, who was in the passenger side of Billy's truck, grabbed his night vision binoculars and pulled them up to his eyes. As they drove slowly past the motel, Swifty scanned the vehicles parked in front of their respective rental units.

"'Bingo," said Swifty softly.

"Did you spot them?" asked Billy.

"Sure did. Late model dark sedan with Utah plates in front of the three units at the end of the motel," said Swifty. "My guess is they rented the three units on the end. I'd bet money they used phony ID to rent the vehicle."

"Any lights on?" asked Billy.

"Nope," replied Swifty.

"Let's go pick up Big Dave and Thor," said Billy.

"Works for me," replied Swifty.

Billy drove back to the triangle park in the middle of the small town. He drove slowly past the Stockman's Bar, and Swifty immediately identified Big Dave and Thor standing outside the bar on the poorly lit sidewalk. As Billy drove toward the two men, he flashed his headlights. At that prearranged signal, Big Dave and Thor immediately walked briskly to Big Dave's trucked parked in front of the old saloon.

"Are they coming?" asked Billy.

"Does a bear shit in the woods?" replied Swifty.

Billy grinned and drove at a steady pace to the rear of the old bank building that housed Rocky Mountain Searchers. As he approached the entrance to the large garage on the side of the building, Swifty hit the button on the door opener he had taken out of his jacket pocket.

The large double door began to open. When the door was fully up, Billy drove his truck into the structure. Three minutes later Big Dave's truck drove in next to them, and Swifty hit the button and the door began to descend.

All the men exited the two trucks and gathered at the end of the big garage. After some hand shaking and muffled greetings, Swifty called the small group to order. He turned to Big Dave and asked, "Are we all set up?"

"There's a cattle truck full of beef parked out behind the Stockman's bar. The driver is in there having dinner and a few beers. I chatted him up, and he's headed for Montreal," said Big Dave.

"We need to move fast," said Swifty. "We don't want these boys to miss their ride to the great white north."

Billy looked at his watch. "Those three yahoos should be headed for bed. Big Dave, you and Thor go park across the road from the Antler Inn and call us when they return to their rooms."

"What about the cattle truck?" asked Swifty. "What if that driver finishes up his dinner and hits the road before we're done?"

"He told me he's gonna park down by the old lumberyard

and sleep for a few hours before he hits the road," said Big Dave. He knows the cops don't mind, and they won't hassle him if he's parked there.

"Here's the plan," said Billy. "Swifty, me, and Chief will each move to the door of one of the three units at the motel. At a hand signal by me, each of us will knock on the front door and when the occupants open the doors, we hit them with these."

Billy pulled out three dart guns loaded with tranquilizer darts like the vets use. "These will knock those old boys out for at least twelve hours. Once they're out cold, we drag them to the truck and load them in the bed. Then we remove all their stuff from the rooms and toss it in the truck bed with them. We drive to the parked livestock truck, strip the thugs naked, and Chief will hold them up while we tape them to the inside walls of the semi-trailer. Any questions?"

There were none, but there were more than a few grins.

Swifty hit the button and the big door began to open. When it was up, Big Dave backed his truck out of the garage, and he and Thor headed for the motel. Swifty hit the button again, and the door began to descend.

"What now?" asked Chief?

"We wait, just like when we were in the army," said Billy. "We hurry up and wait."

Ten minutes later Billy's phone came to life. It was Big Dave.

"There's lights on in the three units. Them boys are in their rooms," said Big Dave.

"We're on our way," said Billy. "Let's go," he said to Swifty and Chief.

A few minutes later they were parked next to Big Dave's

truck across the street from the motel. The five men exited their trucks and met behind the parked vehicles.

"Are we ready?" whispered Billy.

"Here's the plan," said Big Dave. "You three will move to the doors of each of the three units. I'll stand watch by the highway. Thor will stay in the truck with the motor runnin'. When you three are in position, I'll check for any traffic. If there is none, I'll signal with my flashlight. As soon as you three knocks on their doors, I'll head your way and Thor will bring the truck up to the motel." Big Dave looked at the four men. "Got it? Then let's move."

The other four men nodded their heads in agreement. Then all four men slipped on black ski masks. They waited until they were sure there was no traffic to observe them and then all, but Thor slipped across the silent highway onto the parking lot of the Antler Inn. The motel was typical of old-style motels, shaped like a big U with the open end of the U facing the highway.

Billy, Swifty, and Chief each stood in front of a motel door. Each man held a loaded tranquilizer gun down by the side of his leg. Big Dave stood out near the highway. When he gave the signal by turning his now lighted flashlight in a circle, each of the three men knocked on the respective door of their unit. Thor crossed the highway and quietly pulled up in the parking lot area in front of the three end units.

The result was like watching some form of synchronized activity. Almost simultaneously each of the three hired thugs opened their motel doors and received an immediate dart to the chest. All three had words die in their throats as their systems shut down and they slumped to the ground, half in and half out of their motel rooms.

Quickly Swifty, Billy, and Chief dragged their victims to Thor's parked truck. They tossed all three unconscious men in the bed of the waiting truck. Big Dave had quickly entered each of the motel rooms and scooped up all the men's possessions he could find, dumping them in a garbage bag. He then tossed the bag in the bed of the truck and jumped in the passenger side. Thor quietly and deliberately drove the truck off the parking lot and down the highway.

Billy, Swifty and Chief all removed their ski masks, still holding their dart guns down by their legs. They waited until they were sure here was no traffic and then casually walked across the highway and slipped into Billy's truck.

When the three men reached the street next to the old lumber yard, Thor had already parked his pickup truck right behind the rear of the parked tractor trailer truck.

Billy parked his truck behind Thor's and the three men exited the truck and moved quickly to the back of Thor's truck. Big Dave positioned himself on the street side of the trucks as a lookout. If any vehicles appeared on the street, he would give them a warning and they would stop work and slip into hiding until the threat was gone.

The other four men split into two teams. Each team took an unconscious thug and carried him to the back of the cattle trailer. When they had all three of the men on the ground behind the cattle truck, they stripped them naked and then quietly and carefully opened the rear door to the cattle truck.

Chief slipped inside and one by one, the three unconscious men were handed to him. He easily lifted each of the men up against the slats of the sides of the cattle truck trailer and Billy and Swifty used lots of heavy tape to secure their arms and legs to the slats. Lastly, they gagged the men and taped over the gags.

When they were finished, Swifty was about to close the door to the rear of the cattle truck trailer when Billy stopped him.

"Wait a minute, Swifty," said Billy. He took out his iPhone and took several pictures of their evening's handiwork. "O.K. close it up," he said.

Ten minutes later, Billy, Swifty and Chief were on their way back to the ranch. Big Dave and Thor would remain in town and report in the next day if anything had gone wrong.

Once they were driving down the highway toward the ranch, none of the men said a word for about ten minutes. Then all three men looked at each other's grim, serious faces, and they burst out laughing.

CHAPTER THIRTY-FOUR

When they reached the ranch, the three of them realized they were a little too high on adrenalin to try to sleep. So, they gathered in the great room and regaled Kit with the events of the evening as they each had a large glass of whiskey. Kit laughed along with them as they described the night's events and again when Billy displayed his photos of the taped up naked men.

They were joined in the great room by Doc Charlie and Woody. Both asked no questions, but it was obvious they were curious about what had happened in Kemmerer. After giving the two of them a brief summary of the trip into Kemmerer, Kid addressed everyone in the room.

"I'm glad things went so well, and nothing went wrong, and no one got hurt," said Kit. "But I want you to understand that this was the first crew doing recon. They were not special forces troops. They were not trained forces. They were hired thugs. This one was easy. Our opponent will learn from this mishap. They will regroup. They will plan and campaign for how to root us out somewhere around Kemmerer, and they will bring enough muscle and power to the next attempt to inflict some real damage. Remember this, someone powerful wants Doc Charlie silent. That means they want her dead. We've got to be vigilant. We've got to be ready, because the next time will be one hell of a lot tougher to deal with."

Kit stood up and looked carefully at Swifty, Billy, and Chief. "So, tell me, what did we really learn tonight?"

The three men sat in their chairs, all three looking at the floor or the wall as they considered Kit's question.

Finally, Billy broke the silence.

"We learned this team was far from professional. They were careless and sloppy. I agree our opponent, whoever that is, will learn from their mistakes and they won't repeat them on their next try. And there will be a next try," said Billy.

"Did any of you try to question the prisoners before you taped them to the wall of the cattle truck?" asked Kit.

"We did not," said Swifty. "It was my observation they were all out cold from the drug darts

. I doubt they had any idea who they were working for anyway. Whoever is in charge of this gig is too smart to leave a path back to them."

With that, Swifty reached down by his leg and pulled out a small garbage bag. He opened the bag and emptied the contents out on the surface of the coffee table in front of him.

Out of the bag poured three wallets, one set of car keys, three different knives, and three cell phones. Swifty reached down and produced a larger sack and emptied it on top of the small table. Out came three handguns and three silencers plus five extra loaded magazines for the handguns.

Swifty reached down and grabbed the three wallets. One at a time he emptied the contents of each wallet on the tabletop. There were credit cards, driver's licenses, cash, and some miscellaneous plastic cards.

"It looks like these yokels were hired out of Vegas, and they were dumb enough or cocky enough to be carrying their real I.D. I doubt any of this is fake," said Swifty.

"I suggest we run these three through Sheriff Nystrom and see what we come up with," said Kit.

"Works for me," said Billy. Chief just nodded his head in agreement.

"You guys did a great job tonight, but now the game is different. The stakes are higher and much more dangerous. Everyone still in?" asked Kit.

"Yep," said Swifty.

"I'm in," said Billy.

"I'm in, too," said Chief.

"Count me in," said Woody.

"I'm in," said Doc Charlie with a hard tone in her voice.

"All right then," said Kit. "You all get some shuteye. I'll relieve Bushrod up on the ridge in about an hour. See all of you at breakfast."

The five shook hands with Kit and headed for their sleeping bags. Kit got a fresh cup of coffee and sat down and pulled out his pocket notebook. He wrote down information from the driver's licenses and credit cards and then entered the information on his laptop and sent it to Sheriff Nystrom in Sheridan.

When he was done, he sat back in his chair and started thinking about what might come next and how he might be able to prepare for it. He was still thinking about it when his small alarm went off. It was time to relieve Bushrod up on the ridge. He got up, grabbed his coat and hat and went to the camera room. There he told Doc Charlie he was headed up to relieve Bushrod and he headed out the door.

CHAPTER THIRTY-FIVE

The next morning found Woody busy in the kitchen preparing breakfast. The first one to join him was Billy, who grabbed a cup of hot black coffee and sat down at the kitchen table without uttering a word to Woody.

"You're damned unsociable this morning," said Woody.

"I never speak until I've had my first cup of coffee," said Billy. "Until I get some caffeine in me, I can never be sure how I might react to anything or anyone. Until I have coffee, I'd just as soon shoot as talk."

"Good to know," said a now nervous Woody, and he began making scrambled eggs.

They were soon joined by a hungry Bushrod, who had interrupted his hard-earned sleep time when his nose smelled bacon cooking.

"Oh my, is that bacon and eggs I smell?" said Bushrod. "If It is, I think I've died and gone to heaven."

"You're still vertical, old timer, but it is bacon and eggs your nose detected," said a smiling Billy.

Bushrod grabbed a mug of black coffee and then filled a plate with bacon and eggs. "Tell me about last night. I hope I didn't miss anything good," said Bushrod.

Billy told him the events of the previous evening.

Bushrod listened and kept shoveling hot food into his mouth as he listened. When Billy had finished his story, Bushrod wiped his mouth with a paper napkin.

"Damnit, I knew I should have gone," he complained. "You boys are havin' fun, and I'm freezin' my ass off up on that ridge. At my age, that ain't fair."

"I wouldn't worry about missing out on the action," said Billy. "My guess is this is just the first wave. I expect this is just a short-term defeat that will only piss off the opposition even more than they are now."

"Maybe so, but I'd have loved to have seen those rascals taped up naked as jaybirds to the slats on that trailer's walls," said Bushrod.

"Have a look," said a smiling Billy. He took out his phone and pressed a few buttons and there in living color were the three hired thugs strapped to the trailer walls buck naked.

"I'll be damned," said Bushrod as Billy scrolled through the photos they took.

"Them boys ain't gonna be very happy by the time they get to the Canadian border," said a smiling Woody. "Did you happen to take their fingerprints while you had them all trussed up?" he asked.

"We thought about it but decided these three were probably just thugs hired through some third party. I doubt they had any idea who really hired them," said Billy.

"I'd bet you're right about getting ready for the next attempt," said Bushrod as he helped himself to a second plate of bacon and eggs. If the guy behind this is military, he'll learn from this and do a better job next time, even if he is an Air Force puke."

"Good lord, you assholes are making more noise than a bunch of Democrats attendin' a rally for more free shit from the government," said Swifty.

All three men's heads turned to face the source of the voice. Swifty was lumbering into the dining area, dressed in jeans and nothing else. He stumbled to an empty chair and said one word, "Coffee."

Woody quickly got to his feet and snatched a mug from a cupboard and filled it with hot coffee. Then he carried it to the table and placed the mug in front of Swifty. Swifty never looked up from having his head face down on the table, but his hand magically found the handle to the mug and pulled it near his face. His nose twitched and as he smelled the caffeine. He raised his head like Lazarus from the grave and lifted the mug to his lips without ever opening his eyes.

"I believe he's done this before," said Woody as he watched in admiration.

"Many times," said a grinning Billy. "Swifty could find a cup of hot coffee in a manure pit."

Ten minutes later Chief emerged from his room, and he joined the four men at the table. He grabbed a mug of coffee and a plate of bacon and eggs. He sat next to the still mostly semi-conscious Swifty and acted as though nothing was unusual about Swifty's seeming incoherence.

"Is he always like this in the morning?" asked a curious Woody.

"Depends on what happened the night before," said Billy as he sipped coffee.

"He must have tied one on last night," said Bushrod.

"Did he walk in here or was he on his hands and knees?" asked Kit.

"He sort of walked in here," said a grinning Billy.

"Then it was a pretty mild night," responded Kit.

Everyone at the table laughed.

When everyone, including a late arriving Doc, had eaten, Billy and Woody cleaned up the kitchen while the rest of them had coffee in the great room. When the kitchen was shipshape, the two men joined the others.

"Any questions about what happened last night?" asked Kit.

He was answered with silence from the assembled group.

"This was the first try and it was both easy and foolish," said Kit. "The next one will use the information gained from this one and be a lot better and a lot tougher for us to deal with. I plan to keep Big Dave and Thor in Kemmerer as scouts. We will maintain our guard hours, and I recommend you keep any weapons and gear you might need by your beds. If we get hit here at the cabin, there won't be any spare time to go grab something you need."

"You think they will hit us here?" asked Woody.

"I have no idea what they will do next," replied Kit. "But, sooner or later, they are gonna figure out where we are and then we will get hit here."

"So, what do we do to get ready now?" asked Bushrod.

"We wait," said Kit. "We stay alert, we listen to our sources, and we wait."

CHAPTER THIRTY-SIX

Big Dave was sitting at a small table against the front window of the cafe where he had a good view of Triangle Park. He was just lifting a cup of hot coffee to his mouth when he paused, the cup still in midair. Driving slowly around the Triangle Park was a large black Range Rover. A sighting of a Range Rover was rare in Kemmerer. The nearest Range Rover dealership was about five hundred miles either south or north.

Although Kemmerer was a small and isolated town, the occasional foreign car was not an unusual sight. Usually, it belonged to a tourist who had gotten lost. Kemmerer had both a Ford and a GM dealership. Both were owned by the same family and the dealerships stood side by side in Diamondville. The owners were Italian and came from a family long settled in Big Piney, Wyoming, a small-town north of Kemmerer.

If you owned a foreign car in Kemmerer, you were a long way from any authorized dealership. A Range Rover in Kemmerer was a sure sign of a tourist or someone who definitely was not a local.

The Range Rover went around Triangle Park for a second time. As it approached the café, it slowed almost to a stop and then pulled into a vacant parking space. Big Dave watched as three doors opened and three men got out of the vehicle. They stopped on the sidewalk and had a brief conversation. Then all three of them entered the café. They took a booth in the back of the café and the waitress brought them steaming hot cups of coffee.

Big Dave finally unfroze his arm and brought the still hot coffee mug to his mouth. He sipped the coffee, never taking his eyes off the strangers. They were all big men. All of them were white and looked to be in their early thirties. They wore painfully new looking flannel shirts and jeans. All of them were wearing sunglasses when they entered the café and had now slipped them in their shirt pockets. All of them had close cropped hair.

"Military or ex-military," thought Big Dave to himself. He pulled out his cell phone and tapped out a short text to Kit.

"Three military lookin' dudes havin' coffee in the café. Drivin' a black Range Rover," he texted. He added the Utah license plate number to the text. Then he copied the text to his son Thor, who was parked in his truck on the west end of town. When he was finished, Big Dave slid his phone into his shirt pocket.

Big Dave took his time drinking his coffee. He said hello to a couple of old ranchers he knew who walked into the café. He chatted with them for a few minutes, and they wandered back to a table of their own. During the entire time, Big Dave kept his eyes on the three men in the back booth.

The men's waitress returned shortly to refill their mugs of coffee and about ten minutes later she returned with a tray of plates laden with hot breakfast food. The three men talked quietly among themselves. When they finished their meal, they went to the counter and paid their bill with cash.

Big Dave watched the three men leave the café. They walked to their truck and two of them got in. The other man walked across Triangle Park and crossed the road to the old bank building that now housed Kit's business, Rocky Mountain Searchers. He tried the front door, which was locked, and then stood there for a few minutes. The man disappeared around the side. A few minutes later, he reappeared on the other side of the building. As he approached the street, he was shaking his head as if indicating the place was locked up and no one was home.

He returned to the parked Land Rover and got into the front seat on the passenger side. The men remained in the parked Land Rover for about five minutes. Then the driver started the vehicle and backed out of the parking slot and drove to the end of the park. He stopped for the stop sign, and then signaled and turned right on the highway and headed west.

Big Dave got his phone out and called Thor. "They're headed your way," he said. Then he replaced the phone in his shirt pocket, paid his bill, and left the café. He walked directly to his pickup truck. Then he leaned against the front fender of the truck and waited.

About fifteen minutes later, Big Dave's phone rang. He answered it. It was Thor.

"That Range Rover drove to the cemetery and turned in there. They parked by the entrance and they're just sitting there," said Thor.

"Keep an eye on them," said Big Dave. "Let me know if they start to move."

"Will do," replied Thor, and he hung up.

Big Dave put his phone away and pushed himself off the truck's fender. He was about to open the driver's side door when he caught something in the corner of his eye. He stopped and turned until he was facing the front of the old bank building where Kit had his office.

"What the hell is that?" he said. He began walking across Triangle Park to the old bank building. As he was crossing the highway in front of the old bank building, he got a good clear look at someone standing in front of the building, trying to peer in the big front window.

When Big Dave got about ten yards away from the man, he said, "Can I help you, mister?"

The man turned to face Big Dave. He was a small man, with the almost stark white skin of someone who never ventured outdoors. He was young, somewhere around Kit's age, and he was dressed in a somewhat outrageous manner.

He wore a pair of bright red high-top sneakers, a pair of brown cargo shorts, a somewhat white t-shirt under a colorful serape, and a large Mexican sombrero on his head. He wore glasses, which gave him kind of an owl-like look.

The look on his face was a combination of high intelligence, mixed with a lot of "where the hell am I?" mixed in.

The man used a finger to push up his glasses which had ridden down on his nose. "I'm looking for Mr. Carson Andrews. I've driven all the way from California to see him. He's my cousin. I believe he goes by the nickname Kit, but I have no good idea why? Do you know him?"

Big Dave broke out a big smile. "I sure do know him. Did he know you were coming to visit him?" asked Big Dave.

"Oh no, he didn't know I was coming. I wasn't really sure I was coming. I wasn't even real sure when I'd get here," replied the man.

"I'm Dave Carlson," said Big Dave. "My friends call me Big Dave. And you are?"

"Oh my," said the man. "I can certainly see why they call you Big Dave. My goodness. You are one very large man."

"You didn't mention your name," said Big Dave.

"Oh my, forgive me. I sometimes get flustered and forget my manners. My mother would be so ashamed of me," said the man. "My name is Thomas P. Main. Most folks call me Tom. I don't know you very well, but you can call me Tom, if you'd like," said Tom.

Big Dave scratched his head for a moment. Then he smiled at little Tom. "Your cousin Kit is out of the office today. Can I interest you in a cup of coffee?" asked Big Dave.

"Coffee? Certainly. I like a good cup of coffee. Is there a Starbucks near here?" asked Tom.

"Nope. There's no Starbucks in Kemmerer, but there is a place with pretty good coffee. We can go there, get some coffee and get acquainted," replied Big Dave.

"I love a good cup of coffee," said Tom. "Let's go."

Big Dave smiled, looked up at the sky for a moment, and said, "Let's go."

Big Dave led the way, and they crossed the highway and entered the Triangle Park. As they were walking through the park, Big Dave saw the Black Range Rover return from its trip to the west end of Kemmerer. It drove slowly through the downtown portion of Kemmerer and then disappeared.

"Something wrong, Mr. Dave?" asked Tom.

"What do you mean?" asked Big Dave.

"You were looking over your shoulder like you were expecting something bad to happen," replied Tom.

"Nah," said Big Dave. "I just had a crick in my neck, and I was trying to stretch it out."

"Oh," said Tom and they continued walking to the café. Once there, Tom stepped ahead and opened the front door and held it open for Big Dave.

"Thanks," said a surprised Big Dave.

"You're welcome," said Tom.

Big Dave led the way to his favorite table which was unoccupied this late in the morning. The waitress came and took their order and promptly returned with two large mugs of hot black coffee. Tom promptly added two little bags of sugar and poured in some cream, then stirred his coffee until the black had turned to a creamy brown.

"Good lord," thought Big Dave. "Little Tommy is just like his cousin when it comes to their coffee."

"So, tell me about your trip to Kemmerer," asked Big Dave. "Did you say you came from California?"

"Yes sir," replied Tom. "I grew up on a farm in Illinois. Then I went to Knox College in Galesburg. That's a city in Illinois. Well, it's not actually a city, more like a larger town. Then I went to graduate school at Dartmouth. That's a college back east. Then I got a job in California. I guess I've been there ever since."

"What have you been doing since you got out of this here Dartmouth?" asked a curious Big Dave.

Tom smiled. "I went back to school for a while and then got a job with a large defense contractor. Are you familiar with defense contractors, Mr. Big Dave?"

"I've heard of them," said Big Dave. "They make stuff for the military, I think."

"You are correct, Mr. Big Dave. I worked on developing weapons systems for the military," said Tom.

"Instead of calling me Mr. Big Dave, how about you shorten it to just Big Dave?" said Big Dave.

"I can do that," replied Tom.

"So, what kind of weapons systems did you work on for the military?" asked Big Dave.

"I worked on many systems," replied Tom. "But, if you're trying to put some kind of label on what I did, I guess you could best call me a rocket scientist."

"A rocket scientist!" exclaimed Big Dave. "You mean like moon shots and missiles and stuff like that?"

"Well, I'm not really allowed to say much about my work, so let's just settle for rocket scientist," said Tom.

"Works for me," said Big Dave. "Let's finish our coffee, and I'll take you to see your cousin."

"Great," replied Tom.

Over the next fifteen minutes, Big Dave heard more unfamiliar big words that he ever imagined existed in the English vocabulary. Finally, he put up his hands in surrender.

"I'm just a poor uneducated sheep herder," said Big Dave. "You're gonna hafta simplify what you say to me if you expect me to understand half of it."

"I'm sorry," said a chagrined Tom. "I sometimes forget where I am when I talk and to whom I am talking. I meant no disrespect."

"None taken," replied Big Dave. "Just try to keep it simple for a simple guy like me."

"You are too modest, Mr. Dave," said Tom. "My cousin has written me letters telling me of your exploits. He described you to me as 'larger than life,' and even then, he did not do you justice."

"He did, did he," said Big Dave with a large grin on his face.

"Yes, yes he did," said Tom. "He also wrote that if the late movie actor John Wayne had been a real person, he would have been you."

"I'll be damneded," said Big Dave.

"May I see your hands," asked Tom.

Big Dave looked at Tom for a moment and then he put his hands on the table in front of him.

"Oh my, they are huge," said Tom. "They are as big as my cousin Carson described to me."

"Out here we call your cousin Kit," said Big Dave.

"I heard that, but I do not understand why," said Tom.

"When he first came out to Wyoming, he got caught in a spring snowstorm and got stuck in a drift," said Big Dave. "I found him and pulled him out. His car was damaged and not fit to drive, so I took him into Kemmerer. When he told me his name was Carson, I told him that kind of name would just get him beat up in every bar in Wyoming. So, I told him I'd call him Kit, after Kit Carson. He liked it and it stuck. He'd probably be dammeded surprised if anyone here called him Carson."

"I shall endeavor to call him Kit when I see him so as not to cause him any discomfort," said Tom.

"You know, you talk too damneded fancy to be walking

around with a handle as simple as Tom. I think you need a good nickname too," said Big Dave.

"Nickname?" said Tom, quizzically.

"Yep, a nickname that suits you," said Big Dave. "Let me puzzle on it for a bit."

"Puzzle on it?" asked a bewildered Tom.

"Yep, think on it," replied Big Dave.

Not knowing how to respond, Tom lapsed into silence. Something he often did during his life when he was unsure as how to respond.

"I got it," said Big Dave. "Tom is too simple for a guy like you. From now on your nickname is Flash."

"Flash?" said a puzzled Tom.

"Yep, Flash. You know. As in Flash Gordon, the rocket man from the old comic books," said Big Dave.

"I think I am vaguely familiar with the name and his comic book," replied Tom. "But it was a long time ago."

"Don't matter none," said Big Dave. "From now on, your first name is Flash."

After looking into the eyes of the huge man sitting across from him, Tom made a wise choice. From now on he would respond to Flash as his first name. When they finished their coffee, Big Dave paid the bill and they walked outside. When they reached Big Dave's pickup truck. He turned and looked at Flash.

"Where are you parked?" asked Big Dave.

"I parked around the corner," said Flash, pointing to the corner of Triangle Park to the left of them.

"What kind of rig are you drivin'?" asked Big Dave.

"Rig?" asked Flash.

"Yeah, rig. Car or pickup truck?" asked Big Dave.

"Oh, neither one," replied Flash.

Big Dave stared at Flash like he was a creature from outer space.

"Oh, I'm driving a special kind of van," said Flash.

"A van?" said Big Dave incredulously. "You mean one of them things those soccer moms drive?"

"Well, not exactly," replied Flash.

"Not exactly like what?" asked Big Dave.

"It's one of those customized vans built to go cross country and off road," answered Flash.

"I don't believe I ever seen one of those things," said Big Dave.

Flash thought for a moment and then said, "It's one of those big Ford one-ton vans that's been customized for off road activity," he said carefully, trying not to make his explanation any more detailed or confusing than possible.

Big Dave looked hard at Flash, decided he was not funnin' him and turned to his truck.

"Get in and I'll take you to your van. Then you can drive it and follow me out to the ranch," said Big Dave.

"Great," said Flash and he climbed in the passenger seat of the truck.

Big Dave drove around the triangle to where the van was parked. The van was black, with smoked windows, with a ladder attached to the back and several strange looking antennas on the roof. The tires were big and designed for off road work. Upon a closer look, the vehicle was once a Ford E-350 before being heavily adapted for off road work.

Big Dave let Flash out and then he led the two-vehicle caravan out of town, headed west for the ranch.

CHAPTER THIRTY-SEVEN

A few minutes later, Big Dave pulled out his phone to call his son Thor. When Thor answered, Big Dave asked him about the status of the Range Rover. Thor replied that the Range Rover had left Kemmerer and was headed south toward Evanston. Satisfied, Big Dave put the phone away and headed for Kit's father's ranch house west of town.

After a couple of miles, Big Dave dug out his phone again and called Kit. When Kit answered, Big Dave smiled.

"This is Big Dave. I'm on my way out to the ranch. I'm bringin' you a little surprise," he said.

"Surprise? What kind of a surprise?" asked Kit.

"I'd tell yah, but that'd ruin the surprise," said Big Dave, and he disconnected the call.

A puzzled Kit looked at his now dead iPhone and then stuck it in his pocket. With Big Dave you never knew what was coming until it arrived. Usually, it arrived right between your eyes.

Kit got his answer about twenty minutes later when Big Dave's truck arrived in front of the cabin. Kit was out on the front porch having coffee with his half-brother Billy, and Bushrod, Swifty's grandfather.

Before Big Dave even opened the driver's side door to

the truck, Kit was on his feet, curious to see the surprise Big Dave had promised.

Big Dave got out on the driver's side and stood there expectantly. A large black van with huge off-road wheels and tires with several antennae on the roof pulled in next to Big Dave's truck. After a moment, the driver's door opened and out popped a strangely dressed smaller man.

The small man stood next to Big Dave's truck. To say he was dressed in an outrageous getup for a man in Wyoming was a major understatement.

He wore baggy cargo shorts, bright red high top tennis shoes, white socks, a plain t-shirt, a multi-colored poncho, and a huge sombrero on his head. His skin was a pasty white and his brown eyes were focused behind a pair of large black rimmed glasses. Kit had seen a lot of outrageous getups worn by tourists to Wyoming, but this one definitely made the top ten list.

Big Dave confidently walked up to the three men on the front porch with the small, younger man in tow behind him.

"Howdy, boys," said a smiling Big Dave. "I want you to meet my new friend I found wanderin' around in front of Kit's office building, Tom Main. I decided Tom was too common a name and after learning that his real job was a rocket scientist in California, I decided Flash would be a good nickname for him. After the comic book guy, Flash Gordon."

When he was finished with his small monologue of introduction, Big Dave's grin got even bigger.

The three men on the porch were stunned into unnatural silence. Finally, Bushrod broke the silence. "Come on up here, boy," he said. "Let's have a good look at you."

Big Dave led the way up the steps to the front porch and each of the three men shook hands with Flash and introduced themselves. Kit was the last to do so.

"I'm Kit Andrews," he said. "I'm your cousin."

"My goodness," said Flash. "I haven't seen you in years. You've gotten bigger and taller and stronger than I remember."

"Not to mention a lot dumber," added a grinning Billy.

"This smart ass is my half-brother, Billy. I guess that makes him your half-cousin," said a still surprised Kit.

"Pleasure to meet you, Cousin Billy," said Flash as he enthusiastically pumped Billy's outstretched hand like the handle on an old water pump.

"This here is Swifty's grandpa, Bushrod," said Billy.

"Good to meet you, youngster," said Bushrod as he sized up the outfit Flash was wearing. "Who the hell dressed you this morning? You look like a refugee from a Mexican traveling circus."

"Oh this?" said Flash. "I can explain why I am dressed like this."

"Pull up a chair and fill us in," said Bushrod.

"This I gotta hear," said Billy.

The five men grabbed chairs and sat on the front porch. Then Bushrod got up and said, "I need a beer before I hear a long story. Anybody else want one?"

All remaining four men raised their hands, including Flash.

"Five beers coming up," said Bushrod. "Thank god the kid didn't ask for a sarsaparilla," he muttered to himself as he made his way to the kitchen.

Soon, Bushrod returned with five cans of Coors and

passed them out to the other men. For the next few seconds, the only sounds heard were the soft pops as beer cans were opened.

"You were about to tell us how you managed to get those strange duds you're wearin'," said Bushrod.

Flash put down his beer on the small table next to him and said, "Oh yes, I was."

Each of the other four men paused in their beer drinking. No one wanted to miss a word of how and why Flash accumulated such a strange outfit.

The story they heard from Flash was not a disappointment.

"I was driving here from my home in California in the Enterprise," said Flash.

"The Enterprise? What the hell is the Enterprise?" asked a puzzled Bushrod.

"The Enterprise is what I call my van," said Flash. "Originally it was a Ford F-350 van I had specially customized for off road adventures. It's equipped like a small home with all the technical gear I thought I might need. So far, it's worked exactly like I designed it to."

"So, you drove your van from California to Wyoming," said Bushrod. "Lots of folks do that, including a whole bunch of yahoos we'd just as soon stayed in California. I don't see how that connects with the goofy outfit you're wearing unless you ran over a souvenir stand in New Mexico."

"Oh no. Nothing like that," said Flash. I was driving through southern Utah. It's a strange state. Have you ever been there? It's full of these Mormons. They're a strange people. I read where they wear some kind of holy underwear. Why would they do that?"

"I ain't never seen a Mormon wearing a sombrero," said Bushrod.

"Oh yes. You're right Mr. Bushrod. Sometimes I get a little off track," said Flash.

"Off track is one word for it," muttered Billy under his breath.

Big Dave was the only one prepared for Flash's sometimes strange soliloquies, having listened to him for almost two hours. He just sat there drinking his beer, grinning like a large Buddha wearing a cowboy hat.

"Back to my story," said Flash. "I was driving in southern Utah. It's a strange part of the country. Lots and lots of desert and lots and lots of sand and sagebrush."

"And Mormons. Don't forget about the Mormons," added a smiling Billy.

"Actually, I hadn't seen any Mormons for a couple of hours," said Flash. "As I recall I didn't see anybody or even any animals. All I recall seeing were some big birds who seemed to be following the Enterprise."

"Did those birds happen to be buzzards?" asked Billy.

"Buzzards?" said Flash. "I'm not sure what they were."

Billy pulled out his phone and punched in some letters. When he found what he was looking for he showed the screen to Flash. "These are buzzards," said Billy.

"Yes. Yes, those were the birds," said Flash. "Buzzards, you say. I may need to look them up."

"Go on with your story," said the ever-patient Bushrod.

"I finally came upon this tiny roadside stand," said Flash. "It was just a little bit of canvas and sticks, but a sign said they were selling burritos. I stopped the van, got out, and asked to see one of their burritos. There was an older

Hispanic lady there, and she had a small blue cooler. She reached in the cooler and gave me a burrito wrapped in aluminum foil. I asked her how much and she held up two fingers, so I paid her two dollars and took the burrito. I went back to my van and got two bottles of cold water from the frig and returned to the stand. I offered one of the bottles of water to the lady. She seemed shocked, but she took it. Then the two of us sat on two small boxes in the shade. I ate my burrito and drank my water. She drank the water I had offered her. The lady didn't speak much English, so I tried talking to her in Spanish."

"You speak Spanish?" asked Bushrod.

"Yes, I do," replied Flash. "I actually speak six languages. Every time I got sent to a foreign country by my employer, I learned to speak the language before I flew to that country."

"Once I began speaking in Spanish, the lady got very excited and began to talk to me a mile a minute. It was hard for me to keep up with what she was saying, and I asked her to please slow down so I could understand her," said Flash. "She did slow down, and I learned she was part of a big family. Most of them lived in a nearby village that doesn't show up on any map I could find."

"Did this village have a name?" asked Billy.

"I never heard her mention a name. She just referred to it as their village," replied Flash.

Flash seemed to pause, almost as if to catch his breath. The ensuing silence only lasted a few seconds, but it seemed like several minutes to the men listening to Flash's story.

"What happened then?" asked Kit, as his curiosity overcame his patience.

"I asked the lady how she got from her village to this

spot on the highway because I couldn't see any form of transportation she could have used," said Flash.

"What'd she say?" asked Bushrod.

"She told me she got dropped off by her uncle and he would be back to pick her up in time for supper," replied Flash. "I looked at my watch and saw it was about two in the afternoon. I felt sorry for her, so I asked how much she usually made selling burritos and water in a day. She told me she usually made about twelve dollars. So, I took out a twenty and gave it to her and offered to take her home to her village. She was incredibly grateful and thanked me over and over. She gathered up her things, and we loaded them in the back of my van. She got in the passenger seat and gave me directions as I drove her to her village."

"Was the village close by?" asked Bushrod.

"It was about ten miles away," said Flash. "I had noted the milage on the van and then checked it when we arrived at her village."

"What was the village like?" asked Kit.

"It was small and very, very poor," said Flash. "There were maybe five or six small huts and two tents. Bianca, that was the lady's name, introduced me to all her relatives. I think everybody there was somehow related. All together I think there were about twenty-five people in the little village. A few children, but mostly adults and some of them pretty old."

"What happened then?" asked Bushrod. "Were they all right with her bringing a gringo like you to their village?"

"They were all friendly and seemed glad to see me," said Flash. "They invited me to stay for supper, and I accepted their invitation. I didn't want to be impolite."

"Of course not," muttered Billy in a low voice.

"Their meal was meager, but very tasty," said Flash. "It was some kind of stew, I think."

"Most likely roadkill special," Billy muttered again.

"I ended up spending about a week with them," said Flash. "I added some frozen chickens and hamburger to their communal dining efforts, and they were very appreciative."

"Why would you stay a week with a bunch of wetbacks you knew nothing about?" asked Bushrod.

"I took this trip to learn more about the country I live in and the people who live in it," said Flash. "By people, I mean all kinds of people. I mean rich people, poor people, white people, brown people, black people, legal citizens, and illegal aliens. In one week, I learned a good deal about that Mexican family. I spent a few hours a day teaching the five children there some basic English. It was also good practice for my limited Spanish. I learned how they lived in such a desolate part of our country and were still happy to be here. I was also able to improve my conversational Spanish and to help an extremely poor family. I learned a great deal and the cost was only my time and some groceries."

Flash paused, not a natural thing for him, and waited for some response from the other men. There was none.

"When I left the village, they gave me the sombrero and the serape as a gift. I thanked them and left the village, headed for Wyoming," said Flash.

"Now I understand your outlandish getup," said Bushrod.

"Outlandish?" said Flash. Then he took off his sombrero and the serape and held them at arms-length, staring at them. "Ahh, I see what you mean," he said as he stared at the other men's dress and recognized the obvious contrast with his costume. Then he sat them down on the floor of the porch.

Kit rose from his seat and disappeared into the cabin. While he was gone, Flash asked about the cabin and the small ranch. Billy explained to him that Kit's father, who was Flash's uncle owned the ranch, but was down in New Mexico on a visit.

When Kit returned to the porch, he was carrying an old, slightly worn, grey Stetson cowboy hat. He handed it to his cousin and said, "Try this on for size."

Flash was delighted and promptly tried on his new headgear. The fit was not perfect, but it was close. Flash pulled out his phone and punched up a photo ap and took his own picture. Then he grinned when he saw his photo with his new hat.

CHAPTER THIRTY-EIGHT

"I'll be damned," said Bushrod. "With that hat, the kid actually looks like a cowboy."

The rest of the men broke out in laughter. Flash grinned and joined in the laughter.

"Welcome to Wyoming, Flash," said Kit. "Why don't you have another beer, and I'll try to explain what's going on here and why all of us are together on my old man's ranch."

Kit went inside and returned with a twelve pack of Coors and opened the cardboard container and handed out cold cans of beer.

When everyone had a beer in their hands, Kit proceeded to tell his story of fleeing from a vengeful mob in Chicago and winding up as a temporary sheepherder for Big Dave in Wyoming.

"I have to admit," said Kit, "Working as a sheepherder took me completely off the grid and until I bought an old truck from Mustang Kelly and registered it, I left no digital footprints for anyone to follow."

"But they did follow," said Big Dave, between sips of beer.

"Yes, they did," said Kit. "Two guys showed up in Kemmerer and Big Dave and old Woody ambushed them in a restaurant parking lot. They stripped them naked and then taped them to the inside of a cattle truck headed for Mexico. I would have loved to have a camera taking pictures when they were discovered by the Mexican border guards."

"But there is more to the story," said Billy, with a grin on his face.

"Yes, there is," said Kit. "The next time they sent a whole crew including two women. They set up an ambush and Swifty and I drove right into it. After the dust had settled, the five assassins were gone, and we were still standing."

"I'm puzzled," said Flash. "You said they were gone. How did they get gone?"

Flash's question was met with a stony silence. He looked around at the other four men with puzzlement in his eyes.

Finally, Big Dave broke the silence. "Let's just say them five assholes went on an extended vacation, and they ain't comin' back."

Flash got the message. "Oh, I see," he said. He still didn't know exactly what happened, but he got the picture when Big Dave said they weren't coming back.

Kit was relieved. He did not enjoy talking about or reliving what happened back then, but he was happy to fill Flash in on the backgrounds of each of the men present.

"You'll meet Swifty, Thor, The Chief, and of course, Doc Charlie. She's the reason all of us are here," said Kit. Then he went on to tell the story of how they took on the case of finding Doc Charlie for her natural mother.

When Kit had finished his story, which included the recent situation where they sent three hired thugs to Canada in a cattle truck, sans their clothing, Flash's eyes were as big as pie plates.

Finally, Flash spoke. "Isn't what you just described against the law? Couldn't you go to jail for what you did to those men?" he asked.

"I think that's a question for Big Dave," said Kit as he tried to suppress a grin from taking over his face.

"Why me?" said Big Dave as he spread his huge arms and hands in front of him as if in a form of supplication.

"Because you are the grandson of true Wyoming pioneers who homesteaded not far from here," said Kit piously. "Who better to explain the culture of Wyoming to a newcomer?"

Big Dave let out a loud snort and rubbed his huge hands together. Then he looked up and stared straight at Flash.

"Let me tell you a story about the law in Wyoming," said Big Dave. "I think it'll help you understand how things get done in this state. We're big on self-help out here. We don't involve the law or any legal authorities unless there is no other option. We believe in solving our own problems. Some years back there was a ranch north of Kemmerer that belonged to a pioneer ranching family. They had a piece of the Fontenelle Creek runnin' through their ranch and sometimes folks just climbed over the barbed wire fence that surrounded their ranch and helped themselves to some fresh trout from the creek. The family got tired of all that trespassin' and thievin' and put up a sign to post their property against trespassers. The sign read, 'NO TRESSPASSING, PRIVATE PROPERTY, SURVIVORS WILL BE PROSECUTED.' One day some fool who worked at the post office in Kemmerer decided to ignore the sign and climb over the fence and go fishin'. He got shot in the leg by one of the family."

"Oh my God," said Flash. "What happened to the man? Did the family get arrested?"

"Well, not exactly," said Big Dave.

"What exactly did happen?" asked Flash.

"The rancher took the wounded trespasser to the hospital in Kemmerer, and they patched him up," said Big Dave. "Then the trespasser sued the rancher."

"Did he win the suit?" asked Flash.

"Yes, he did," said Big Dave. "He got a small settlement awarded by the court that covered his medical expenses, and the judge scolded the rancher in court."

"Did the rancher have to go to jail?" asked Flash.

"No, he did not," said Big Dave. "He told the judge he yelled at the trespasser to get off his land, but the dummy kept fishin', so the rancher shot him in the leg to get his attention."

Flash looked confused. "I guess I don't understand," he said.

"It's simple," said Big Dave. "The rancher made sure everyone knew about what happened when the postal worker trespassed on his ranch. Since that day, no one has ever trespassed on that ranch again. And that, my young friend, is how the law works in the great state of Wyoming."

"So, if someone breaks the law, you don't call the police, you just handle it yourself?" asked a still puzzled Flash.

"Sometimes you do and sometimes you don't," said Big Dave. With that said, he cracked open another cold can of beer.

"In Wyoming, it's a big state with not a lot of people in it," said Kit. "Some folks say our laws are forty years behind the times, and that's fine with most of the folks in the state.

Most of the time bad things happen a long way from any kind of law enforcement people. People in this state are used to being self-reliant."

"What happens when you are in the wrong?" asked a still puzzled Flash.

"You man up and admit what you did and if there is a price to pay for what you did, you pay it," said Billy.

"Oh," said a slightly overwhelmed Flash.

"Have another beer, kid," said Big Dave, and he tossed Flash a new can of Coors.

CHAPTER THIRTY-NINE

The beer ran out, and the five men went in the cabin to the great room. Doc Charlie and Woody were busy in the kitchen. They both came out to the great room to meet Flash. Doc took a few minutes to tell Flash her story and how she came to be sharing the cabin with eight men. When she was finished with her story, Flash had his mouth hanging open and a shocked look on his face.

"You mean to tell me some senior general in the United States Air Force is plotting to have Doc Charlie killed to keep her from telling what happened one night at his orders at the air force base in Cheyenne?" asked a shocked Flash.

"Exactly," said Kit. "Plus, according to Big Dave, three more hired thugs showed up in Kemmerer today driving a black Range Rover. Big Dave's son Thor is keeping an eye on them. So far, it seems they drove out of town and haven't returned."

"But they'll be back," said a grim-faced Billy.

"When they do, we'll be ready for them," added an even grimmer Bushrod.

"They're coming here?" said Flash in a panicked voice. "With guns?"

"If they show up here, they won't be trying to sell us Girl Scout cookies," said Kit.

"We won't be in a buying mood," added Swifty. The other men in the room joined in voicing their agreement with Swifty.

"Let me get this straight," said a now calmed down Flash. "Some general in the United States Air Force had his men kidnap some alleged terrorist. They secretly brought him to the air base in Cheyenne and imprisoned him in some empty hangar and then tortured him for information he did not give up or never had in the first place. When they went too far in their torture, they grabbed Doc Charlie out of her quarters on alleged official business and had her treat the prisoner to keep him alive, but it was too late, and the prisoner died. No records were kept, and no official reports were ever made, and Doc was told to keep her mouth shut under punishment of death?"

"That's a pretty good summation," said Kit.

"So that's why Doc Charlie made plans to disappear when she retired from the Air Force," said Flash. "She planned to disappear to keep from being found as a civilian and probably murdered to keep her silence intact."

"Again, pretty good summation," said Kit. "She had a pretty good plan, but we kind of ruined it when we went looking for her after we got the request from her birth mother."

"And so now this general and his people are looking for her," said Flash.

"Based on the last three who showed up in the Range Rover, I don't think they were discouraged when we sent the first three guys on a special guided tour of Canada," said Kit.

"What happens now?" asked Flash.

"We have no idea how many there are, who they are, where they are, or what they plan to do," said Kit. "So, we sit tight and wait for them to make the next move."

"I see," said Flash, as he scrunched up his forehead and seemed to be trying to digest all the information he had just received.

The ensuing silence lasted for about five minutes. It was broken when Bushrod announced he was making another beer run to the kitchen and asked who wanted another beer.

"Who's up on the ridge?" asked Big Dave.

"Chief is up there, and the Doc is in the com room," said Kit. He was about to say more when he was interrupted by the deep voice of Woody from the kitchen.

"Supper's ready. Come and get it," said Woody in as loud a voice as he could muster.

There was a lot of noise as chairs were pushed back and boots hit the wooden floor of the cabin. In less than two minutes the men were all seated at the table as Woody delivered several large dishes and pots to the table. Doc turned up the volume in the com room, set the acoustic alarms, and joined them.

The evening menu consisted of Woody's version of goulash, which consisted mostly of hamburger, noodles, onions, and God knows what else. There were also baked potatoes clad in aluminum foil along with butter, sour cream, and shredded cheese. There were a few moments of noisy exchange as dishes and pots were passed and when everyone had served themselves, silence ensued. The only noises were sounds of chewing and silverware scraping against dishware.

CHAPTER FORTY

Kit had invited Flash to share his room and the next morning, after a quick breakfast, he took Flash on a tour of the ranch and took time to explain in detail the fortifications they had installed. At each point they encountered a claymore or camera or other device, Kit took care to explain why they were placed where they were. Flash said little, but Kit noticed nothing seemed to escape his sharp eyes.

They finished up the tour on top of the ridge. Swifty had now replaced Chief on duty, and he gave Flash a good explanation of the surrounding topography and detail on all possible approaches to the ranch house.

When he was finished, Swifty looked at the short scientist and asked if he had any questions.

"I have just one question," said Flash.

"Shoot," replied Swifty.

"Everything I have seen is based on defense of the ranch house from attack," said Flash.

"You are correct," said Swifty. "We assume eventually the opposition will figure out we have Doc located here at the ranch and then they will come and try to take her."

"I see," said Flash. He then walked around the perimeter

of the ridge and took in every angle, using the binoculars loaned to him by Swifty.

"You appear to be well defended," said Flash when he finished his examination of the surrounding countryside.

"If you see something we've missed or have a solid suggestion on improving our position, I'm all ears," said Swifty.

"I need to think about what I have just seen and heard," said a studious looking Flash. "Thank you for the tour."

Flash followed Kit down the trail back to the ranch house.

"Is there someplace quiet where I might sit and think?" Flash asked Kit.

"You can use our room, or you can use the barn," answered Kit. "Nobody is likely to disturb you in either one of those locations."

"Thank you," replied Flash.

When they reached the area of the ranch house, Flash stopped at his van, grabbed his laptop and then had Kit take him to the barn. Once there, he went into the tack room and sat on an old bench. As Kit was leaving the barn, Flash opened his laptop and began to punch at the keys.

Big Dave had returned to Kemmerer, so Kit grabbed his half-brother Billy and they sat alone on the front porch of the ranch house. Billy looked around and said, "Where's Swifty?"

"He's got ridge duty for the next two hours," replied Kit. "I wanted to talk to you about the defense we've set up here at the ranch."

"I'm all ears," said Billy.

"How good is our defensive setup?" asked Kit.

Billy paused before answering Kit. His gaze took in the area of the ranch below him and then to the west and then to the east.

"Our defensive setup is pretty good, considering," he replied.

"Considering what?" asked Kit.

"Considering we have limitations on manpower and weapons and equipment," answered a serious looking Billy. "The other guys have a lot of resources we don't. But they can't use most of them without tipping their hand to a completely illegal operation on U.S. soil."

Kit did not respond to Billy's comments. He waited. He knew this was a good time to let his half-brother think and when he did, he would tell Kit what he really thought.

"Do you want some bullshit full of military jargon, or do you want the hard, cold facts?" Billy asked Kit.

"I want the truth," replied Kit.

"The truth is always the simplest, but it's what you rarely get to hear," said Billy.

Again, Kit did not respond and remained silent.

Billy looked at Kit and then broke into a faint smile, a rarity for him. "Playin' poker with me, Kit?"

Kit just smiled back at his half-brother.

"Just like old Jack Nicholson said in that movie line of his, 'Most people can't handle the truth.' They want some soft soap crap about truth, justice and the American way, or so they say," said Billy. "They're afraid of the truth."

Then Billy paused, as though he was not sure or not ready to continue.

"I want the truth," said Kit.

Billy looked hard at Kit. Then he spoke.

"We are up against an enemy of unknown numbers and weaponry. All we really know is the enemy wants to find and kill and eliminate Doc Charlie as a potential witness who could discredit some Air Force asshole general and keep him from getting a promotion and possibly get him tossed out of the military on his fat ass. Therein lies our strength in this situation," said Billy.

"Strength?" asked a puzzled Kit.

"This asshole general can't come out in the open. He must operate in the shadows and in secret. He can't issue orders in official channels. He cannot use normal Air Force systems or weapons. He can't use highly trained Air Force personnel and weapons," said Billy.

Kit waited and kept his mouth shut. He knew Billy would continue, but not until he was good and ready.

Billy looked down at the ground and studied it for a moment. Then he looked up at Kit and continued.

"This general has to hire mercenaries to do his dirty work. He has lots of contacts through his job. There are lots of ex-servicemen who try their luck at being killers for hire. But most of them get jobs working in third world countries, not gigs in the U.S. He can also find ways to provide them with classified information about us. What he can't do is use Air Force staff and weapons against us," said Billy.

"That's a relief," said Kit with a sarcastic grin on his face. "I can stop looking for B-52 bombers every time I go outside to take a leak."

Billy looked at Kit with a mixture of amusement and concern. "Just the kind of smartass remark I would expect from you," he said, shaking his head slowly.

"All this is very educational, but it doesn't begin to answer my question," said Kit.

"Just what is your question?" asked Billy.

"What do we do now?" replied Kit.

"One of the things I learned in the military was this. The best defense is a good offense," replied Billy.

"You're suggesting we go on offense?" asked Kit. "Against whom? With what?" he asked.

"That's in your department. You're the brainy one in the family. I'm just the better muscle," replied Billy with a sardonic grin on his face.

"You're the one with military training," said Kit. "What would you do?"

"Are you sure you want to know?" asked a suddenly grim-faced Billy.

"I think I'm out of good options," said Kit.

"I don't think you'll like my idea, but I have a few questions first," said Billy.

"Shoot," replied Kit.

"You could have used a less offensive word," said Billy with a grin on his face.

"Explain," countered Kit.

"Let's bring the situation up to date," said Billy. "We are protecting a witness some hot shit general in the Air Force wants silenced. He can't use official channels or forces. He must rely on hired help to silence Doc Charlie. He's not sure where she is, but it won't be long before he finds us. There's always some brown nose shithead trying to win favor from a high -ranking officer who will break the rules for him. We have a good defense plan, but we have no idea how much force he can muster against us. Nor do we know where his base or bases of operations are located. Are we clear so far?"

"Crystal clear," replied Kit.

"We need to do several things as quickly as we can," said Billy. "First, we need to find out where these assholes are set up in some kind of camp. We can check all the motels within a reasonable distance and see if they have several rentals that are ongoing. If we strike out on that, we need to put out feelers for anyone who might have seen and noticed these guys. There's got to be more than a few of them and they need bunks, and they need to be fed."

Kit was taking notes. "I can check on motels. How about fast-food places that deliver?"

"Good idea. I knew there was a reason you're in charge of this screwed up operation," said Billy. "We need to check out trailer parks as well. Some of them have permanent rentals."

"I'll have Big Dave and Thor look into that," said Kit, as he made more notes.

"We need to check out all the official campgrounds and as many unofficial ones as well," added Billy.

"I can check with the state boys and the Forest Service, but there's a ton of spots used for camping in the upper drainage of the Ham's Fork River," said Kit.

"Are any of them large enough for a sizeable encampment?" asked Billy.

Kit thought for a minute and then shook his head. "I'm not sure. There are some that are like large circles with slots for individual campers. But. . .."

"But what?" asked Billy.

"Most of those are full during the weekends at this time of year," said Kit.

"Checking with the state and fed boys should clear that up," said Billy.

"How about all the unofficial campsites? What about some rancher who rents out a pasture along the Ham's Fork?" asked Kit.

Billy paused and leaned down to pluck a long blade of grass, studied it for a moment, and then stuck it in his mouth like a tiny green cigar. "If we put out the word we're interested in a sizeable encampment of strangers, we're just liable to get some input from folks who know Big Dave and you," said Billy.

"You're probably right about that," responded Kit.

"I wish we had some good old fashioned aerial surveillance of the surrounding area," said Billy.

"Yeah, just call up the CIA and ask for some good satellite coverage of Lincoln County," said Kit derisively.

Both men laughed at the idea.

Then Kit stopped laughing.

Billy noticed his half-brother's face suddenly grow serious. "What's up, Kit? Did you get one of you brain fart flashes?" asked Billy.

"Do you remember that drone we borrowed from Sheriff Nystrom when we were looking for those bad dudes who were hired to eliminate you up by Sheridan?" asked Kit.

"I do," replied Billy. "He sent that Indian deputy to fly it for us and we used it to locate the campsite of the opposition. I also remember we needed some kind of balloon to go up to control it as it was one of those line-of-sight deals."

"Do you remember what kind of drone it was?" asked Kit.

"It was good sized, but it was one you could launch by hand, and it came apart to store and you could put it in the bed of a pickup truck," replied Billy. "Give me a minute and I'll see if I can find it."

With that Billy took out his phone and began an internet search. After a few minutes, he looked up at Kit and smiled. "Bingo, little brother. It was an RW-11 Raven. Only now they have one that has solar panels on the wings, and it can stay up longer than 90 minutes. Plus, it now has both day and night cameras that deliver real time images to the ground operator."

"I wonder if the Raven Sheriff Nystrom got has been upgraded?" asked Kit.

"I'm sure it has," said Billy. "When it gets upgraded in the military, they pass the upgrades on to law enforcement as well."

"Will we need the balloon?" asked Kit.

"I don't think so," said Billy. "If I remember correctly, most of the county is flat or valleys. We launch it from the high ground and control it from there."

"Will we need to ask Sheriff Nystrom for the operator?" asked Kit.

"I qualified to fly both this bird and the bigger one, the RQ-20 Puma. The military doesn't require a special qualification to fly them. They are quite simple to fly and control," said Billy.

"Do we tell Sheriff Nystrom why we want to borrow it?" asked Kit.

"Plausible deniability," replied Billy with a grin.

"Knowing him, if he gets asked about the drone, his response would be, what drone?"

"Anything else you can think of?" asked Kit.

"We need to find these assholes," responded Billy. "Once we do, then we have to plan an attack."

"I'm on it," said Kit and he headed up to the cabin to make some calls.

CHAPTER FORTY-ONE

After dinner that night, Flash put his hand on Kit's shoulder. Kit stopped and turned to see who had stopped him.

"Oh, it's you, Flash. What can I do for you?" asked Kit.

"I'd like you to accompany me to the barn," said Flash. "I have something to show you, and I have some thoughts I'd like to share with you," replied Flash.

"Of course," said Kit, and he followed the smaller man out the front door of the ranch house and across the ranch yard to the barn. Once they were inside, Flash turned on the lights and led Kit into the tack room. Kit was surprised to see some diagrams taped to the outside wall of the room.

"I hope you don't mind that I borrowed some things from your office, but I think you'll be pleased with what I have discovered," said an apologetic Flash. "I got most of what I needed from my trailer, but I had to borrow a few items. I promise I'll replace them or repay you."

Kit just grinned at his cousin. "Look, Flash, I'm happy to get your help. I need all the help I can get. If you need anything of mine, help yourself. I'm bettin' you'll put it to better use than I ever would," he said.

"Thank you," said Flash. "I was worried you would be angry with me."

"As you get to know me better, you will find I only get angry with people who agree with me and then disobey me or who attempt to cheat me," replied a still grinning Kit.

A visible wave of relief passed over Flash's face.

"Now, what do you have to show me?" asked Kit.

"Please have a seat," said Flash. "This may take a bit of time. I hope you don't mind."

"Not at all," said Kit. Flash sat on the bench, and Kit grabbed a metal bucket and turned it upside down and sat on it.

"So, what do you have?" asked Kit.

"I'm not sure how to begin," said Flash.

"Just start where you are comfortable. If I get lost, I'll interrupt you," said Kit warmly.

"Great," said Flash. Then he hesitated. He picked up his iPad and punched in some keys and then he found what he was looking for. He set the iPad on the rough table in front of them so both men could see the screen clearly.

"What you see on the screen is a brief outline of my thoughts concerning the situation with Doctor Charlie," said Flash.

"We just refer to her as Doc Charlie, and I think she is comfortable with that," said Kit.

"Right, I'm sorry," said Flash.

"Nothing to be sorry about, Flash. I'm just trying to bring you up to speed with what's been going on here," said Kit.

"Quite right," said Flash. He hit a button, and the outline print became larger and easier to read.

Kit looked carefully at the screen and read the first line.

It read as follows: "Alternatives to neutralizing threat to eliminate Doctor Charlie."

"What I am proposing is a less violent and less illegal strategy to thwart the efforts of the misguided Air Force general to illegally take the life of Doctor Charlie," said Flash.

"I'm all ears and eyes," said Kit.

"One of my concerns about your plan to fight it out here at the ranch with the forces this maverick general has assembled is it's reactive, not proactive. It's an old problem of using seemingly easy solutions of obvious problems," said Flash.

"What do you mean?" asked Kit.

"Have you heard the phrase, unintended consequences?" asked Flash.

"Yes, I have," said Kit. "I worked for a consulting company right out of college. It was a problem that kept cropping up when we tried to apply simple solutions to what we felt were simple problems."

"Good. Then you understand my concern," said Flash.

"I understand the concept, but I'm not sure what exactly your concerns are," said Kit.

"My concern is fairly simple, but I will do my best to make them clear to you," replied Flash.

"Please do," said Kit.

"If somehow you are able to successfully withstand an armed assault on your father's ranch, what then?" asked Flash.

"What do you mean?" asked Kit.

"If you vanquish one set of scoundrels, what prevents this mentally unstable Air Force general from just hiring another bigger and better armed group of thugs and send them to Wyoming?" asked Flash.

"Your point is well taken," said Kit. "I assume you are not asking an empty question. What strategy would you propose if you were me?" he asked.

"I know my proposal is a bit iffy, and I am rather naïve in the rough and tumble world of combat. I think I have a plan that might achieve your goals and in addition forever neutralize this out-of-control Air Force general," said Flash.

"You have my undivided attention," said a now profoundly serious Kit.

"My analysis told me eventually you will decide you have to leave the safety of the ranch and find your enemy. Once you have located him, you must devise an attack to neutralize him. That can be both dangerous and costly in human life," said Flash.

"What do you propose?" asked a very curious Kit.

"I am not sure how to obtain all the items I feel would be necessary for my plan, but I will give you the raw outline I have come up with and see what you think," said Flash.

Kit now remained silent and waited for Flash to continue and explain his plan.

"First of all, we need to find where the enemy is located," said Flash.

"I'm working on that," said Kit. "I have Billy and Big Dave checking with all the hotels, motels, official camp sites, and unofficial ones as well. It was Billy's idea as he said the enemy needs beds and food."

"He is absolutely correct," said Flash.

"I hate to tell him he is right," said Kit. "I'll never hear the end of it from him."

"A small price to pay for his assistance," said Flash.

"Did we leave anything out in our plan to search for their camp?" asked Kit.

"It would be very helpful if we had access to satellite imagery of the area to assist in locating them," said Flash.

"We obviously don't have access to a satellite, but I might have access to a military drone with both day and night real time cameras," said Kit.

"Really," said Flash. "What kind of drone?"

"My friend, the sheriff up in Sheridan, has an RQ-11B Raven drone in the latest version," said Kit. "I'm about to call him and see if we can 'borrow' it for a few days."

"How much range does the Raven have?" asked Flash.

"This version has solar collectors on the wings and can fly for about two hours and travel over a dozen miles," replied Kit.

"That would be excellent," said Flash. "I doubt these mercenaries have camped very far from Kemmerer."

"My thoughts exactly," responded Kit.

"When can you bring the Raven here?" asked Flash.

"I was about to call the sheriff. My best guess is I could drive there and back with the drone tomorrow and be back here by dark," said Kit.

"Excellent!" exclaimed Flash.

"Did you have more in mind than using a drone?" asked Kit.

"I did. I am so sorry," said Flash. "Sometimes I get so excited I forget the rest of my train of thought."

"And?" asked Kit.

"Oh yes," said Flash. "We need a weapon that will

neutralize the enemy and allow us to disarm and capture them without harm."

"We used tranquilizer guns before, but you need to be pretty close to the target and they are a single shot device and take time to reload," said Kit. "They are hardly practical for the terrain and number of the enemy we are likely to encounter."

"Exactly!" said Flash. "I have a much more practical and efficient method in mind."

"Like what?" asked Kit.

"Like this," said Flash. He punched a few keys and a picture of a strange device with wires appeared with a caption below it. The caption read, Taser XREP.

"What the hell is that?" asked a bewildered Kit.

"That is a Taser XREP, a 12-gauge, non-lethal round that delivers an electric shock to the target it hits. It is the most complex shotgun bullet ever made. Unlike a regular taser which only has a range of up to 35 feet, this is a projectile fired from a shot gun with a range of over a hundred feet. It sails through the air like a normal shotgun slug but induces muscle paralysis on impact. When contact with the target occurs, barbed electrodes pierce the skin and sends just 500 volts into the body. The waveform created current is shaped to mimic electrical signals in the body and jam the nervous system. The wave form is the secret to the weapon's efficiency," said Flash.

"I've never heard of such a thing," said Kit incredulously.

"It's been around for a while and is in use by some law enforcement and the military," said Flash.

"How much do these things cost?" asked Kit.

"They're not for sale to the public for obvious reasons," said a smiling Flash.

"Can we get some?" asked Kit.

"I actually have some in my trailer," said Flash. "I've been working on some improvements to the current version and forgot to take them out of my trailer when I left California."

"How many do you have?" asked Kit.

"They come in packs of five, and I have three packs," said Flash. "Or is it four packs? I'm not really sure. I'd have to look and check," he said.

"Can you get more of them?" asked Kit.

"Of course," said Flash. "I could order them and have them delivered in a couple of days. Sooner if we were willing to pay extra for air freight."

"How many can you order?" asked a now excited Kit.

"I can order as much as you want," replied a puzzled Flash.

"Can you order a gross of them?" asked Kit.

"A gross? You mean 144 of them?" asked Flash.

"Yes," replied Kit.

"As I explained, they come packed in units of five so no, I could not order a gross. But I could order 150. Would that be all right?" asked Flash.

"Absolutely," said Kit.

"They are quite expensive," said Flash. "I could call and get a quote; including shipping and let you know."

"I don't care what the cost is," said a grinning Kit. "Here, take my American Express card and order 150 of those shotgun bullets and get them here by the quickest means possible."

"You're sure. They are quite expensive," said a concerned Flash.

"I'm sure," said Kit. "And do it as soon as possible."

Flash looked at Kit's credit card, then at Kit. He could see the fire in Kit's eyes. "All right," he said. "I'll do it right away. But before I do, I have one more issue to discuss about the plan."

"Let's hear it," said Kit.

"If you are able to locate the camp of the enemy force, organize an attack and neutralize them using these electronic shotgun bullets, what then?" asked Flash. "How do you prevent this obviously unstable general from simply sending for more hired thugs to attempt to kill the good Doctor Charlie?"

"I have a plan," said a suddenly smiling Kit.

"May I hear it?" asked Flash carefully.

"You may," said an incredibly pleased Kit. He then proceeded to share the plan he had just formed in his head with his cousin Flash.

Flash listened intently. When Kit was finished, Flash smiled.

"Did I forget anything?" asked Kit.

Flash thought for a moment and then spoke.

"I might have a few questions and maybe some suggestions," he said.

"Let's hear the questions first," said Kit.

"If your plan is successful and you have subdued the enemy team without loss of life, what do you do with them then?" asked Flash.

"Good question," said Kit. "I guess I hadn't got that far in my plan."

"I would think it an important item in the plan," said Flash. "Even if you have videoed the encounter and then handed the prisoners and the video over to law enforcement authorities, what's to stop this obsessed Air Force general from just sending a new and larger batch of mercenaries after Doc Charlie?"

"I see your point," said Kit. "The last thing I want is to have to deal with more problems sent here by this nutcase general in the future."

"I concur," said Flash.

"Do you have more questions?" asked Kit.

"Perhaps, but that was the big and most important one," replied Flash.

"Do you have any suggestions or ideas of how we can bring this whole mess to a satisfactory conclusion?" asked Kit.

"I have spent some time cogitating on the issue, and I believe I may have a suggestion for a plan to bring this Air Force general to his knees and out of Doc Charlie's life forever," said Flash.

"You mean kill him?" asked Kit with surprise in his eyes.

"Heavens no!" retorted Flash. "I abhor violence and cannot stand the sight of blood."

"What do you mean?" asked a puzzled looking Kit.

"We need a plan to publicly disgrace this evil general and get him forcibly removed from his position as a general in the Air Force and then get him imprisoned and stripped of all of his worldly possessions," said a calm Flash.

"I get we need a plan to get this dude kicked out of the

Air Force and maybe sent to prison, but how do we strip him of his possessions, namely his money," said Kit.

"Separating the general and his money will be child's play," said a smiling Flash. "Just leave that part to me. If he has no money, he has no power whether he is a free man or stuck in prison."

"All right. I'll leave the stripping of his possessions to you," said Kit. "Now how do we get him kicked out of the Air Force and sent to prison?"

"The general has hired several hooligans and sent them to Wyoming to eliminate Doc Charlie," said Flash. "Someone hired them, and someone has supplied, equipped, and paid them. While you work on your plan to subdue his hooligans, I will trace the money back to the foolish general. When I am finished, we will provide the authorities with the hooligans and their weapons, copies of how the money changed hands, and the sworn testimony of Doc Charlie on what happened that night on Warren Air Force base in Cheyenne. I will also provide the same information to each of the Joint Chiefs of Staff in Washington, D.C."

Kit was speechless. When he recovered from his initial shock, he asked, "How long will this take?"

"Not long," replied Flash. "The oldest solution to a situation like this is almost always the same and it is usually the simplest solution."

"What solution?" asked Kit.

"Follow the money," said a smiling Flash.

"Do you see any holes in my plan to deal with the mercenaries?" asked Kit.

"Only one," replied Flash.

"What's that?" asked Kit.

"Some folks could get hurt, wounded, or killed," replied a calm Flash.

"I'll take that risk," said Kit. "Let's join the others in the cabin."

Flash nodded and the two men rose from the bench and the bucket and made their way to the cabin.

CHAPTER FORTY-TWO

The next two days sped by quickly. Neither Big Dave nor Thor had any sightings of the black Land Rover, nor did they get any reports from any of their friends they had alerted to be on the lookout for the large foreign SUV.

Billy drove to Sheridan after getting a green light from Sheriff Nystrom. After the Indian deputy who was the drone's handler finished helping Billy load the disassembled drone and equipment into the back of Billy's pickup truck, Billy went into the sheriff's office to thank Sheriff Nystrom.

"I want to thank you on behalf of my brother Kit for the loan of the drone, Sheriff," said Billy.

"What drone?" replied Sheriff Nystrom. "I don't know what the hell you're talkin' about. Now get the hell out of my office before I have you arrested for vagrancy or littering," said the straight-faced sheriff. Billy grinned and left the office. As soon as he was out of Sheridan, Billy hit the gas, only pausing when he needed to as he negotiated the twisting roads going over the Big Horn Mountains.

Billy reached the ranch just before dark. Kit and Swifty helped him unload the drone and took it into the barn.

"Shouldn't we test fly it first?" asked a too eager Swifty.

"We'll test fly it in the morning," said Kit, cutting off

his friend in mid-protest. "Let's go have supper and then we need to have a meeting and go over a new plan."

"New plan!" exclaimed Swifty. "I'm just starting to understand the old plan and now you've come up with a new plan. Good lord."

Billy just smiled and led the way to the cabin where the smells of a good supper wafted on the slight breeze.

Everyone but Chief was at the supper table. When they finished the meal and cleared off the table, everyone took a seat to hear what Kit was proposing.

Kit waited until everyone was seated and quiet. Then he looked at each of his friends and felt a wave of confidence. Being surrounded by loyal friends is important to anyone faced with making difficult decisions. Kit took a last look around the room, and then he began to deliver his plan.

"After talking things over with Billy and Flash, I have decided to make a change in our plan and our tactics," said Kit. "Sooner or later the thugs this Air Force general has hired are going to figure out where we are. When they do, they will do reconnaissance on our position and then devise a plan to eliminate Doc Charlie. Any plan they come up with won't be extremely healthy for any of us. Or anyone else between them and Doc."

"Are you suggesting we turn tail and run?" asked Bushrod with a strong note of defiance in his voice.

"No, I'm not suggesting we run. I'm not suggesting we surrender or do anything else to help these criminals in their effort to kill a friend of ours," replied Kit.

"What are you suggesting?" asked Bushrod.

"It was recently mentioned to me that a strong military axiom has always been to rely on a strong offense rather than a strong defense," said Kit. "I intend to go on offense. I have a plan, but it's not foolproof and there is obvious risk to life and limb for anyone who agrees to participate in my plan," said Kit. "So, before I continue with details, is there anyone who wants out now. I'm not trying to embarrass you. This deal is dangerous. If you participate, you could get killed or maimed for life. I want to make that clear up front. The reason I want to know now is simple. It's better for you if you know nothing about the plan if you choose not to participate. It's also better for the rest of us who do go ahead with the plan. You can't be tried or convicted of something you knew nothing about. Is that clear?"

Kit waited and slowly scanned everyone at the table. No one moved. No one spoke.

"If you want out, speak up now," said Kit. "There is no shame in avoiding violence. I will think less of no one who chooses to take a pass on this."

Kit paused and waited for a response. There was none.

"No one has spoken out," said Kit. "May I see the hands of everyone who is volunteering for this plan to take the attack to the enemy?"

Every person at the table raised their hand. No one spoke.

"Good. You're all in. I can't tell you how much I appreciate your support," said Kit.

"Let's hear the plan," said Swifty.

"My conclusion is that staying here and waiting for the enemy to find and attack us is not the brightest plan in the world," said Kit. "My new plan is for us to find, attack, neutralize, and eliminate the enemy." Kit paused to let that part sink in.

"Does anyone have any questions so far?" asked Kit. "I should have said this first, but if any time during this meeting any of you have a question, just raise your hand and we will stop our discussion and deal with your question. Any of you except Swifty, of course. Swifty doesn't ask questions, he just likes to make degrading comments about my speaking ability."

Everyone broke out in laughter. No one laughed louder than Swifty.

When the laugher stopped, Big Dave had his hand up. With the size of his hands, it was hard to miss.

"You have a question, Big Dave?" asked Kit.

"I do," said Big Dave. "If we're all out attacking these bozos, what happens to Doc Charlie? Are we leavin' her here unguarded?"

"Good question," said Kit. "Although Doc Charlie has become pretty damn proficient with a .45 semi-auto, I think the best plan is to hide her in plain sight."

"Explain?" asked Billy.

"Doc Charlie will be wearing a dark brown wig and have tinted contact lenses. She will wear glasses with plain glass in them. She will be the new assistant in Woody's law office. She will work there during the day, and she will be driven to and from work by Big Dave's wife. Doc Charlie will be staying out at Big Dave's place," said Kit.

"Hells bells," said Big Dave. "Nobody tells me nothin' anymore. Did my wife agree to all this?"

"Of course, she did," said a grinning Kit. "She not only agreed to the plan but told me she will be heavily armed the entire time she is responsible for Doc Charlie's safety."

"God help the poor dumb bastard who tries to take on my wife," muttered Big Dave.

"I think it's a good example of hiding in plain sight," said Kit.

"Any time you get a plan and Big Dave don't know nothin' about it, you done somethin'," said a grinning Bushrod.

"I made up a list of places to check," said Kit. "Motels, rooming houses, campgrounds, and apartments. I divided them up geographically as best I could, and each of you will have a list to check out. You can make phone calls, you can drive by the places, you can stop in and chat with the owners or landlords, and you can be plain nosy when talking to anyone you know."

"What about campgrounds on private land or government land not monitored by the state or the feds?" asked Woody.

"We got the drone from the sheriff up in Sheridan," said Kit. "We used it once before up in the Big Horns. It can take photos and video during the day or night. It can stay up for almost two hours."

"Don't you need a balloon up in the air to keep in contact with the drone?" asked Bushrod.

"We plan to launch it from high ground and maintain contact with it by line of sight," answered Kit.

"It might be tough finding all of them," said Billy. "They might be spread out in several locations."

"You could be right, Billy," said Kit. "But we need to try to find them first. If they are spread out and we can't pinpoint all their locations, we will have to go to plan B."

"What in the wide, wide world of sports, is plan B?" asked Swifty.

Kit smiled. This time he had thought about an alternative plan, and he had come up with one.

"Plan B is one of the oldest hunting tricks in the book," said Kit. "Whether hunting lions in Africa, grizzly bears in the Rocky Mountains, or wild pigs in Texas, hunters have used bait to draw their prey to them."

"Do you remember the box canyon I had to hide out in when those hired guns from the Chicago mob were hunting for me?" asked Kit as he looked directly at Big Dave and Swifty.

"I sure as hell do," said Big Dave. Swifty nodded his head in agreement.

"We're going to set up a tent camp in the canyon, complete with a small supply wagon. Then we'll make it look like its being lived in, with things like stacked firewood. Once that's set up, we'll send someone there as if they were resupplying it and they will try to hide their tracks, but be a bit clumsy at it," said Kit.

"So, we lure them in and once we have them in the box canyon, we close the only entrance, and we shoot them with the new shotgun shells and the tranquilizer darts from the top of the canyon walls and the blocked entrance. We'll start out with tranquilizer guns because they are almost silent. But, if the need arises, we'll use the shotgun shells. When all of them are immobilized, we tie their hands and feet with plastic ties and strip them," said Kit.

"Why the hell do we strip them. Isn't zip tying them up enough?" asked Bushrod.

"We're going to question them and find out who is in

charge. Being naked helps to break down their reluctance very quickly," said Kit.

"Not to mention its downright unhandy to be naked and trying to make your way out of that country if one of them should manage to escape," said Billy.

"Why question them?" asked Bushrod. "We know they're just asshole mercenaries who are only loyal to the almighty dollar. They'd be lucky to know who really hired them."

"Probably true," said Kit. "But one or some of them are in charge of their part of the operation, and we need to find out which one or ones for the next part of our plan."

"Next part? You mean there's more of this goddamneded plan?" said Big Dave.

"These men work for money. They have no loyalties. We find out who is in charge of this outfit. We get them to contact their boss to let him know they have taken Doc Charlie prisoner, but she is demanding to talk to the general. Even though they plan to kill her as they were ordered, they think, as former soldiers, her request is righteous," said Kit.

"Righteous?" asked Flash in a puzzled voice.

"Righteous as in a legitimate request from one soldier to another, especially when one of them is going to be killed," said Billy.

"Ah, I see," said Flash, although his expression said he clearly had no idea what Billy was talking about.

"Questions?" said Kit.

There were several questions. Most of them dealt with who was going to be doing what and when they would have the drone, the special shotgun shells, and the tranquilizer guns.

"What about shotguns?" asked Bushrod.

"Another good question," said Kit. Between Billy, Swifty, Big Dave, me and my father's armory, we have enough. Some over and under, some side by side, and some semi-automatic. Billy also has contacted our old friend in Buffalo, and he has five, like-new Benelli M4 semi-auto shotguns. Billy will be making a run to Buffalo to pick them up."

"Are we allowed to carry our own personal weapons?" asked Chief who had remained silent until now.

"I'd like to believe we won't need them, but I know better," said Kit. "Every plan is always a good plan until the first shot is fired. Then everything goes to hell in a handbasket. Everyone is to be armed." Kit knew Chief would be carrying several edged weapons as well as firearms, but he chose not to mention it.

Kit paused and looked out over the group of men around the table. Every man returned his stare. No one avoided it. They were all on board.

"Now, I'm going to hand out assignments for tomorrow to try to find where these mercs are holed up. If you have any more questions after getting your assignments, I'll be sitting here for the next hour," aid Kit. "Line up, and let's get this show on the road."

CHAPTER FORTY-THREE

After the sheets were handed out and the group had disbursed, Kit was picking up his notes from the old dining table when he sensed someone standing in front of him. He looked up to see Doc Charlie.

"Can I help you, Doc?" asked Kit.

"I heard you give out assignments to everyone here," said Doc Charlie. "But I didn't hear an assignment for me. Since I am the object of this crazy person's search, I think it's only right I take part in the operation. I'm not some scared woman, Kit. I'm a trained officer in the military. I'm perfectly capable of doing any job you assign to me."

Kit paused and then responded to Doc's issue.

"I'm sure you can handle yourself in a sticky situation, Doc," said Kit. "I was fairly sure of that when I first met you and my opinion hasn't changed since then. But, having you exposed is a risk I'm not willing to take. The whole objective of this rogue military operation is to silence you forever so some butt-brained Air Force glory hound can get promoted to a position he is unfit to fill."

"I listened to your plan, and you didn't disclose what happens if your raid is successful and you capture or eliminate the opposing force. Even if you are completely successful, what's to stop this nutcase general from just hiring more mercenaries?" asked Doc Charlie.

"I have a part B to the plan," said Kit.

"Just what is part B?" asked Doc Charlie.

"It's a combination of things I'm setting up and a few things I haven't figured out yet," replied Kit.

Despite her reservations, Doc Charlie could not help herself and burst out laughing.

"What's so funny?" asked Kit.

"You. You're what's funny," replied Doc Charlie.

"How so?" asked Kit.

"You may be the most honest man I ever met and certainly one of the most direct. You certainly don't mince words, do you?" responded Doc Charlie.

Kit smiled, and his face seemed to relax.

"Back in my previous life I worked for a consulting company in Chicago," said Kit. "Every year we had a performance appraisal and review. Each year my review had the same comment, sometimes on the positive side and sometimes on the negative side."

"What was the comment?' asked Doc Charlie.

"Mr. Andrews is brutally honest," replied a grinning Kit.

"I certainly would not argue with that evaluation," responded Doc Charlie.

"Look, I know you're antsy and want in on the action," said Kit. "But I see it as too dangerous for this mission and I promise you, when I finally figure out Plan B, you will have an active part in it. In the meantime, I need you to stay with the Olson family, and go to work in Woody's office helping his legal assistant. It's the perfect cover. You'll be hiding in plain sight. Best of all, you'll be on the outside looking in and are likely to see more of these mercenaries than we are. Anything you see or hear, you are to tell Big Dave's wife Connie, and she'll pass it on. Are you clear on this?"

"Crystal clear," replied Doc Charlie. "I don't like it, but I see the logic in your plan."

"Good," responded Kit. "You will be wearing a wig. You will get a ride from Connie Olson to work and then back home. Connie will tell people you are a distant cousin's daughter. Does that work for you?"

"Yes, it does, but, when this thing is coming to a close, I want to be in on it," said a determined looking Doc Charlie.

"I promise," said Kit. "Boy Scout's honor."

Kit held up three fingers in a mock salute.

Doc Charlie burst out laughing again. When she stopped laughing, she managed to achieve a more mature composure. Then she spoke.

"If I'm not in on the end of this deal. If I'm not allowed to confront this chickenshit general who tried to ruin my life and now is hiring people to kill me. I promise you I will hunt you down to the ends of the earth and neuter you without the aid of painkillers or antiseptics. Is that clear?" she said.

"Crystal clear," replied Kit as an unconscious wince went through his entire body. "I promise you will be in on the end of this mission, and you will have your time with the general."

Doc Charlie held out her hand and Kit shook it. Then she smiled at him, turned, and walked out of the cabin.

"I'm pretty damn sure she meant every word of it," said Kit to himself.

'Bet your ass', but that's the first time I ever heard of bet your manhood," said a grinning Swifty, who had been standing in the hallway, out of sight of the dining room.

"You heard?" asked Kit.

"I wouldn't have missed hearing that for all the tea in China," said Swifty.

"You hate tea," said Kit.

"Doesn't matter," said Swifty. "It was the first thing that popped into my mind. Besides, you know I'm the guy who always tells you some version of the truth."

"I plan to put that on your tombstone," said Kit.

"That assumes you will still be around when I go to the great beyond. And after that little speech from the Doc, I'm glad I never tried to sell you life insurance," retorted Swifty.

"I need a drink," said Kit. "I feel a bit woozy."

"Coming right up," said Swifty. He strode into the kitchen, opened a drawer and took out a box labeled 'snake bite cure'."

"What the hell is that?" asked a startled Kit.

Swifty opened the box and extracted a full bottle of Buffalo Trace Bourbon. He grabbed two glasses from the cupboard and set the glasses on the counter. He opened the bottle and paused before he began to pour whiskey into the glasses.

"How much?" asked Swifty.

"Start pouring and don't stop till you filled it to the brim," replied a still shaken Kit.

Swifty filled both glasses to the brim. He put the top on the bottle and slid it back in the case. Then he handed a glass to Kit.

Swifty raised his glass in a mock toast. "Here's to your health, which ain't lookin' too damn good right now."

CHAPTER FORTY-FOUR

When Kit strolled into the kitchen at six the next morning, it was already full of people. Doc, Bushrod, and Woody were busy in the kitchen. Everyone else was drinking coffee in the great room and out on the front porch. It was obvious everyone was anxious to head out and get their assignments completed as soon as possible.

When Doc, Woody, and Bushrod started to bring food to the table, it seemed like an invisible vacuum cleaner was sucking the food right off the serving dishes and causing it to disappear. Kit rapped on the table with his fist to get everyone's attention.

"When you're done with your assignments, head back here and report to me. We'll get together right before supper and go over what we have learned and see if we can agree on a plan of action," said Kit. "See you then."

The room was full of the noise of chairs scraping over the wooden floor of the dining room and the somewhat muffled sound of clips of several short conversations. In five minutes, the dining room was empty except for Kit, Swifty, and Billy.

Swifty rose from his chair and walked into the kitchen. He returned with a pot of coffee, three empty mugs, and the bottle of whiskey. He poured hot coffee into each mug, added a shot of whiskey, and slid mugs across the table to Kit and Billy.

"Let's talk," said Swifty.

"Talk? About what?" asked a puzzled Billy.

"If we manage to neutralize and capture all or most of the current gang of hired assassins, I see nothing to prevent this deranged general from simply hiring another crew of mercenaries," said Swifty as he pickup up his mug and took a swig.

"Good point," said Billy. Then he turned to face Kit. "What's my brother's clever plan to taking this idiot general out of the game permanently?"

Kit took a sip of the alcohol infused coffee. He stared at his mug for a few seconds. Then he set the mug down on the table.

"The truth is, I don't have a plan for what to do next. Everything that has come into my mind doesn't pass the what if test," said Kit. "I'm open to suggestions."

"Wait, just a minute," said Swifty. "I need a paper and pencil."

"What for?" asked Kit.

"This is the first time in my life I've ever heard you admit you're stumped for an answer to a problem. I need to write it down along with the date and time, so I have something historic to show my grandchildren," said a grinning Swifty.

"The scary thought is Swifty might actually have grandchildren," muttered Kit.

"Only God knows how many and where they might be located," added a grinning Billy.

"Well, I've been a lot of places and been with a lot of women," said Swifty sarcastically.

"This discussion is a long way off from answering my question," said Kit.

The laughter suddenly stopped.

"Well?" asked Kit.

No words were spoken for a few minutes as Billy and Swifty considered Kit's question.

Kit broke the silence.

"Let me try to set the stage for this," said Kit. "Our plan works, and we manage to lure the mercenaries into the small box canyon and disarm and capture them. Now what do we do?"

As if to improve their thinking process, both Billy and Swifty took a long drink of their whiskey laced coffee.

A long silence ensued. Finally, Billy broke the silence.

"Didn't this Air Force general put out some kind of request to all the law enforcement offices in Wyoming asking for any leads to the whereabouts of Doc Charlie?" he asked.

"Yes, yes he did," said Kit. "That was a while ago, and I had forgotten about it."

"Let's just suppose the mercenaries took the bait and entered the small box canyon, and we captured and disarmed them. Once we had them captured, any communication contact with them would be shut down. The general would not know what happened because no one would be responding to any calls for updates," said Billy.

"My guess is that the general is not communicating directly with the mercenaries," said Kit. "I'd guess he has some middle-man or intermediary who keeps his name out of the chain of communication."

"I buy that," said Billy. "That means the general might contact the intermediary, but the intermediary is as clueless to what happened as the general."

"All the general knows is something happened and now all he's got is radio silence," added Swifty.

"What if the general gets a call from a law enforcement officer telling him he has arrested Doc Charlie based on the call he got from the general. The officer tells the general he is holding Doc Charlie in their jail," said Billy.

"The general doesn't want to have Doc Charlie in jail and certainly doesn't want to have real Air Police go to the jail and pick her up. That leaves too much of a trail back to him," said Kit.

"What if the arresting officer asks the general if this arrest is a matter of national security? Wouldn't the general say it was, so he can keep everything under wraps? If the arresting officer asks the general how he wants this handled and suggests he can quietly deliver the prisoner to a neutral location out of public view, known only by the arresting officer," said Billy.

"The general would leap at that suggestion," said Kit.

"We need to have the arresting officer demand he will only turn the prisoner over to the general in person," added Swifty.

"Then we set up the meeting and arrange to have it recorded," said Billy. "We need to have the arresting officer leave the general and Doc Charlie alone in a room where we can record it."

"We can neutralize any guards or assistance the general

brings with him and then get Doc Charlie to piss off the general and get him to admit on film what he was trying to do," added Kit.

"What if he doesn't admit his guilt on tape?" asked Billy. "What if the general pulls a weapon on Doc Charlie?"

"I'm fairly sure someone as cocky and prideful as this general will be no match for Doc Charlie in a one-on-one conversation. I'd bet on her getting him so outraged he admits what he was doing," said Kit. "In addition, Doc Charlie will be armed, and we can have the arresting officer search the general for weapons before allowing him in the room with the prisoner."

"Yeah, but what if the general clams up and refuses to talk? What do we do then?" asked Billy.

"We keep our mouths shut and wait," said Kit. Most guilty people can't stand the silence and I'm counting on him to open his mouth and say something his lawyer wouldn't want him to," said Kit.

"What if the general brings armed thugs with him and plans to kill both Doc Charlie and the arresting officer. Leave no evidence or witnesses?" Said Billy.

"We make sure the arresting officer is not alone, and we are backing him up as well," answered Kit.

"Do we use Sheriff Nystrom up in Sheridan?" asked Swifty.

"Sheridan is too dang far away," said Kit.

"How about we use Detective Parcell in Laramie?" offered Swifty.

"That would work. We could set up the meeting at one of those cabins my dad and I rented in Centennial. It's outside of Laramie and nice and isolated," said Kit.

"How do we get access to the cabin?" asked Billy.

"I know the owner, and I'll arrange to rent it from her," said Kit.

"Will Detective Parcell go along with this ruse?" asked Swifty.

"I'll give him a call and sound him out," said Kit. "I'm pretty sure he'd love to be a part of this plan."

"What do we need to do to make this happen?" asked Billy.

"Let's go over the plan, and I'll take some notes. We need to make sure we haven't missed something important," said Kit.

"Let's do it over a fresh cup of coffee," said Swifty. He poured fresh coffee into each of the three mugs, adding a shot of whisky to each mug.

Swifty sat at the table and took a healthy swig of hot whisky-laced coffee and gave out a big sigh. "Much better," he announced.

"Are we all ready now?" asked a slightly annoyed Kit.

Billy and Swifty both grinned and nodded their assent.

"First, we abandon our attempts to locate all of the mercenaries," said Kit. "Agreed?"

"Yep," said Billy and Swifty, almost in unison, but not quite.

"Second, we send Swifty to the small box canyon and have him pitch a Baker tent and set up enough gear to make it look like it's currently in use," said Kit. "Agreed?"

"Wait! Me?" asked Swifty.

"Yep," said Billy and Kit in perfect unison.

"Dang it. I always get all the crap details," muttered Swifty.

"Bushrod will go with you and help set it up. He'll be the one making trips to the site on fake supply runs so we can entice the mercenaries to follow him. Then, once a day, we send Bushrod on horseback leading a pack horse into the box canyon, where he appears to be unloading supplies and taking them into the tent. Then he rides out of the box canyon and back to the nearest hard road where he has a parked pickup truck and horse trailer," said Kit. "Agreed?"

"Yep," said Billy, and Swifty just grunted something unintelligible which both others took for his agreement.

"We station Chief up on the rim of the box canyon where he can stay hidden and see the canyon floor and the entrance clearly. We supply him with a satellite radio to keep in touch with us," said Kit. "Agreed?"

This time both the other men just nodded their heads in agreement.

"We leave Woody, Doc, and Flash here at the ranch to man the communications and keep watch," said Kit. "Agreed?"

Again, both men nodded yes.

"We set up a small camp in this little valley the creek runs through. It's about two miles south of the small box canyon. The camp is to be manned by Swifty, Billy, Bushrod, Big Dave, Thor, and me," said Kit. "Agreed?"

Again, both Billy and Swifty nodded their heads in agreement.

"We keep two satellite radios in the camp, along with horses, tack, feed, food, water, and weapons," said Kit. "Agreed?"

"What about weapons?" asked Billy. "Which ones? We have to be able to transport them on horseback."

279

"We each bring a shotgun, a dart gun, a pistol, and a handful of zip ties and gags," said Kit.

"Then I agree," said Billy.

"Me too," said Swifty.

"Once we know the mercenaries are at the entrance or just inside the box canyon, we move in," said Kit. "We neutralize any rear guard with dart guns and then immobilize them with quick ties and gags. We leave Thor and Bushrod to guard the entrance. Then the rest of us climb the trail to the top of the ridge on two sides of the box canyon and start using the shot guns until all the mercs are down. Did I leave anything out?"

"I think you nailed it," said Billy.

"If and that's a big if," said Swifty. "If the plan goes as you just outlined, what the hell do we do with all those mercenary prisoners?"

"Good question," said Kit with a smile. "We strip them of all their clothes so the only thing they're wearing is the zip ties on their hands behind their backs and their ankles, plus the gags in their mouths."

"How do we move them out of the box canyon?" asked Billy.

"We pack them out on our horses to the road where Chief will have driven a big, staked farm truck," said Kit. "Then we drive them out to the ranch and dump them in the corral."

"Who tends to them there?" asked Billy.

"Woody and Doc will oversee the prisoners," said Kit.

"So how do we get through to this greedy Air Force general?" asked Swifty.

"Are we assuming no one has time to send out any kind of alarm?" asked Billy.

"I don't think so," said Kit. "During our search and stripping of the prisoners, we identify which one is in charge and we tag him with a red bandanna tied on his ankle zip ties," said Kit. "Then we check his phone to make sure he wasn't able to get a call out."

"Unless the guy has a satellite phone, it's unlikely he could make a call from that remote canyon," said Billy. "The longer I think about it, the more sense it starts to make. I must be losing my grip on reality."

"It's pure human nature, playing to what a person wants to believe," said Kit.

"So, we set the hook in the general's mouth," said Swifty. "What then?"

"We set up a meeting at Swifty's friend's cabin up in Centennial, a small town just up and west of Laramie," said Kit. "We have Flash set up sensors, and sound and video recorders hidden in the cabin and when the general gets there, we spring a little surprise party."

"What if the general shows up with a whole bunch of Air Police?" asked Swifty. "They can be unpleasant at times."

"He won't," replied Kit.

"Why won't he?" asked Swifty.

"He can't afford to have any witnesses from the Air Force to what he is doing," replied Kit. "If he brings anyone, he'll bring some more hired guns. And if he does, it's open season on them."

"What about Doc Charlie?" asked Billy. "We can't put her in the middle of all this danger!"

"She'll be there in the cabin," said Kit. "She'll be wearing a bullet proof vest and we'll make it look like she's tied to a chair, but her hands will be untied, and she will have easy access to a weapon."

"Why put her there in what could turn into a gunfight?" asked Billy.

"Because I promised her that she could be there when we snapped the trap shut," said Kit. "And even when I regret it, I keep my promises."

"Who will be in the cabin?" asked Swifty.

"Doc Charlie. Detective Parcell will be outside the cabin when the general arrives, and he will let only the general in. No one else but the general and Parcell goes into the cabin," said Kit. "When the general and his friends arrive at the cabin, they will be greeted by an armed Detective Parcell, who will ask for the identification and then let only the general into the cabin," said Kit. "It will all be recorded by cameras outside the cabin."

"What happens when the general goes in the cabin?" asked Swifty.

"Once they are inside the cabin, if the general refuses to talk and trying to wait him out doesn't work, Detective Parcell will pull a gun on the good general and inform him he is under arrest for the attempted murder of Doc Charlie and other war crimes. Detective Parcel's deputies from Laramie will have surrounded the cabin, and we will be backing them up as concerned citizens," said Kit.

"I've always wanted to be one of them "concerned citizens," said Swifty with a snort.

"I admit it sounds like a good plan," said Billy, "but I have a question."

"Let's hear it," asked Kit.

"What do we do if some part of this plan falls apart?" asked Billy. "I'm no lawyer, but it sounds like we have hearsay and second-hand evidence at best."

"Falls apart?" asked Kit.

"What if the general confesses to nothing. Everything we have on him is what they call circumstantial on TV," said Billy.

"We wing it," replied Kit. "Just like we usually do. Almost no plan goes exactly as it was laid out. When it goes off the rails, we improvise."

"Works for me," said Swifty.

"Me too," added Billy.

"I think I have a better idea," said Flash who had quietly moved into the room unannounced.

All three men turned to look at Flash who helped himself to a chair and sat down and pulled it up to the table.

CHAPTER FORTY-FIVE

"I think I have some news that might alter your well thought out plans," said Flash.

All three men at the table turned and focused their attention on Flash.

"I'm sorry to so rudely interrupt your high-level strategy meeting, but I have some facts you will need to make any final decisions on how to deal with the rogue Air Force general," said Flash.

"We're all ears," said Kit. Billy and Swifty both had puzzled looks on their faces.

"Kit, you may remember when we last chatted, I told you I would look into the general's finances and try to discover a link between him and these hooligans we are dealing with that are threating our well-being," said Flash.

"I do remember," said Kit.

"I was able to discover wire transfers from the general's personal account to the account of a Mr. Waverly of Butte, Montana," said Flash. "Although I can't imagine who in their right mind would want to reside in some awful place named Butte. The name of the place is just too close to butt and just saying the name makes me uncomfortable."

"Who is this Mr. Waverly?" asked Kit.

"Mr. Waverly is a disgraced accountant who was found guilty of fraud, stripped of his CPA certification, and spent five years in a federal prison," said Flash. "He has been out of prison for about three years and began a fairly lucrative practice as a broker of services between dishonest people and criminals of all stripes. To simplify his occupation, he is a crime broker."

"Crime broker?" asked Swifty.

"He gets requests from dishonest people, who wish to employ thugs to carry out illegal and nefarious deeds to their benefit," said Flash.

"I see," said Swifty, although it was clear he did not.

"Mr. Waverly then contacts mercenaries or other criminal specialists and issues instructions. He then provides them with one third of the fee up front, again using wire transfers," said Flash. "Any questions so far?"

There were no questions. Just three cowboys with their mouths hanging open as they sat rather spellbound by Flash's presentation.

"I was able to penetrate Mr. Waverly's computer files, although I must admit using the word penetrate gives the appearance of some difficulty and I assure you, this was mere child's play," said Flash. "I was able to obtain emails and texts between Mr. Waverly and General Ventura and Mr. Waverly and two gentlemen of dubious reputations. One was a Mr. Bannion, an ex-convict out on parole, and the other was a Mr. McIntyre, a rather well-known leader of a group of ex-military louts carrying on as mercenaries for hire. I have reasonable assurance that Mr. Bannion is one of the unseemly gentlemen you ambushed, stripped of their clothing and tied them to the slats of a cattle trailer bound for Canada. I traced Mr. McIntyre's whereabouts to Rock Springs, Wyoming, as of four days ago. I think it is safe to assume his hirelings are the gents we are currently dealing with."

"So, let me get this straight," asked Kit. "We have proof linking the general to a crime broker and then proof linking the crime broker to two individuals who sent or brought criminals here to Kemmerer to capture and eliminate Doc Charlie?"

"An excellent encapsulation of my comments, Kit," said a smiling Flash.

"That's great news," said Kit. "We can use this information to get a warrant for the slippery general's arrest. Can we get copies of these wire transfers and emails and texts?"

"I've made copies of all of them," replied Flash, and he handed Kit a thick file.

"Thank you," said a surprised Kit.

"But wait, there's more," said a smiling Flash.

"More?" said a surprised Kit.

"Two days ago, I was having coffee with Doctor Charlie, and she mentioned the incident with her iPhone the night she was forced to attend to the injured detainee who died," said Flash. "I asked her to loan me her phone, and I spent some time examining it and was able to find the recording she had made that night. I've spent a bit of time cleaning it up so it's clearer and easier to hear by removing some background noise. Would you gents like to hear it?"

"Yes!" said all three men loudly, almost in unison.

"Goodness," said Flash, as he was slightly taken aback by the men's enthusiastic response.

He went on to explain the original recording was intact on Doctor Charlie's iPhone, but he had made a copy and cleaned it up and he set his phone down and hit play.

The recording was surprisingly clear and while it was not word for word as Doc Charlie had recounted to Kit back when he had questioned her about it, it was awfully close.

"Does this assist you in any way?" asked Flash.

"This, my little genius cousin, is what we like to call a game changer," said Kit.

After breakfast the next morning, the next few hours were a flurry of activity. Kit had made a master checklist and by suppertime, almost all the items on his list had been checked off.

After supper was finished and the dining table was cleared off, Kit gave the group the outline of their plan and an update on their progress.

"It appears we have assembled everything we need, and we are ready to initiate the plan," said Kit. "Tomorrow morning, Bushrod will trailer his horse and a packhorse near the small box canyon. Then he will ride in, set up the phony camp, and then return to the ranch. Then each following morning, he will repeat the trip and take a few supplies to the tent site. Anyone keeping an eye on the ranch will notice him and then follow him to the box canyon. Most of us will drive to a site near the box canyon tomorrow and set up our camp. Chief will set up a cold camp on top of the rim of the box canyon and keep in touch with the rest of us by satellite radio. When he sees unwanted company approaching the camp, the rest of us move in. Only Woody will remain here at the ranch. Doc Charlie will be in disguise at either Woody's office or home with Big Dave's wife."

Swifty looked perplexed and then spoke up.

"I thought I was going to set up the fake camp?" he asked.

"I need you at the main camp," said Kit. "Bushrod will not arouse any suspicion."

"Cause I'm a geezer?" asked a grinning Bushrod.

"No," replied Kit. "You're more seasoned and experienced," he added diplomatically.

Everyone hooted and hollered at that. Even Swifty.

"What about Flash?" asked Billy.

"Good question, I almost forgot about Flash. He will be up on the box canyon wall with Chief. Flash will be operating the drone and sending it out to give us an early heads-up of any approach to the canyon by the mercenaries," said Kit.

Kit paused and looked out over the faces of the men seated at the table. "Is there anyone here uncomfortable with what we are about to do? If so, speak up and let me know. This plan is dangerous. If anyone wants out, now is the time to tell me. There is no shame in skipping this caper. I only want you there if you want to be there."

Kit paused again and waited. He was greeted with silence.

CHAPTER FORTY-SIX

By dawn, everyone at the ranch was up, dressed and eating breakfast and drinking coffee. Then, except for Doc Charlie and Woody who were cleaning up the kitchen, the rest of the men began running over their checklists and gathering their weapons, ammo, and gear.

Connie, Big Dave's wife showed up in her Cadillac and picked up Doc Charlie along with her packed bags and headed for Kemmerer and Woody's office.

Chief and Flash and the drone headed for the canyon. So did Bushrod in his pickup truck and horse trailer. Big Dave, Swifty, Billy, and Kit headed for the campsite they had picked out. That left Woody to man the ranch and the communications room. By ten in the morning, Woody was by himself.

On the way to the campsite, Kit called Detective Parcell on his cell phone. After a brief introduction to the current situation, Kit went on to explain his plan and his need for Parcell's assistance.

When Kit had finished explaining his plan, Parcell seemed to pause before speaking. Then he spoke.

"It sounds like a plan to me," said Detective Parcell.

"But I need to get some clearance from the sheriff first. I'll talk to him and get back to you."

"Will that be a problem?" asked Kit.

"The sheriff is a politician first," replied Detective Parcell. "This sounds like the kind of deal which could get him tons of headlines and tons of great publicity. I can't see him saying no to this, but he will probably want to be here when we take down this crooked general so he can take credit. And he will want lots of photos and video."

"Is that a problem?" asked Kit.

"Not as long as you are all right with him hogging the spotlight and taking the lion's share of the credit for this arrest," explained Parcell.

"I could care less who gets the credit and publicity," said Kit.

"Same for the rest of your team?" asked Parcell.

"I can't speak for them, but I really doubt they give a crap who gets credit for bringing this asshole down," responded Kit.

"I'll get back to you in a couple of hours," said Parcell.

"Thanks," said Kit. "I'll owe you."

"Nope," responded Parcell, "I'll owe you."

Kit laughed and broke the connection.

"Are we good to go?" asked Billy who was driving his truck and listening in as Kit talked to Detective Parcell.

"So far, so good," replied Kit. "Parcell has to check with the sheriff to get permission for this operation, but he can't see why the sheriff would pass up a chance for a big-time collar and get himself on television."

"Politicians are all the same," replied Billy.

"Are we there yet?" asked Swifty from the back seat of the truck.

"Shut up, Swifty," said both Billy and Kit in unison.

～

Chief drove Kit's pickup truck to a wooded spot next to an old two-track. The old road was more of a trail than a road. It led to the creek and then turned south. Chief parked the truck deep in a grove of Aspen trees and sagebrush and the two men got out. Chief hefted a large pack on his back. He added his rifle and a shotgun on slings, along with a bow and a quiver of arrows. He handed the packed-up drone to Flash who eased it onto his back. Then Chief led the way on a faint game trail. They hiked three miles to the creek and the entrance to the small box canyon. There he stopped and turned to face Flash. He paused as his eyes scanned their surroundings and as he listened carefully. He spoke softly, with his back to the prevailing wind.

"We go west from here and then up a trail to the west rim of the box canyon. Keep silent and place your feet where I place my feet," said Chief. "Understand?"

Flash nodded he understood.

"Say nothing and make no noise unless I speak to you," said the Chief.

Flash again nodded his understanding.

Chief began to follow the edge of the box canyon's outer wall as they moved to the west. Flash was careful to keep silent and tried his best to place his feet in each of Chief's footsteps. An hour later they had climbed to the west rim of the box canyon. There, Chief found a large natural pocket in the rocks and placed their gear in the pocket. Then he motioned for Flash to stay put. He did.

Chief returned about twenty minutes later. He paused by the pocket and extracted a canteen of water from his pack. He handed it to Flash who took a long drink. Then Chief took a drink and replaced the canteen.

"This is a good spot. We can sit on those rocks over there," he said as he pointed to a small line of rocks near the edge of the box canyon rim. "We cannot be seen by anyone in the canyon or anyone on the ground outside the canyon. We also have a good view of the area to the south and east. Do you need my help to launch the drone?"

"No," said Flash. "I can handle the drone. When do you think I should launch it?"

Chief thought about Flash's question for a bit. Then he spoke.

"Not until Bushrod has made at least one trip to the canyon," replied Chief. "It is unlikely they will notice Bushrod until at least tomorrow, but anything is possible. I will keep watch and alert you if I see anything. Otherwise, we wait for a call on your satellite phone."

"What if I launch the drone when Bushrod is heading back to his truck. Kind of a trial run?" asked Flash.

"Good Plan," said Chief.

"What do we do now?" asked Flash.

Chief smiled at the younger, much smaller man. "We wait," he said.

CHAPTER FORTY-SEVEN

Two hours later, Chief tossed a pebble at a napping Flash. Flash was instantly awake, and he frantically looked around.

"Relax," whispered Chief. "I can see Bushrod and his packhorse approaching the canyon entrance."

Flash crawled forward and peered over the rim of the canyon, taking care to stay low, as Chief had directed him. When he reached the rim, he slowly moved his head up until his eyes could see below and beyond the rim of the box canyon. At first, he could see no movement of any kind. He wondered if Chief was mistaken about Bushrod. He lay there motionless for several minutes. Then he saw a flash of movement in the trees and brush to the southeast of his position. After another minute he saw Bushrod on horseback, leading a packhorse, suddenly appear from behind a stand of willow trees along the creek bed. Flash silently watched as Bushrod rode to the entrance of the box canyon and then entered it, leading his packhorse.

Flash turned his head until he was facing a prone, silent, and motionless Chief. "Should we go down and help Mr. Bushrod set up the camp?" he whispered.

Chief looked at Flash and frowned. He shook his head slowly side to side to indicate they should not. Flash turned his head and watched as Bushrod reached a site near the back of the box canyon and tied up his horse and the packhorse. Then he began to unload the packhorse. Flash watched as Bushrod expertly erected a sizeable Baker tent, and then began to move items inside and outside the tent.

When Bushrod had finished unpacking and moving things inside the tent, he then walked around the area and began to pick up dead wood. He collected rocks and built a fire pit about fifteen yards from the tent. Bushrod placed some firewood in the pit and lit a small fire and then added wood until the fire was burning briskly. He walked around the tent in circles, beating down the grasses and kicking at a few loose rocks. He grabbed his canteen from his saddle and took a long drink of water. When he was finished, he walked over to the small fire and poured water on it to extinguish the blaze. Smoke rose from the wet ashes, and Bushrod waited until the smoke ceased. Then he swung into the saddle of his horse and led the packhorse as he rode back out of the box canyon, crossed the creek, and disappeared into the trees and brush, as he headed toward his truck.

Flash didn't want to make any noise, so he picked up a pebble and tossed it at Chief, hitting him on the neck. Chief turned his head and looked hard at Flash.

Flash then whispered, "Now would be a good time to test out the drone and use it to watch Mr. Bushrod make his way back to his truck."

Chief thought about it for a minute and then nodded his head in agreement with Flash's suggestion. Flash carefully crawled back to the ledge where he had placed the drone. He quickly and expertly assembled the drone and checked the controls. Satisfied, he looked up at Chief. Chief nodded his head, and Flash stood and picked up the drone. It took both of his hands to hold the drone, and he took a long step forward and threw the drone into the air, launching it on its maiden flight in Lincoln County, Wyoming.

Flash picked up the control box and was quickly able to adjust the drone's flight and head it toward the area where he was sure Bushrod had left his truck and trailer. The video screen depicted the tops of pine trees mixed with the occasional stand of quaking aspen. Occasionally he could see parcels of green grass in the open spaces between stands of trees. After a few minutes he spotted Bushrod on horseback, leading a pack horse.

He then vectored the craft towards where he thought Bushrod's truck and trailer were parked. In a few minutes, he found the truck on the side of a barely visible two-track in a rocky clearing, bordered by large clumps of sagebrush.

Flash had the drone circle the truck and trailer and then he took the drone higher, so he could see the truck and Bushrod on horseback at the same time. Bushrod was coming out of the heavy forested area near the box canyon, so both he and the truck were easy to see clearly. As Flash circled the area, moving the drone-based camera to pan the surrounding landscape, he saw a flash of color that did not seem natural. He remembered what Big Dave had told him about using his eyes. He had instructed Flash to look for what does not belong there. A flash of a bright blue color certainly did not belong in the area he was circling. The lone possible exception was the creek, but he had never seen water in that shade of bright blue. It had to be man-made.

He maneuvered the drone back to where he had seen the flash of blue and directed it lower to take a closer look. Flash moved the drone lower, but not too low. He did not want to alert anyone on the ground of the drone's presence. He got flashes of blue as the subject moved. Flash then realized, the flashes of blue were following Bushrod's horses trail, keeping a distance of about fifty yards behind him. Flash brought the drone to a close, but safe distance, zeroed in on the blue spot and saw a man in a camo shirt, cargo pants, and a bright blue ball cap following Bushrod on foot. The man was at least six foot tall, broad shouldered, with long blonde hair that fell below the blue baseball cap. He also wore sunglasses and carried what looked like an AK-47.

Flash motioned Chief to come to him and look at the screen of his control unit. Chief complied and his eyes got wide as he saw the image of the armed man in the bright blue hat following Bushrod back to his truck.

As the two men watched via the drone's video feed, Bushrod reached his truck. He loaded the horses in the horse trailer and then got in the truck and drove back toward Kemmerer. The man in the bright blue hat stopped in a clump of pine trees and watched until Bushrod drove off. Then he pulled out what looked like a satellite phone out of a pocket in his cargo pants and held it to his face as he waited for it to connect with a satellite. When it connected, the man raised the phone to his face and seemed to speak into it. A few seconds later, the man put the phone back in his pocket and disappeared back into the trees. Flash brought the drone back to the edge of the ridge where he and Chief waited.

They retrieved the drone and sat down on a flat rock where they could not be seen by anyone in the canyon or from any of the approaches to the canyon entrance.

"Call Kit," said Chief.

Flash pulled out his satellite phone, waited for it to make a connection, and then hit a preprogrammed button for Kit's phone. When Kit answered, Flash gave him the details of what he and Chief had seen from the drone. He then forwarded the video he had taken of the stranger to Kit's iPhone as well. When he was done, he put away the satellite phone. Then he set up the drone's battery to be recharged by the solar collectors he had spread out on the flat rock near the top of the canyon rim. When he was finished, he looked over to find Chief to talk about what they had just seen. Chief was sound asleep.

CHAPTER FORTY-EIGHT

After getting the call from Flash, Kit grabbed Swifty and Billy and had a quick council of war. Kit filled the two men in on what he had learned from Flash. When he had finished, he looked Swifty and Billy in the eyes.

"What do you think?" Kit asked them. The look in his eyes was as forceful as the tone of his voice.

Neither Swifty nor Billy spoke up immediately. Both men had some questions, most of which Kit had no answers for.

"I wish I knew more, but now you know what I know. What should we do next?" he asked his two friends.

Billy spoke first.

"If I were that scout, I'd hightail it to a place where I had cell phone connection or use a Sat phone and I'd call whoever my boss was and let him know about the camp being set up in the box canyon," said Billy.

"But does the scout know if Doc Charlie is in the camp?" asked Swifty.

"Maybe and maybe not," replied Billy. "Either way it's likely they will assume she will be there if she ain't there now."

"Makes sense to me," said Kit. "What about you, Swifty?"

Swifty had been uncharacteristically quiet. He picked up a small stick from the ground and examined it carefully. Then he broke the stick in half and tossed the two pieces away in the nearby weeds.

"I think Billy's right. I'd bet good money that scout's report will bring those bad boys to the canyon like a bear on the scent of honey," said Swifty.

"How long do you figure it would take us to get to the box canyon and get in position?" asked Kit.

"Maybe half an hour or forty minutes," replied Billy.

"Why take a chance on timing?" asked Swifty.

"What do you mean?" asked Kit.

"Let's have half our guys stay at this base camp and the other half set up on the rim of the box canyon. When we see these yahoos show up, we call the base camp and bring the rest of our guys up. When they arrive, we have them set up behind the mercenaries and block their escape out of the canyon," said Swifty.

"I hate to admit it, but that idea does make one heck of a lot of sense to me," said Billy.

"Me, too," said Kit. "Let's consider it a plan. Who makes up the first group?" he asked.

"How about the three of us on the rim with Chief and Flash," suggested Billy. "Then keep Big Dave, Thor, and Bushrod in the base camp as the second unit."

"Sounds like a plan to me," said Kit. "How about you, Billy?"

"I'm in," replied Billy.

"Let's get everyone together and fill them in on the plan," said Kit.

Twenty minutes later, the small meeting broke up. There had been a few questions, but not many and they were all very technical in nature. Everyone in the meeting knew this moment would come. They were here to do a job and had come prepared. Now they were ready.

It took Kit, Billy, and Swifty about fifteen more minutes to pack their essentials and weapons and then they were ready to go. The three men shook hands with Big Dave, Thor, and Bushrod and headed out on foot towards the box canyon.

Before they were out of sight, Big Dave was on his satellite radio, calling the ranch to let Woody and Doc Charlie know the plan and give them the timing.

As they walked out of camp, Kit was the last in line. Just before they entered the tree line next to the creek, he stopped and turned around. Big Dave, Bushrod and Thor were all standing at the end of the camp watching them leave. It was a comforting sight to Kit.

CHAPTER FORTY-NINE

Flash had dozed off in the warm sunlight and woke up to Chief's huge hand silently shaking his shoulder.

"Put drone up," whispered Chief. Then he crawled up to the rim of the canyon and used the binoculars to study something down below him and out toward the horizon.

Flash checked the drone. The battery was fully charged. He disconnected the charger and checked his controls. Satisfied, he then picked up the drone and with his left foot forward, he used both hands to launch the drone into the air.

As soon as the drone was airborne, Flash picked up the control box and got down on his knees, facing the Chief's prone back.

"Now what?" asked Flash in a whisper.

Chief pointed a finger on his right hand at a small clearing about half a mile from the box canyon on the other side of the creek. Flash strained his eyes but could not see what Chief was pointing to. Chief silently handed his binoculars to Flash. After peering through the binoculars and making a slight adjustment, Flash could see two men dressed in camo standing under a large fir tree. One was gesturing with his hands and then pointing in the direction of the box canyon. Both men carried what looked like AK-47 automatic rifles.

"Good lord," muttered Flash, which drew a stern look from Chief who made a clear sign that Flash was to remain silent. Both Chief and Flash watched the two men as they continued their argument or discussion and then began moving closer to the entrance of the box canyon. Flash watched through the binoculars as the two men made their way to a grove of willow trees that grew thickly for about forty yards, ending about ten yards from the far bank of the creek. Once there they found positions where they had clear fields of fire to the entrance of the box canyon, they settled into position and remained there.

After almost an hour had passed, Chief motioned to Flash and they both crawled backward down the rim of the canyon until they were sure they were out of sight of anyone outside the box canyon entrance.

"What do we do?" whispered Flash.

"We wait," Chief whispered back. "Those two were sent to watch the entrance to the box canyon the first scout noticed when he was shadowing Bushrod. In an hour or so, I will slip down into the box canyon and light the campfire. Then I will return. When the two scouts see the smoke from the fire, they will assume the tent is occupied by their target."

"Doc Charlie?" whispered Flash.

"None other," Chief whispered back.

Flash used his controls to move the drone above the hiding spot occupied by the two enemy scouts. He kept the drone high enough to avoid attracting the scout's attention, but low enough to get good video of them and their position.

Then he directed the drone around to the back side of the box canyon and brought it in from the north where it could not be seen or heard by the two scouts. Flash retrieved the drone and forwarded the video the drone had recorded to both Kit and Swifty. Then he removed the battery and hooked it up to the solar panel charging station. He placed the drone further down the box canyon wall where it was available but hidden from prying eyes.

His drone chores completed. Flash looked over at Chief.

"Now what?" he whispered.

"I call Kit with sitrep," Chief whispered back.

After Flash saw Chief pull out his satellite phone and speak softly and briefly into it, Chief put his satellite phone back in his pocket and resumed his surveillance.

"Now what?" whispered Flash.

"We hurry up and wait," Chief whispered back with a sly smile on his face.

CHAPTER FIFTY

Chief slipped down into the canyon two more times and added wood to the small campfire by the tent to keep alive the illusion the camp was occupied. Each time he ignored Flash's imploring looks for new information. Chief said nothing, but his stern eyes send a firm message to Flash. "Shut the hell up."

Chief and Flash took turns keeping watch through the binoculars on the approaches to the small box canyon. Occasionally they caught glimpses of the two mercenaries set up as scouts to watch the canyon.

Noise seems to travel farther in the mountains. When a person takes the time to pause and listen for a while, nature has a way of letting you know how things are around you, even in places you cannot see.

Suddenly Chief's head snapped up, and he seemed to cock his ear. He looked directly at Flash and whispered, "Launch the drone."

Flash scrambled over to the drone, inserted the freshly charged battery, and then got to his feet on the rock ledge and launched the drone. Then he slipped back to a higher position on the canyon wall and began to operate the drone controls. He could neither see nor hear anything unusual from his position on the canyon wall.

Chief snapped his fingers to get Flash's attention. He raised his hand and used it to point in the direction he wanted Flash to maneuver the drone. After a couple of adjustments, Flash could see in the viewfinder what Chief had noticed with his naked eye. Two black SUVs were coming down the same dirt track that Bushrod had used. They were not moving very fast due to the surface of the old two-track, but they were still kicking up a lot of dust.

Chief pulled out his satellite phone and punched in a number. He waited for a few seconds and then he said one word in an exceptionally soft voice. "Attack."

He put the satellite phone back in his pocket and brought the binoculars up to his eyes and began to scan the forested area opposite the entrance to the small box canyon.

Flash continued his surveillance of the two SUVs with the drone. He watched the two vehicles until they parked on the side of the two-track not far from where Bushrod had parked his truck and trailer.

Kit heard the buzzer on his satellite phone and pulled it out of his small backpack. He powered it up and then as soon as it acquired a signal, he heard Chief's one word message. He held up his hand as a signal to halt to Swifty and Billy. Then he punched in the number for Bushrod's satellite phone. When Bushrod answered, Kit explained his message from Chief and the urgency of the current situation at the small box canyon.

Bushrod's response was brief. "Roger. Out."

Kit put the phone back in his pack and used an arm

signal to start the three of them on their trek to the box canyon. They moved quickly, but as quietly as possible.

In a short time, they reached the edge of the small box canyon. Kit led the others up a narrow game trail to the lip of the west end of the box canyon. When they were about fifty yards from the summit, Kit held up his hand for a halt. He and the other two men went to one knee and carefully listened, sniffed the air, and carefully surveilled their surroundings.

Sensing nothing alarming, they rose to their feet and proceeded up the game trail to where they found Chief and Flash waiting for them just below the rim of the canyon.

Kit moved up the trail until he was next to Flash and Chief.

"Any update?" he asked softly.

Flash pointed to the monitor on his drone. Kit could see the men from both SUVs had emptied the SUVs of weapons and gear and were gathered in a semicircle around one of the mercenaries. Kit studied the images carefully. He counted eight heavily armed men, dressed in black. Then handed the control box back to Flash.

Kit turned to Chief. He whispered, "I count eight bogies."

Chief held up two fingers and pointed down just beyond the creek in the tree line.

"Two more?" whispered Kit.

Chief nodded in the affirmative.

"Should I bring the drone back in?" whispered Flash.

Kit thought about his question for a moment. Then he looked at both Chief and Flash.

"Nope, leave it up and keep us informed of their progress.

When they get a quarter of a mile from the mouth of the box canyon, bring the drone back and retrieve it," he said. Then he looked Flash directly in the eyes. "Don't forget what you need to do when the tent blows," he said very carefully.

"I won't. I promise," replied Flash.

Kit motioned for Swifty and Billy to join them. When all five men were huddled together, Kit looked each man in the eye and then spoke. "I count a total of ten armed men, dressed in black. Billy, Swifty and Chief will deploy to the other side of the box canyon on the east rim. When Big Dave, Bushrod, and Thor get here, I'll have Big Dave join me up here and leave Bushrod and Thor down on the ground where they can close the entrance to the box canyon. Anybody got a better idea?" Kit asked.

"Works for me," said Billy.

"Me, too," said Swifty.

Billy paused, looked around to make sure the five of them were alone.

"After we lure these assholes into the box canyon, what do we wait for before we open up on them?" whispered Billy.

"We wait until they are within about fifteen yards of the tent," replied Kit. "When they get that close, I press this," he said. He produced a small object like a garage opener in his open hand.

"What the hell is that?" asked a puzzled Swifty.

"This sets off a charge of plastic explosive I had Bushrod rig in the tent," replied Kit. "When the charge goes off, we open up on them and then Flash provides some aerial confusion."

"Aerial confusion? What the hell is that?" asked Billy.

"Flash brought some small fireworks to set off and create confusion," replied a grinning Kit.

"Fireworks?" said Swifty. "You mean he is gonna set off firecrackers eighty yards away from these yahoos? What the hell good would that do?"

"Not firecrackers," said Kit. "He'll set off a type of bottle rocket he made just for this occasion."

"He made them. Where the hell did he make them and when?" asked a stunned Swifty.

"He made them in the shop back at Dad's place," replied Kit. "He showed them to me and gave me his word they would be helpful in creating confusion down in the box canyon. I thought even if they didn't work very well, we had nothing to lose."

"I guess that's true," said Billy. "But I'm glad you told us. Rockets going off in the middle of a firefight would have scared the crap out of me, not knowing where they were coming from or who was shooting them off. Won't this be a big surprise for Big Dave, Thor, and Bushrod?"

"Flash should be telling them about the fireworks right about now," said Kit as he glanced at his watch.

"I got another question," said a still skeptical Swifty.

"I'm not a bit surprised," said Kit.

"If we have some leakers who get out of the box canyon, what do Bushrod, and Thor do to stop them?" asked Swifty.

"They use the same shotgun shells we have and hopefully will incapacitate them," said Kit.

"And if they don't?" asked a grim faced Swifty.

"Bushrod will permanently eliminate them," said Kit in an unnaturally cold voice.

Swifty and Billy fell silent.

"Any more questions?" asked Kit.

Both Swifty and Billy both shook their heads in a negative response.

"Then you three need to get moving and make your way to the rim on the other side of the canyon," said Kit.

Swifty, Billy, and Chief slipped away from Kit and Flash and soon disappeared below their position on the rim of the canyon. Kit turned and stared intently beyond the entrance to the small box canyon. He was looking for what did not belong.

CHAPTER FIFTY-ONE

Kit's phone rang softly. He answered it. It was Chief calling him.

"Bogies at six o'clock," said Chief.

"Roger. Out," responded Kit.

Kit pulled out a small pair of binoculars and began to slowly scan the approaches to the box canyon from the south. At first, he saw nothing. He continued to scan the wooded area on the other side of the creek. Then he saw movement. He focused on that area and within seconds, he could see the approaching raiders.

A quick look at the opposite rim of the canyon revealed his three men making their way up to the rim.

Satisfied with their position, he shifted his binoculars back to the approaching mercenaries. They were moving in single file with about five yards between each man. They were probably ex-soldiers, Kit thought to himself.

Kit shifted his position and began to scope the banks of the creek to the west. At first, he saw nothing. Then he caught a flash of movement and after concentrating on that area, he could make out Thor prone on the ground behind a big clump of buffalo grass. He slowly scoped the area around Thor and could see Big Dave, but not Bushrod. The old jungle fighter knows how to blend into his surroundings, thought Kit.

He could see the three men were in position along the undergrowth on the north bank of the creek as it ran in a southeasterly direction following the base of the box canyon. They were in a good, hidden position where they could observe the entrance to the box canyon without being discovered.

Kit checked the opposite rim of the box canyon once again. Chief, Swifty, and Billy were all in position, lying prone on the rock surface with their shotguns next to them. Then he looked at Flash. His cousin was watching the monitor of the drone. He had the drone flying in a pattern circling the box canyon, high enough to be almost silent, and yet low enough to send good pictures of the ground of the box canyon. Kit noticed Flash had laid six bottle rockets on the ground next to him. He also noticed Flash held a butane lighter in his right hand.

We're ready as we're ever gonna' be, thought Kit. He also remembered an old military axiom. "Every plan is a good one until the shooting starts. Then all hell breaks loose."

Kit motioned to Flash to keep low. Then he crawled up to the edge of the canyon rim and slowly lifted his head with the binoculars already in place. The ten-armed mercenaries were crossing the creek. They crossed the creek without incident and with little noise. At the entrance to the box canyon, they halted. Kit watched as each of the mercenaries did a weapons check. They were carrying M-16 rifles, capable of fully automatic fire, and illegal as hell for them to possess. Kit smiled as he remembered a sign he saw in a Kemmerer bar. It read "When guns are outlawed, only outlaws will have guns."

"Ain't that the truth," Kit whispered under his breath.

He watched as the men broke into two columns of five men each. One column moved to the left side of the box canyon entrance, the other column to the right side. One of the mercenaries looked over at the lead men in each column and lifted off his black baseball cap. Both lead men in each column slipped inside the entrance to the box canyon.

Kit saw the other men move up slightly and resume their wait. After about three minutes, the remaining men slipped into the box canyon.

The scouts took the bait, thought Kit.

He scanned the creek to the west and saw Bushrod and Thor move from their cover and take up positions on the creek bank with a commanding view of the entrance to the canyon. Kit moved his binoculars to see where Big Dave was, but he was unable to catch even a glimpse of him.

Five minutes later, Big Dave crawled up next to him. Kit hadn't heard any sound of Big Dave's approach. Big Dave turned to look at Kit and gave him a thumbs up sign.

Kit looked over at Flash. His cousin had set the drone controller on the ground and was holding the first of the bottle rockets in one hand and the lighter in the other.

Show time, thought Kit.

CHAPTER FIFTY-TWO

Kit had shifted his binoculars to the floor of the box canyon. The ten men clad in black had formed a loose skirmish line as they moved forward into the box canyon and toward the tent site at the north end. They moved slowly and silently. Kit admired their skill in moving in an orderly fashion and managing to remain silent.

The air was still. Kit neither saw nor heard any birds or insects. The sun was slightly above the north rim of the canyon and only the tent was in the shadows. The rest of the box canyon was illuminated with bright sunlight.

Kit found himself holding his breath and forced himself to take a deep breath and continue to breathe normally. He pulled the small transmitter from his shirt pocket and checked it to make sure it was right side up so he could place his finger on the button.

When the line of mercenaries was twenty yards from the tent, Kit saw the same man in black begin to lift his black ball cap. Kit knew it was going to be a signal to attack and he pressed down on the transmitter button with his finger.

The resulting explosion was larger than Kit expected. He knew that was a result of Billy making the package a bit bigger than it needed to be. The sound of the explosion echoed again as it bounded off the walls of the box canyon. The energy had no place to go except up. The fireball was large and impressive. Kit could feel the heat way up on the rim of the canyon and feel the blast of super-heated wind the blast created.

Most of the mercenaries were either knocked down by the force of the blast, or they instinctively had thrown themselves on the ground in a natural reaction. Seconds later, as a few of them raised their heads and then got to their knees, Flash sent the first bottle rocket directly at their position at the north end of the canyon.

When the rocket exploded, the result was amazing. Some of the mercenaries kept flattened out on the ground, but most of them got to their feet and began to run back towards the entrance of the box canyon in an obvious panic. The tent was gone, smoke was everywhere, and the mercenaries found it hard to see or breathe.

More rockets followed and then the blasts of shotguns began. The loud sounds of shotgun blasts and the hiss and explosions of the bottle rockets were all captured inside the box canyon and the noise was louder and more terrifying than Kit was prepared for. He and Big Dave rose to their knees with shotguns mounted and began picking out moving targets and accurately shooting their paralyzing ammo into the unarmored chests and backs of the black clad mercenaries. As Billy would later describe it, "It was like shooting fish in a barrel."

The entire gun fight lasted less than five minutes. As Kit gazed out over the floor of the box canyon, he began to count the prone bodies of armed men he saw. He quickly reached the number ten and none of them were moving.

He and Big Dave rose to their feet. Kit looked across the canyon to the east rim and saw Swifty giving him a grin and a thumbs up. He looked back down at the floor of the canyon and saw Bushrod and Thor had come through the entrance. As they reached a prone mercenary, they checked him and then zip tied his hands behind him and did the same with their ankles.

"Search them for identification and more weapons," Kit yelled down to Bushrod.

Bushrod acknowledged Kit's request by waving his hat up at the west rim of the canyon.

Kit waited until Flash retrieved the drone and packed it up. Then he led his cousin down the game trail to the path along the base of the canyon wall. When they reached the entrance, Big Dave was nowhere in sight. But Kit and Flash were soon joined by Chief, Billy, and Swifty.

They entered the canyon and Kit made it a point to check each of the ten mercenaries. As he reached the last one sprawled on the ground not thirty yards from the tent, Bushrod joined him.

"All ten of these rascals are all right," said Bushrod. "Of course, they're gonna have one hell of a headache when they do wake up," he said with a big grin on his face.

Bushrod led him over to one of the prone mercenaries and rolled him over on his back with the toe of his boot. "This one was in charge," said Bushrod.

"How do you know?" asked Kit.

"He was carrying this," said Bushrod. In Bushrod's hand was a satellite phone. Bushrod pushed the button to activate the phone and once it was powered up, he scrolled through the saved number section and pointed his finger at the screen. There was only one number saved. The number was marked as 'Boss.'

As Kit looked at the man's face, he recognized him as the one who had lifted his cap as a signal to the others. He knew Bushrod was correct.

Kit got to his feet and looked around the box canyon. The smoke from gunpowder and the bottle rockets had cleared and the ten unconscious and bound mercenaries had been dragged into a line near the entrance to the box canyon.

"What do we do with these yahoos?" asked Billy.

"Oh crap," said Kit. "I forgot we had to transport these boys out of here. We'll have to send someone for pack horses."

Just then he heard some voices at the entrance of the canyon. Kit turned to look and saw Big Dave on his pinto horse, leading a string of three pack horses.

Big Dave rode up to where Kit was standing. He pulled the pinto to a halt and looked down at Kit.

"I knew you'd forget something important," said Big Dave. "I brought these horses up to the tent camp yesterday. Goddamneded tenderfoot."

CHAPTER FIFTY-THREE

Over the next forty-five minutes, Kit and his men methodically searched each of the ten mercenaries. They collected wallets, cash, credit cards, spare ammo magazines, knives, and lots and lots of guns. Kit directed the searchers to put the wallets and money and credit cards in one big canvas bag and the rifles, pistols, knives, and ammo went into several big canvas packs used on the pack horses.

"How will we know whose property belongs to whom?" asked a puzzled Flash as he observed the nonchalant mixing of weapons, ammo, wallets, and money.

"We'll let the Lord sort that crap out," said Bushrod as he shook his head in wonderment at this display of Flash's innocence.

The unconscious mercenaries had their hands cut loose and then retied in front of them, after they were hoisted up over the backs of the pack animals like so many sacks of flour. Then ropes were tied under the pack horses' bellies, connecting the tied wrists to the tied ankles to secure them on the horses' backs. The result was two mercenaries strapped to each pack horse.

Big Dave, Bushrod, and Thor mounted saddled horses and led the pack train of bound men out of the box canyon and back toward the two-track road where the mercenaries' trucks were parked. Once there, they left Bushrod and Flash to guard the prisoners and went back for another load. It took a total of three trips to pack all the unconscious bodies out of the box canyon.

Kit, Billy, Flash, and Swifty hiked back to the base camp they had set up west of the canyon. Once there, they broke the camp down, packed it up, and hiked out to where Billy's pickup truck was parked, about four miles away.

It was almost three hours before everyone arrived at Kit's father's ranch. Big Dave, Thor, Bushrod, and Chief had erected a sizable metal cage made of metal ranch gates they had wired together. The cage was about twenty feet by ten feet and barely six feet high. As the prisoners were unloaded from the horses, their hands were cut free and then resecured with zip ties behind their backs. By the time they had finished the cage and carried the prisoners inside, a few of the mercenaries were beginning to wake up. When they did manage to open their eyes, they were not happy with their situation nor their new accommodations.

After one prisoner cut loose with a string of profanities at Bushrod, he just looked at the guy and shook his head.

"Jesus Christ. You're alive, you ain't hurt bad. By all that's right in this world you should be dead. Shut your trap before I shut it for you," snarled Bushrod.

Bushrod and Chief took the first watch overseeing the prisoners. As each mercenary came to his senses, he joined in the moaning chorus.

Bushrod was disgusted. He looked over at Chief.

"Don't this damned ruckus piss you off none?" he asked Chief.

"Nope," said Chief in a loud voice. "Sounds like sheep right before we slit their throats."

Suddenly the prisoners became quite silent. Chief grinned and Bushrod grinned back at him.

~

Inside the ranch house, Kit, Woody, Swifty, Billy, Big Dave, Thor, and Doc Charlie sat around the dining room table. Flash had made a pot of coffee and was filing everyone's empty mugs. When he was finished, he took the pot back to the stove and then grabbed a chair at the table.

Kit looked around the table. What he saw was a group of his friends who were feeling pretty good about themselves. Now he had to remind them that their job was only partly done and the most important, and probably the most difficult, was still in front of them.

"Good job, everyone," said Kit. "Today went better than I could have ever hoped for. We got all of them and none of us got so much as a scratch."

"I gotta say, I loved Flash's idea of bottle rockets," said Billy. "After the planned explosion, it was a great second strike and one that unnerved some of those bastards."

"Hell, it looked like the damn Fourth of July out there," said a grinning Big Dave.

Others at the table openly agreed with Billy and Big Dave, and it got quite noisy at the table.

"Quiet down," said Kit. "We got more to do, so listen up."

The room became completely silent. Kit continued.

"I'm gonna make a call to our friend Detective Parcell in Laramie. I've set up a scam with him so we can get face to face with this asshole Air Force general who's paying all these thugs to kill our friend Doc Charlie," said Kit.

The room broke into a chorus of cheers and clapping. Kit waited for the hubbub to settle down.

"Detective Parcell is gonna call the general and tell him he got the APB from the general's office. He's calling to inform the general he picked up Doc Charlie and has her in the back of his squad car," said Kit. "Of course, that's a bald-faced lie, but we need it to lure him in. Parcell is gonna suggest to the general that he can turn over the prisoner directly to him and avoid all the paperwork in processing her through the county facility in Laramie. Since the general's orders to pick her up are fraudulent, he can't afford to have anything go through official channels, so I'm sure he's gonna jump on the idea."

A murmur of approval ran around the dining room table. It was obvious to Kit everyone there was on board with the idea, even Swifty, who almost always disagreed with everything he heard.

"I told Parcell to arrange to meet the general at a cabin in Centennial, which is just west of Laramie. The cabin belongs to a friend of Swifty, and she has agreed to lend it to us for the day," said Kit.

"A she who is a friend of Swiftys?" asked Billy. "Sounds like an oxymoron to me."

Everyone at the table laughed.

"Your track record with females is not exactly bulletin board material," snorted Swifty in response.

More laughter ensued. Kit waited for it to die down, and then he resumed his explanation of the plan.

"Parcell will tell the general where and when to meet him at the cabin and to only bring one other person. He'll explain to the general that it's a small town, and he doesn't want to draw any more attention to this meeting than is absolutely necessary. He will further tell the general he will have Doc Charlie in handcuffs and held inside the cabin. When the general and his assistant show up, Parcell will demand identification papers and then turn the prisoner over to them," said Kit.

"The general is gonna think he's died and gone to heaven when he hears this deal," said Bushrod.

Everyone at the table nodded their agreement.

"What happens when the general and his aide show up?" asked Billy.

"Detective Parcell will meet them outside the cabin. After he sees their ID, he'll let them in the cabin. Doc Charlie will be in a chair in handcuffs that are not locked. She will be wearing a bulletproof vest. And she will be armed," said Kit.

"You think this idiot general will try to kill her there?" asked Bushrod in surprise.

"No, I don't," said Kit. "He's got what he wants, and all he has to do is take Doc Charlie out of the cabin, put her in his vehicle, and drive away. Otherwise, he has a law enforcement officer to deal with, and I'm more than sure he wants to avoid that."

"What if he is that stupid?" asked Swifty.

"Detective Parcell is prepared to shoot both the general and his aide to defend Doc Charlie. Plus, Doc Charlie is also armed, and her hands will be free," said Kit. "Plus, we will be out behind the cabin listening in under the open window."

"Who is we?" asked Swifty.

"You, Billy, and me," said Kit.'

"Works for me," said Billy.

Swifty grudgingly nodded his head in approval.

"Before any of this happens, Flash will be wiring the cabin for video and sound, so we capture anything said or done in the cabin," said Kit. "Any questions?"

"I got a question," said Bushrod.

"Fire away," said Kit.

"What happens to this dufus after Parcell drops the hammer and arrests him and his dumb ass aide?" asked Bushrod.

"They both go to jail, and Parcell notifies the Air Force and turns both of them over to the Air Police in Cheyenne," replied Kit.

"I'd prefer we give both of them a long walk off a short pier over shark infested waters," said Bushrod.

"We're a little short on sharks in Wyoming," replied a smiling Kit.

"Well, they got that damn alligator farm down in southern Colorado. We could offer them two up as a donation and make those hungry critters plum happy," suggested Bushrod.

Everyone broke out in laughter, but Kit kept a grim face. In truth, he knew nothing was certain when it came to justice and the government, particularly the military. It was still the best and the proper legal way to proceed.

CHAPTER FIFTY-FOUR

Kit had arranged for Parcell to call the general at one o'clock the next afternoon. By seven that morning, he had the keys to the cabin in Centennial and had taken Flash there to install the recording equipment. Billy and Swifty had accompanied him and had hidden themselves in the surrounding forest, each armed with a sniper rifle.

It took Flash less than an hour to install hidden cameras and microphones in the small log cabin. He ran several tests and then set up a control point in an old woodshed located about fifty feet behind the cabin. When he was ready, he came and got Kit and ushered him into the small confining space. In the woodshed he had set up a tiny monitor and a box with two headsets attached to it.

Kit shot Flash a puzzled look. "How does it work?" he asked.

His cousin Flash spoke softly, as though he might be overheard, even though he and Kit were the only ones within any logical earshot distance.

"I will activate the system as soon as Detective Parcell and Doc Charlie arrive. It will run continuously until shut off here in this woodshed," replied Flash.

"Does this system record everything seen and heard by the cameras and the mics?" asked Kit.

"The system records everything and automatically sends the recordings to the cloud," replied Flash. "That way, any evidence is preserved, no matter what might happen here."

"You mean it's safe even if all of us are shot and killed and the cabin and woodshed and everything in them are destroyed," said Kit grimly.

"Exactly," said Flash excitedly, not catching the sarcasm in Kit's voice.

Kit rolled his eyes and left Flash to do some final testing, which included having Kit walk in the cabin and talk to make sure the equipment was working and picking up everything it was supposed to.

When the testing was finished, Kit and Flash drove to a café and picked up some sandwiches and coffee and drove to a remote spot near the woods behind the cabin. There they met Swifty and Billy. The two men piled into the back of the truck and the four men ate a quick lunch and went over the plan for the general's visit. After going over the plan and getting all the questions answered as best as he could, Kit watched as Billy and Swifty melted back into the woods.

Kit drove back to the cabin and let Flash out of the truck to take up the station in the woodshed. When Flash moved out of sight, Kit sent a text to Detective Parcell. Parcell immediately texted back he was on his way to the cabin with an ETA of about an hour and a half.

Kit then drove his truck about three blocks away and parked next to an unoccupied cabin. There were about eight cabins in the area. One family had owned the land and built the cabins for their family members. As time had gone by, family members married, divorced, got older and generally lost interest in the cabins. Several years before, they had subdivided the land with each cabin on a plot of land and sold them off. One of Swifty's lady friends had bought one of the cabins, and she rented it out to tourists. As far as she knew, the cabin was being used by Swifty. And very indirectly, it sort of was.

Kit left the truck and worked his way across the clearing in front of the cabins until he found a good spot across the access road. He moved into the woods next to the road where he could clearly see the cabin and the woodshed. He found a good spot about twenty yards deep in the bordering woods. He sat down in the shadows with his back up against a big pine tree. He pulled his Kimber .45 caliber semi-automatic pistol from his holster and did a press check. A bullet was resting in the chamber, waiting for the impact of the pistol's hammer. He replaced the pistol and checked his pockets for two more magazines of ammunition. He slapped the magazines against his hand to make sure the bullets were properly seated. He remained seated on the ground with his back to the pine tree and did what he needed to do. He waited.

An hour passed. Then twenty minutes more. Some black ants became curious about Kit's butt sitting on top of territory they obviously wanted to explore. He got up and moved to a different tree, surrendering the site to the unhappy ants.

Finally, after almost two hours of waiting, Detective Parcel pulled up in an unmarked patrol car and parked in front of the cabin. He got out of the driver's seat and walked back to the rear seat door and opened it. Then he helped Doc Charlie out of the back seat. She wore handcuffs with her hands in front of her. Kit knew the cuffs were not locked.

After a quick look around, Parcel led Doc Charlie to the door of the cabin. He opened the door for her, and she entered the cabin, followed by Parcel.

Kit heard a soft buzz on his communicator earpiece. He pulled out the tiny radio and whispered into it.

"What?" he asked softly.

"Action?" came the soft voice of his half-brother Billy.

"Nope," was Kit's reply.

The radio went silent.

Kit heard the sound of a vehicle's engine as it increased its whine as it began its ascent up the drive to the row of cabins. Soon the vehicle came into view. Kit could see it was a late model four door Jeep. As the Jeep drew closer, he could see two women in the front and an empty back seat. As the women passed by, he used his small binoculars to study the Jeep. Both women were likely in their late thirties. One was a brunette, and the other was a redhead. Then they were out of sight. He watched the rear end of the Jeep as it seemed to turn into the next to last cabin on the driveway.

Kit put the binoculars away and resumed his vigil of Doc Charlie's cabin. After he head the cabin door shut behind the two women, he heard nothing. He waited for another ten minute and then decided to try to get an update on Parcell's progress.

Kit texted Parcell. "How long."

Parcell immediately texted back, "No word from the general."

Kit readjusted his position against the trunk of the pine tree and again checked his pistol.

"Nervous is normal," he thought to himself.

CHAPTER FIFTY-FIVE

Ten minutes passed. The woods were now somewhat noisy with the sound of birds. Overhead a squirrel came part way down the tree to check out the strange creature seated on the ground below it. Kit moved his head and the squirrel shot back up the tree. He sped out on a limb, jumped to the next tree and was gone.

The wooded area was quiet. Kit could occasionally hear motorized traffic on the highway down below him. Other than traffic noise, he could hear the wind in the pine trees above him and the occasional call of a bird. Except for those sounds, the area was as quiet as a tomb.

Kit became alert as he heard a big powerful motor roar as a vehicle exited the main road and began the climb up the dirt road to the cabins.

"Showtime," thought Kit.

A big, black Chevrolet Suburban, the huge urban car gorilla so loved by government officials came into view. The big car seemed to pause for a moment, then slowly moved forward toward the cabin with Deputy Parcell's unmarked police car parked in front of it.

The black Suburban seemed to crawl slowly forward until it finally pulled in next to Parcell's unmarked vehicle.

There was a pause and then a man dressed in military utilities climbed out of the passenger side and immediately moved to the back door and opened it.

A short, heavy-set man stepped out of the Suburban. He was dressed in utilities so crisp and clean they appeared to have just come from off the hanger where it had been covered by a plastic laundry bag. The man had a commanding air about him, and he looked around at the cabin and its neighbors with obvious distaste. Kit had no doubt he was looking right at the general who had created all the trouble, misery, and fear for Doc Charlie. Kit sat up straight and unconsciously dropped his hand down on the butt of his still holstered pistol.

The armed airman stepped up to the front door of the cabin and knocked. The general waited impatiently about five yards behind him. As they waited, the general unconsciously was nervously shifting his weight from one foot to the other.

The door to the cabin opened and Detective Parcell emerged. He stepped up to the shorter general and the two men shook hands. Kit could not hear what they were saying, but he knew what he could or could not hear was not important. What got recorded in the cabin was important.

Kit kept his focus on the front of the cabin. Parcell stepped aside and let the general and his armed aid inside the cabin. The airman who had escorted the general to the cabin door emerged shortly from the cabin and took up a protective position next to the cabin door. Kit noted the airman was wearing a holstered sidearm. He was obviously well trained as he kept his head on a swivel and was careful to take detailed note of his surroundings.

After about ten minutes, the cabin door opened, and Detective Parcell emerged. He took no note of the armed airman and walked past him like he was invisible or unworthy of any notice by Parcell. Kit smiled. That was so unlike Parcell who was exceptionally good at being polite to everyone he encountered, even the thugs and idiots.

Parcell proceeded to his vehicle, got inside, and then drove back out the driveway to the highway below.

Kit sent a text to Billy and Swifty. "Show time."

He received a reply of the image of a thumbs up from both of them. Kit was tempted to rise to his feet but did not want to prematurely alert the armed airman in front of the cabin. He remained seated behind the tree and waited for the general and Doc Charlie to emerge from the cabin. That was the moment he and Swifty, Billy, and Doc Charlie had agreed on for them to spring their trap. Ten minutes went by. Then five more. Kit was getting nervous.

He knew Doc Charlie would not willingly leave the cabin until she had managed to get the general to admit his guilt involving the prisoner who was tortured to death and his attempts to permanently silence her recorded on voice and video tape.

Suddenly he heard the sound of something being smashed in the cabin and the loud angry voice of the general. The airman guarding the front door heard it too as he turned to face the cabin. Kit took this lapse in the guard's attention to get to his feet and draw his pistol. Apparently, Doc had managed to really piss the general off.

Less than a minute later he observed Doc Charlie being

pushed out the door of the cabin, followed closely behind by the general. The general barked some orders at the airman sentry who grabbed Doc Charlie by the arms and began to propel her toward the waiting black Suburban.

He didn't make it.

CHAPTER FIFTY-SIX

"Hold it right there, asshole," boomed Billy's voice as he stepped out from behind the cabin holding an AR-15 rifle. Billy was dressed in camo from head to toe and his size made him an even more intimidating figure.

The airman stopped in midstride and almost fell as he tried to quickly turn to face the threat. His hand dropped to his holstered pistol once he had regained his balance.

"Don't even think about it," shouted Swifty who had emerged from the woods on the side of the next cabin, dressed in camo and holding an M-4 combat semi-automatic shotgun at his hip. "You pull that peashooter, and I'll splatter you all over that nice shiny black Suburban."

The driver in the Suburban was frantically trying to undo his seat belt and get out of the Suburban when his door was yanked open, and Kit dragged him out of the vehicle and dumped him unceremoniously on the ground. The driver looked up into the muzzle of Kit's drawn Kimber .45 caliber pistol and raised his hands while he remained in a sitting position on the ground.

The general had finally realized what was happening and as he whipped his head around from Kit, to Billy, to

Swifty, he was sputtering as he tried to come up with words that seemed to be frozen in his brain.

Finally, he managed to get out a semi-complete sentence. "What are you people? What's the meaning of this? Do you have any idea who I am?"

"I've crapped turds with more value that you," snarled Swifty. "Real men don't make war on women and they sure as hell don't kill innocent people because they might be inconvenient to someone's career aspirations."

The general seemed to regain control of his emotions and recover from the surprise of being confronted by three large and heavily armed men. He looked at Kit, Billy, and Swifty, and he smiled.

"That can't be good," thought Kit. "I hate it when they smile."

The general raised his hands high in the air. Almost immediately, four heavily armed, camouflaged men appeared from the woods running parallel to the road below the cabins.

"Drop your weapons, or I'll have my men kill you where you stand," snarled the general.

Kit looked at both Billy and Swifty. Both men were as surprised as he was. He had to give the general credit. He had planned for every contingency he could think of, and the general's men had the drop on the three of them.

Kit, Swifty, and Billy all dropped their weapons on the ground and raised their hands. Kit was surprised, but he doubted the general would risk shooting the three of them and Doc Charlie in a public place. The cabins were right above a highway lined with homes and shops and stores of the tiny town of Centennial.

As the four armed men got closer, Kit noted they wore camo, but no insignia of any kind. He was pretty sure they were ex-military hired guns. Real airmen would have worn proper insignia on their uniforms. He also noted the four men were carrying AK-47 rifles. Hardly the weapons of airmen of the United States Air Force.

Kit thought hard about his options. Not counting the general, there were six-armed airmen or mercenaries or whatever they were. The driver didn't seem to represent much of a threat nor did the general. The other five mercenaries were another issue altogether.

Kit glanced at Billy and Swifty. They were both angry at being fooled and trapped. Kit knew how formidable both men were in a fight. The dirtier the fight, the more formidable they became. If he could get the five-armed mercenaries close to himself and his two friends, there was a good chance they could jump them. Five to three was not great odds when two of the three were Billy and Swifty. He would have to stall and try and get things maneuvered so they had a chance.

The general walked up to the three men and Doc Charlie. He stood there with his hands on his hips and smiled. It was not a nice smile. "I thought anyone who was smart enough and trained well enough to ambush my other men could not be taken lightly," he said.

"Nice try, but no cigar," said the general. He paused and turned to stare at Doc Charlie. "You've caused me a considerable amount of trouble, not to mention way too much money. I'm going to enjoy taking you to a nice remote spot in the mountains west of here I picked out for just this occasion. You and your three vigilante friends are going to have your legs and arms broken and then your disabled and gagged bodies will be tossed down an old mine shaft my men discovered while camping out of sight of this dog shit little town. Nobody will hear you. Nobody will find you. There are no trails near or anywhere close to the mine shaft. I will be glad to see the last of you, Major."

The general paused for a moment and then ordered, "Tie them up and get them out of here and up to the mine shaft."

The armed man dressed as an airman stepped forward with polymer strips to tie the prisoner's wrists and ankles, while the four mercenaries kept them all covered with their AK-47s.

The airman never made it.

CHAPTER FIFTY-SEVEN

As the airman stepped forward, he was struck in the back by a large rubber bullet fired from a 12-gauge shotgun. The force of the blow knocked him forward on his face, the polymer strips scattered across the ground.

As the general and the four mercenaries attempted to turn toward the sound of the gunfire, two things happened. Kit, Swifty, and Billy hit the ground, joining Doc Charlie who had already arrived there.

Then five more loud shots came from 12-gauge shotguns and the remaining five men who had been standing were suddenly knocked down to the ground.

Before anyone could move or even attempt to rise, six figures appeared from behind trees, shrubs, and the cabin Kit had rented as well as the next cabin down the dirt road.

All six figures were completely clad in black, including helmets, boots, and facemasks. All six were armed with military M-16 rifles. The six were all shorter and considerably slighter than the men they had just felled. They ran to the fallen general and his mercenaries and immediately disarmed them and then used plastic ties to immobilize their feet and hands, making sure to secure their hands behind their backs. None of the six uttered a sound during all of this.

The driver of the black Suburban came out of his shock and started to move to the door of the big utility vehicle. But, before he could pull the door open, he was yanked backwards, and tossed to the ground. He looked up to see Doc Charlie smiling at him as she pointed a .45 caliber pistol directly at his nose.

"Goin' somewhere, honey?" she asked. "I think it's impolite to leave before you've been properly introduced. Turnover on your stomach, you miserable piece of crap, and put your hands behind your back." The frightened driver could not take his eyes off the barrel of her handgun, which looked enormous from a distance of twelve inches. He quicky regained his senses and rolled over on his stomach and put his hands behind him.

Doc Charlie produced a pair of plastic ties and quickly secured the driver's hands and ankles. When she was finished, she stood up and turned to face the baffled faces of her friends, Kit, Swifty, and Billy.

"What the hell just happened?" blurted out Swifty.

"I guess I owe you guys kind of an apology," said the still smiling Doc Charlie. "When I was in the Air Force there were a lot of cases of unjust treatment of women officers as well as enlisted personnel. About ten years ago, a couple of my friends who were Air Force Academy graduates decided enough was enough. They created this little club within the Air Force. Everything about it was kept hushed up. Over time some of the members left the service but kept their ties to the club. They solicited money and funded legal defenses of females in the Air Force that the government wouldn't help. In the last few years some of them created an elite squad of female warriors who were trained for combat."

"Combat?" asked Kit.

"Yes, combat," replied Doc Charlie. "Sometimes even good legal teams run up against politics, prejudice, and in this case, blatant corruption. There is no place for that crap in the United States Air Force and this group represents the armed fist of the group."

"How did you get in touch with them?" asked Kit.

"Actually, they got in touch with me when I was still stationed at Warren Air Force base in Cheyenne," replied Doc Charlie. "The military is no different than any other organization. The rumor mill exists everywhere, and they heard about what happened to me that night the captive was killed on base. When they heard about you guys picking me up and taking me to Kemmerer, they were alerted and headed there to set me free. They got in touch by text, and I told them to back off, that you were the good guys. They did but agreed to keep me under surveillance. When you planned this confrontation with the general, I knew he would double cross you, so I alerted the club in case things went south and here they are."

"I had no idea they were even around," said Billy, shaking his head.

"I can't believe I got snuck up on by a half dozen women," said Swifty incredulously.

"I can't believe you didn't tell me about them and your plan," said Kit with as much false indignity as he could muster.

"Every woman has secrets, Kit. You're old enough to know that by now," said a smiling Doc Charlie.

"What are you planning to do with them?" asked Kit as he pointed to the six shackled men lying prone on the ground.

"If Flash has done his job, there is enough hard evidence to put the general and these hired pukes away for a long time," replied Doc Charlie. "I managed to get the general very pissed off and he took great delight in threatening me and then bragging about what he had done and what he was planning to do with me."

"What was his plan?" asked Billy.

"Suspect shot while trying to escape," replied Doc Charlie. "Not very original, but short, effective, and to the point."

"Speaking of Flash, where the heck is he?" asked Kit.

"I'm pretty sure he is still holed up in that woodshed with his equipment," said Billy.

"What are your plans for the prisoners?" Kit asked Doc Charlie.

"As soon as you have the film and voice tapes of the general, I suggest you call Detective Parcell and tell him you need overnight accommodations for six males," said Doc Charlie. "I'm calling the Secretary of the Air Force and sending him the video and audio evidence we now have of the general's guilt. I'm quite sure the Air Police will be in Laramie in force to take possession of the prisoners by the time the Secretary has finished viewing and listening to the tapes.

"We better give Parcell a call," said Kit.

"He's already been called and he's on his way with some help," said a smiling Doc Charlie. "Don't look so surprised, Kit. These women are very well organized."

Fifteen minutes later, Detective Parcell arrived along with three county squad cars and five deputies and the Sheriff in a freshly pressed uniform. After his men finished rounding up the trussed -up criminals and placing them in the back of the squad cars, Detective Parcel came over to Kit.

I'll need you and your guys to come to the station in Laramie so we can take your statements along with Doc Charlie," said Parcell.

"What about the women soldiers?' asked Kit.

"What women soldiers?' replied Parcell.

Kit looked around and there was no sign of any woman except for Doc Charlie. When the squad cars left the highway and headed up the drive to the cabins, the six black-clad women had melted into the surrounding forest and disappeared.

Kit took another look around and then realization of what had happened dawned on him.

"Never mind me," said Kit. "I'm still kinda shell shocked. For some reason I must have imagined there were female soldiers here."

Parcell laughed. "You're a little young to start hallucinating", he said.

Kit managed a smile and then looked over at Doc Charlie.

She had a big smile on her face. The kind of smile one gets when they've just won a pie bakin' contest at the county fair. Or an ass kickin' contest.

CHAPTER FIFTY-EIGHT

Two weeks had passed since the capture of the general and his hired killers. The reporters had disappeared along with the television trucks with satellite dishes mounted on them and the media had moved on to the next big thing to capture their less than infallible attention.

Kit sat in his office in Kemmerer, sipping on a hot cup of coffee, carefully doctored with cream and honey. He was waiting for Doc Charlie to arrive as well as Big Dave.

The past two weeks had been consumed with military investigators from the Air Force questioning each of Kit's team and Doc Charlie several times. That had taken almost a week. Then there were the reporters. They had descended on Laramie like a horde of starving mosquitoes in search of a fresh source of blood.

They had tried to interview everyone they could find with varying degrees of success. They interviewed Doc Charlie, who was both professional and direct in her interviews. They had interviewed or tried to interview Billy. He had the same response to every inquiry. "No comment."

Swifty had been less diplomatic. His response to one of the first over aggressive female reporters who tried to thrust a microphone in his face had been epic and made television news broadcasts around the country. After scowling at the blonde reporter and trying to ignore her, Swifty finally lost his temper. "Get that damn microphone out of my face before I shove it down your plastic mouth." Then he stormed off. To his credit, no one tried to interview him again for at least forty-eight hours.

Kit had come up with an answer to interview questions that was a tad more polite and professional. "Doc Charlie is my client. Her story is her story, not mine. You need to ask her your questions." The response kept some, but not all the reporters at bay, and was a subtle nod to his business, Rocky Mountain Searchers. As Kit had learned some time ago, a little publicity is generally good for business.

Flash turned out to be the darling of the press. Reporters loved him. They ate up every word he uttered. Flash just smiled at everyone. He said a lot but told them nothing. Even rocket scientists know how to have a little fun with folks who have no idea what you are talking about. His face graced by his cowboy hat was photographed and filmed at least a hundred times and graced the evening news of television stations across the country.

After almost a week, the Air Force and the Sheriff's office were done with them and Kit, Billy, Swifty, Flash, and Doc Charlie drove back to Kemmerer. When they got there, they were met with more reporters including some from foreign countries. They descended on Kemmerer like the legendary hoard of locusts on Salt Lake City.

After two or three days, they packed up their cameras and microphones and left. Kemmerer was suddenly quiet. A person could walk down the street and cross the Triangle

Park to get a cup of coffee and not trip over a reporter or a TV camera.

The front door to the old bank building opened and in walked Big Dave. He ignored Kit and went straight back to the kitchen and came back with a hot mug of black coffee. Then he entered Kit's office and made himself at home on one of the comfortable side chairs.

After taking a long drink from his mug, Big Dave looked up at Kit. "Where the hell is the Doc?" he said.

Kit looked at his watch and said, "She'll be here at ten when Flash drives her here from the motel. Just like I told you on the phone yesterday."

Big Dave ignored Kit's subtle jab at him and just nodded his head. "What time is her flight out of Salt Lake?" he asked.

"Her flight leaves at 3:30 P.M. this afternoon," replied Kit.

"Where the hell is she flyin' to?" asked Big Dave.

"She's flying to see her mom, like I told you yesterday," said a slightly exasperated Kit.

"That's the lady who hired you?" asked Big Dave.

"One and the same," replied Kit.

"How long since she's seen her mom?" asked Big Dave.

"Her mom gave her up for adoption at birth," responded Kit.

"Damn long time," snorted Big Dave.

Kit just shook his head.

The front door to the old bank building opened and in walked Doc Charlie. Instead of being clad in jeans and a denim shirt, she was wearing a black silk pant suit with a creamy white silk blouse. She wore sensible flat black shoes. And a big smile.

Both men jumped to their feet. "Where's yer stuff?" asked Big Dave.

"Flash is moving it from his van to Kit's truck," said Doc Charlie.

"So, you're ready to go?' asked Kit.

"Born ready, Kit," replied Doc Charlie.

The three of them paraded out through the back of the old building and into the attached multi-car garage Kit had built where the old drive-in had been located. Flash was waiting for them, standing next to Kit's truck.

"The Doc's stuff is all loaded in the back of your truck, Kit," said Flash.

"How much damn stuff is she takin'? asked Big Dave.

"Just a suitcase and a carry-on bag," said Doc Charlie with a smile.

"Well," said Big Dave. "Let's get the hell out of here. We're burnin' daylight."

Kit and Doc Charlie laughed. Flash just looked puzzled.

Kit got in the driver's seat with Doc Charlie in the passenger seat and Big Dave settled himself into the back seat. Kit pulled out of the garage and soon they were on their way south on the highway, heading for the junction with Interstate 80.

After they passed Evanston and then the Utah state line, the small talk between the three had died down to silence. It stayed that way for almost half an hour until Big Dave could no longer contain himself.

"Did you tell her?" Big Dave asked Kit.

"No, I did not," replied Kit.

"Tell me what?" asked Doc Charlie.

Her question was followed by silence from both men.

"I repeat, tell me what?" asked Doc Charlie.

Finally, Big Dave spoke.

"You know how you kept in contact with that group of women veterans," he said.

"Yes," answered Doc Charlie.

"You knew what a devious bastard the general was, and you figured he'd have some sort of contingency plan in case picking you up might be a trap," said Big Dave.

"Yes, I did know what a cunning assshole he was," replied Doc Charlie.

"Well, you ain't the only one who don't put all their cards in one pot," said Big Dave.

"Meaning what?" asked Doc Charlie.

"Me and Kit didn't want to show all our cards at once to anyone, least of all that crafty old bastard general," said Big Dave.

"I'm not following," said Doc Charlie.

Big Dave chuckled to himself. Then he spoke. "Did you ever wonder why Kit only brought himself, Swifty and Billy for security to the cabin for you and Flash?" asked Big Dave.

Doc Charlie thought for a moment and then responded. "He needed the rest of you to guard the prisoners."

Big Dave laughed out loud.

"What's so funny?" asked Doc Charlie.

"It don't take four men to guard ten goons hog tied and helpless," said Big Dave.

"What's your point?' asked Doc Charlie.

"If you had bothered to look real hard at the area around

the cabin where they took you, you might, just might, have noticed something out of place," said Big Dave.

"I saw nothing out of place," said Doc Charlie.

"You didn't look hard enough, Doc," said Big Dave. "Me and Chief were behind the second cabin down from the one they took you to. And we weren't armed with no bows and arrows."

"But you didn't come out when it was all over and Detective Parcell and his men arrived and took charge of the prisoners," she said.

"Weren't no need," said Big Dave. "I ain't fond of answering a bunch of stupid questions and Chief, well he ain't fond of answering any questions."

"You were there the entire time?" asked Doc Charlie.

"Me and Chief was settled in them woods about five hours before Parcell showed up with you, Doc," answered Big Dave.

Doc Charlie looked over at Kit in disbelief. "Is he bullshitting me?" she asked.

Kit just smiled and shrugged his shoulders as he kept his eyes on the road.

When they were at the airport in Salt Lake City and had just reached the line to go through security, Doc Charlie turned and faced the two men who had quickly become a big part of her life.

"You boys try to stay out of trouble while I'm gone," said Doc Charlie.

"Fat chance of that happening," said Big Dave.

Doc Charlie smiled and started through the security

line. When she got past the airport security check station, she took a few steps and turned to wave good-by to her friends.

They were gone.

THE END

ACKNOWLEDGMENTS

Every place mentioned in this novel exists. Next time you're in Wyoming, take a few side trips and you will see the same sights that inspired me when writing this story.

After I finished my last novel, I started thinking about ideas for a new yarn to spin. I came up with two ideas. Both of them seemed good, and I couldn't decide. In the end, I took a quarter and assigned heads to one idea and tails to the other. Heads won.

I write from a masculine point of view, and it had been suggested to me I should think about writing about a woman. That stumped me. Then I remembered a line from a Jack Nicholson movie where he wrote women's romance novels. He was in his publisher's waiting room and the receptionist asked him how he, a man, could write like a woman. "It's easy," he said, "I just remove all logic and reason from my mind and start writing."

He lied. It's a lot harder than one might expect. But I focused on my daughter, Christine and tried to create a character who was not her but had strong pieces of Chris in her character. I hope I succeeded.

Recently I compiled a list of characters I had created in my books. I came up with one hundred and twenty-five. To this list, I proudly add the name of my recently deceased cousin, Tom Main. Tom was probably the most brilliant member of my family. He graduated from Knox College in Illinois, then a master's degree from Dartmouth. Tom spent his career and the rest of his life in California as a rocket scientist. He was an avid reader of my books. I took a great deal of pleasure including him in this story. I know he would have loved reading about himself. He died while I was writing this book and when it happened, I decided to include him in the story. When I did it seemed to breathe new life into the story.

I use an unusual cast of characters in my volunteer team of helpers. They all read my drafts and offer corrections, suggestions, and yes, criticism. I couldn't write books without their help. My special thanks to my wonderful wife, Nancy who proofreads and criticizes without any mercy. My helpers are scattered all over the country. Thank goodness for the internet. Marcia McHaffie, Boulder, Colorado; Craig Morrison, Bethel, Connecticut; Mary Marlin, Longmont, Colorado; and my oldest son, Steve Tibaldo, Athens, Alabama.

I'd also like to thank Wade Nystrom, my high school friend, and Bob Parcell, my old college roommate, for allowing me to use their real names for characters in this book.

Please feel free to let me know what you think of this book by contacting me at **rwcallis@aol.com**. If you come up with a good idea for a book, pass it on and I'll see what I can create.

You write because you enjoy writing. I enjoy creating a story about something historic and real and then letting my imagination take over. I get plenty of satisfaction when people read my books and enjoy them. Thank you for being one of my readers. Kit and Swifty exist only in my mind. When I sit down at my computer, they come to life. What could possibly be more fun than that?

ROBERT W. CALLIS

Printed in the United States
by Baker & Taylor Publisher Services